Published by: GladEye Press
Interior Design: J.V. Bolkan
Cover Design: Trask Bedortha & Sharleen Nelson
ISBN-13: 978-1-951289-25-6
Library of Congress Control Number: 2025950568

This is a work of fiction. All names, characters, places, and events are
either a product of the author's imagination or are used fictitiously. Any
resemblance to real persons, businesses, organizations, or events are
totally unintentional and entirely coincidental.

10 9 8 7 6 5 4 3 2 1

The body text is presented in Adobe Jenson Pro, 11 point for easy
readability.

OFF ROUTE

Rick Levin

GladEye Press

Springfield, OR

Dedicated to songwriter, stamp maker, saint—the late, great
Jimmy Silva.

Author's Note

The following work of fiction was written while I was employed full-time as a bus driver in Eugene, Oregon. It has been funded by no grants, nor supported by any organizations, academic or otherwise. My paycheck paid for it, and it was squeezed out and sweated over, word for word, during my days off, which were infrequent

This story, then, is meant to be exactly what it is, and only that—an account of working-class reality, lived and felt and suffered and celebrated at proletarian ground zero. As such, it makes no sociological claims. It speaks from the aching muscles and addled brain of a working stiff, and the only truth it asserts is the truth of how it feels, subjectively, to make a living among the people who actually do the hard, physical work of keeping this god-awful machine chugging down the broken road. And by machine, I mean the gears of capitalism itself, in its final stages.

Rich Bus, Poor Bus

Believe it or not, some of the first motorized buses to make an appearance in public were of the double-decker variety. Fueled by diesel and slow as a horse-drawn carriage, these lumbering beasts were introduced primarily as a luxury of the European gentry, a quaint curiosity for members of the leisure class, who could take them out for revitalizing jaunts into the countryside or whatever it is the fin-de-siècle rich did for fun.

Of course, the wealthy soon grew bored of this fad, which was rapidly being replaced by the irresistible enticement of owning your very own car and thereby driving wherever you wanted, whenever you wanted, with whoever you wanted, thank you very much.

The issue, for Mercedes-Benz and the like, became what to do with all these empty buses, as well as the massive assembly lines designed to produce them. Things so large and expensive rarely just go away.

In a move that has been repeated so often that one is tempted to say it's cooked into the very system of modern industrialism, the former buses of the rich were now shunted off to cities as a means of public transportation—a way to move around the poor and working class, from tenement to factory and back again. In capitalism, ontogeny capitulates phylogeny. Problem solved.

The first question most people ask about a double-decker bus concerns its stability. Isn't that thing going to tip over? Interestingly, rigorous tests on early models were performed with exactly this issue in mind, and they simply couldn't get the buses to capsize, no matter how hard they tried. Turns out there was so much weight so down low that its apparent instability was an illusion—a misperception, if you will.

Every Story has a Lesson

had this one sponsee, he wouldn't stop sleeping around. Just basically screwing his way through all the available women at the recovery club. And some of the unavailable, too. Didn't matter to Craig. They were all fair game. He had the goods, too. He was handsome. He was charming, funny, smooth, he came on all soft and groovy like Sexy Rehab Jesus. Watching him operate gave me the vapors. He was impervious to my warnings. I couldn't get my hooks into him, no matter how hard I tried. Craig was returning from a relapse, so he'd already had some time under his belt. He knew the program well enough, so he should have known better than to substitute one addiction for another—pussy for dope, as they say in the rooms—but, then again, when it comes to addicts, knowing doesn't mean shit. It's not like we don't understand that our behavior is killing us. That's not the real issue.

There are fates worse than death. Like becoming a bus driver, for instance. But more on that soon enough.

Anyhow, I rode Craig pretty hard. Argued with him, pleaded with him, reasoned with him, appealed to his dignity as a man, appealed to his fear of gonorrhea. I quoted the Big Book chapter and verse. In response to my haranguing, Craig would nod and shrug and give me the "yeah, man, I know, I know," seducing me with his sad sexy puppy-dog eyes until at last, inevitably, I'd take my foot off the gas. Because, honestly, his act was irresistible, even if I was hip to every move he was making. I'd made them all myself.

I was far from innocent in all this. Because, truth be told, I was also just a wee bit jealous of his womanizing. It's not quite true that I secretly wanted to do what Craig was doing; more to the point that I envied the pure expression of his demon—a lust-demon more degraded and yet somehow more honest than whatever two-bit apparitions were bedeviling me at the moment.

Life is a pretty vicarious affair—a game of tag and triangulation, mirrors reflecting mirrors—and it was really only a matter of circumstance that prevented me from being his pimp, or him becoming my wingman. The tension was exquisite, and it finally broke.

Craig set his sights on Missy—a smart, pretty single mom who was fresh in recovery and in the process of escaping an abusive relationship with her crank-crazy baby daddy. She was a hot mess. Every guy in the club harbored a crush on her, which—vicariously—probably only increased her appeal for Craig. They started hanging out, spending time together.

The funny thing is, their entanglement was somehow more chaste, more patently traditional than the previous five or six or two dozen tawdry sexual escapades he'd just blazed his way through. It looked for all the world like the early stages of dating, American style. I'm not sure what it was that made it different. I don't know whether it was the unexpected possibility of a future beyond a one-night stand rearing its romantic head for the both of them, or whether my endless bargaining with Craig finally broke through, but all of a sudden he became much more receptive to my warnings about getting into a relationship so early in recovery.

"Listen, man," I said to him one day over coffee. "Seriously, what do you have to offer this girl? You've got no job, you're broke, you're living in a recovery house, you're still shaking off the dope. Look at you. You can barely sit still."

It was the same argument my sponsor had used on me regarding my early incursions on Clare's attention, which was ironic to say the least. Craig squirmed in his seat and took a sip of coffee.

"Harsh," he said, setting his mug down with a sharp clack. "But you're right. I gotta get serious about the program. And she's on the same page. The timing isn't right for either of us. We don't need to be getting all serious when neither of us has even worked the steps. I don't know … I really like her, she really likes me, it's crazy, but I've been here before and so has she, and we both know how this usually goes. Not good, basically."

I nodded. He looked genuinely bereft. For the first time since we'd been working together, I experienced a glimmer of hope. But I also felt really bad for the guy, and I had the immediate urge to tamp down the severity of the very thing I'd been proposing all along and which, at last, he was now taking to heart. Winning arguments would be much more satisfying if the victory lap didn't include hurdling your own guilt.

"Hey, listen," I said. "Nothing is forever, right? It's about taking care of yourself first, and not dragging somebody else into your shit show before that happens. It's about learning to love yourself before getting involved in a relationship. Patience, and all that. Maybe in a year's time, or whatever, after both of you have stabilized a bit, who knows? Boundaries can always be renegotiated. But for right now, I think you're making the right choice. I'm proud of you, man."

An expression of warmth softened the features of his face. He smiled. I took this as a sign that my words had landed.

"Yeah," he said, looking down at the table. "She and I are going to get together later today and talk it through. It's been a good—"

"You're what?" I said. "Talk what through?"

His smile vanished in a look of confusion. "Talk about how we shouldn't be together," he said.

"So wait," I said, "let me see if I have this right. You and Missy are going to get together to talk about how the two of you shouldn't get together?"

Craig nodded.

"You realize how ridiculous that is, right?" I said.

Craig looked like a little kid who'd just been busted, not for all the shit he had done but for the one thing he hadn't. "The talks have been good," he said.

"Talks?" I said. "Like, more than one?"

He nodded, once.

"How many?"

He held up his right hand showing three fingers, looked at each finger individually as though silently counting, shrugged, then flipped up his pinky finger as well.

I fell back into my chair and blew a long, dramatic sigh.

"Dude," I said. "You've got to be kidding me. If you were going to quit a job, would you get together with your boss four goddamn times to talk about how you just weren't a good fit for the company? Come on, man, you're not that thick. Don't you see what's going on? This isn't a breakup. It's a seduction. In the form of a refusal. I mean, it's pretty hot, I'll hand you that, but …"

He stared at me, frowning.

"You two must be about to explode," I said. "How long before the fuzzy handcuffs and leather restraints come out?"

Craig was getting angry, for good reason. He was ceasing to be the subject of my compassion and becoming the object of my derision. I was losing the thread. I was ready to wash my hands of him.

"What do you want me to do?" he said.

"I don't care," I said. "I give up. You guys do whatever you want. It's not my business."

"Don't give up on me," he said. "Please?"

I told my therapist the story of Craig and Missy.

"It pretty much haunts me to this day," I said. "I failed him as a sponsor. I failed him as a friend. Especially as a friend. I stopped working with him. Basically, I fired him, which is completely dumb. You don't fire people in the program. It's the only time I've ever done anything like that. The funny thing is, the two of them are still together, Craig and Missy, which shows just how much I know. She and Clare are pretty tight. Craig and I hang out every now and then. I actually really like the guy."

"So what's the problem," my therapist asked. "Everybody

makes mistakes, right? The point is acknowledging them, fixing what you can and moving on, not dwelling on them forever. Maybe you're being too hard on yourself?"

This was a common refrain, along with her suggestion that I tend to overthink everything. Truth be told, neither of these observations has ever really landed with me.

"I guess the problem," I said, "is that it's not like me to give up on people. Failure seems to be the norm for almost everybody, and it's not like I'm doing any better. So I'm pretty forgiving. I'm not so sure that's necessarily a good quality, either. Empathy doesn't feel like a virtue to me. It's more like a nervous response. I can't detach from it all. I can't let it go. I can't find the humor or the beauty in it like you're supposed to, right? It just upsets me. I've got no Zen. I can't tell where I end and the world begins. I can't tell whether I'm too smart or maybe not quite smart enough. All I see are these subtitles coming out of peoples' mouths when they talk, and I can't read them. There's just all these games of desire and seduction, and they only cause more suffering. It's like there's no upshot. It all feels like a performance. I can't make it stop. I'm performing right now. All I'm ever doing is performing. Who's watching? Who do I think is watching?"

My therapist smiled. "That was a lot," she said.

I laughed. "I think I've had too much coffee," I said.

"Okay," she said.

Rewind a bit: Way back in the long ago, Clare and I found this hip little coffee shop just a few blocks from the recovery club where we met. It was here we could court in private, long before we admitted that's what we were doing.

All this wanting and not having, I wasn't used to it.

"I don't know," I said. "I suppose it's getting better. I slept a little last night."

We were sitting outside at one of the cafe's metal tables. The May breeze blew hot and cold, a hyphen separating the seasons.

"Give it time," Clare said. "Your serotonin's all messed up."

"There's more messed up about me than just my serotonin," I said.

Clare snorted. "Join the club, dude."

"I've never really been much of a joiner," I said.

She took a sip of coffee and grinned. We'd only been hanging out a few weeks, but I already adored the way she constitutionally refused to let me get away with anything. Compliance was not in her nature, and her bullshit detector was top-notch.

"Okay," I said. "I get it. Thanks for pointing that out."

"I didn't say anything," Clare said.

"That's what I like about you," I said. "A woman of few words, but all these incredibly poignant looks that speak volumes."

"Yeah," she said. "I sorta like you, too." Her lower lip trembled. "And you scare the fuck out of me, too," she added.

"Sometimes I scare the fuck out of myself," I said, which was easier than admitting I was scared of everything all the time.

Later, much later, Clare would confess that it wasn't just her desire that scared the daylights out of her—her falling head-over-heels for yet another fixer-upper head case with terminally untapped potential. She was also scared for me.

"I would rather see you cheat on me than relapse," she said a few weeks later. "At least if you fucked someone else, I'd have a fighting chance. But if you start using it again …"

I understood what she meant by that, but it still pissed me off. I did not want her understanding. I wanted her need.

"That's just a really weird thing to say to someone," I said. I heard the anger in my voice. "Why would you say that?" But I was also thinking that it was sort of nice to have permission in advance.

In the end, I believed in Clare, not because I wanted to believe, but because I wanted the forgiveness such believing brings. I told myself I wanted all of her, and in telling myself that, I realized it was true. I loved her. With her, I discovered a better part of myself. That small good thing was where I knew I should live, even if I could only grasp it momentarily. I had no name for it. It appeared in flashes, before disappearing into the tangles of time.

"I love everything about you," I told her, sitting outside that cafe so long ago.

"You don't know everything about me," Clare said.

I felt the blood in my veins go hot. "Yeah, okay," I said. "I don't know everything. We haven't been together all that long. So what? Does that mean I can't love all of you?"

"You don't know all of me," she said, darkening.

I wanted to scream at her; I wanted to fall on her history and ravage it of all its dark energies, and at the same time I wanted to run away, to find a place where my fear could shelter in peace. I wanted to know and not know, which meant that in the vacuum of not knowing I wanted to create my own knowing.

One morning late into the pandemic a sailboat appeared outside our house. I was pulling the garbage to the curb before work and there it was, seemingly levitating in the predawn moonlight: a beat-looking white sloop with a red hull, sitting propped in the bumpers of a trailer parked in the gravel abutting our driveway.

It couldn't have been more surreal, this object so poignantly out of place in the aquamarine glow of the neighborhood. I glanced around, expecting to find someone nearby who could answer for it. The streets at this hour were silent.

When I went back inside, Clare was already huddled on the couch, legs curled beneath her, sipping from a big mug of coffee. She was bundled up in my bathrobe, which I always found ir-resistibly sexy. She didn't look up from her cell phone.

"There's a sailboat in the front yard," I said.

She lowered the phone to her lap and looked at me. "A what?"

"A boat," I said. "I shit you not. There's a big sailboat sitting in our front yard."

Clare is typically low energy, at least until she's not. Her spirit of adventure flips on an invisible switch, a hair trigger of readiness. A devious smile crossed her lips. She jumped up and cinched the belt tight around the bathrobe, took a quick sip of coffee. "Let's go," she said, making a beeline for the front door. I followed.

"What the fuck?" Clare made a slow circuit around the boat. "Do you think it's the neighbor's?"

We lived in a working-class part of town. You might even call it a white-trash ghetto, although the very early stages of gentrification were detectable; small, single-story homes that formerly housed truckers and mill workers now stood in various stages of disrepair or renovation, depending on the owner. A stroll down our street felt like a schizophrenic snapshot of modern America, as falling-down shacks with mossy trampolines and a half dozen busted-up cars in the gravel driveway stood side-by-side with freshly renovated ramblers sporting Black Lives Matter signs and a Prius parked in the newly asphalted driveway.

An elegant austerity in landscaping vied with next-door neighbors whose enormous Trump flag only partially obscured their face-first slide off the socioeconomic cliff. Considering the occasional junkyard feel of our street, it wasn't so strange to find a boat suddenly parked outside our house.

"Yeah, could be," I said. "That was my first thought. Maybe Gary? Still, I mean, who owns a fucking sailboat? Did you see the plates on the trailer? California."

"It does seem kind of druggy, doesn't it?," Clare said.

"Two hundred kilos of coke stashed in the hull," I said, "and a hired killer on his way up from San Antonio to retrieve it."

Clare knocked on the hull. "I don't know why," she said, "but I all of a sudden have Steely Dan playing in my head."

"Yacht rock vibes, for sure," I said. The image of an impossibly tanned and wrinkly old man in tight white shorts popped into my mind's eye, his Bermuda shirt unbuttoned to reveal a hairy chest and bronzed nipples, sailor's cap tilted jauntily on his head as he chewed a cigarillo and wrestled with the rigging.

"I actually hate sailboats," I said. "I especially loathe the people who own them. Rich fuckers. That whole come-sail-away weekend culture is pretty gross."

"Pick your battles, I guess," Clare said.

"I went sailing once in high school," I said. "It was with this friend of mine's family. The sailing part was cool, but his parents were a nightmare. They gave off waves of contempt, like half-baked royalty or something. They were military, and at one point I made some comment about Vietnam, and the mom gave me this cold stare that made me want to jump off the boat."

Clare looked at me. "Leave it to you to ruin a nice outing on the water."

"He became a cop," I said.

"Who did?"

"That friend who took me sailing," I said. "I can't imagine he had any choice in the matter, with mommy dearest throwing daggers of disapproval anytime anyone in the immediate kinship group stepped outside the Republican line."

Clare didn't respond. Since the onset of the pandemic and all the political craziness taking place, we'd somehow scratched a raw spot into our usual ability to discuss anything remotely political. It wasn't that we fundamentally disagreed. The issue was emphasis.

"I'm sorry," I said. "Did I say something wrong?"

I wasn't sure she'd heard me, but she finally spoke: "Did you notice the name of the boat?"

"Hell, I can't remember," I said. "That was more than thirty years ago. The *SV Retaliation*, maybe?"

"No," she said, pointing. "This one."

I glanced at the stern. The name was written in loopy red cursive, with a graphic of a martini glass separating the two words. "*Sea Thru*," I said. "Ironic."

"I like it," Clare said. "It's pretty clever."

"The good ship *Sea Thru*," I said. "My, she was yar."

"I think it's a nice addition to the neighborhood," she said, patting the hull. "Trashy but classy."

"I gotta get to work," I said.

The man charging me is swinging a baseball bat back and forth. His pants have fallen down around his ankles and his flaccid dick flaps in the breeze. The thick, ratty beard on his face grows all the way down his neck, bleeding into a dreadlocked mat of red chest hair. That's what I notice, his body hair. And his skin. His skin is bronzed and leathery. It hangs off his bones like an ill-fitting suit. He looks like a cartoon caveman.

And I, behind the wheel of my bus—I am the woolly mammoth. He is absolutely focused on me, his pupils locked onto mine in unreconstructed predatory hatred. I wonder if the windshield between us is shatterproof. I have no move here. I can only wait. I pop the emergency brake and sit back, watching.

I'm driving the express down 11th. A woman sprints from the Fred Meyer parking lot and makes a wide arc into my dedicated bus lane. Now she's running directly in front of my bus, her arms waving in the air. She keeps looking over her shoulder with a crazy, happy grin on her face—like she's participating in the running of the bulls in Pamplona. Except she's not wearing any pants. Her bare white ass heaves and undulates in the sunshine. All she has on is a yellow T-shirt. I tap the brakes and slow down, moving along with her at a crawl. There's no point in blowing my horn. That only makes it worse.

The ice clicks and tinkles against my windshield. I've already fishtailed this articulated bus twice today—a weird, faraway sensation of being pulled in reverse as the bendy back end jackknifes in the direction opposite your turn. My nerves are strung wire-tight and all I can hear is the beating of the windshield wipers. I can't believe I'm driving in this shit. I can't believe they're letting us.

On Roosevelt I glance to my right and notice a body moving slowly across the open lot next to the used car dealership. A girl, not more than a teenager, barefoot in terry cloth shorts and a Misfits T-shirt cut off at her bare midriff.

Her face is plastered in clown makeup and her hair hangs stringy and damp into her gaunt face. She's tip-toeing across the ground, hunched into herself and soaking wet. She looks like a fairy-tale witch creeping across the arctic tundra of Middle Earth.

I stop the bus in the middle of the street and flip on the hazards. Throw open the front door and start waving frantically at her. "Get on!" I yell. "Hurry up!" She looks up and sees me, pauses a moment, then continues on toward the bus with her head down.

I look into my rearview mirror and notice my passengers staring at me. They look confused, concerned, pissed off. But I don't give a fuck anymore. I'll wait all day. I'm not leaving her out there in this ice storm. No way.

She clambers onto the bus and ducks right past me without a glance. I watch as she finds a bench seat and sits down, muttering to herself. I close the door and move on. Not ten seconds later, I hear the bell ring for the next stop on 11th. I pull in slowly, sliding and bumping into the platform.

I trigger the door open and watch as she jumps off and skitters away down the icy street.

I let everybody ride my bus. Money, no money, pass, no pass, excuse, no excuse, cajoling, begging, justifying, lying—doesn't matter. Get on. It's the least I can do. They are all children of God, aren't they? Aren't we? I'm not sure I believe in God, but other folks do—Jesus, Jehovah, Allah, the god of methamphetamine, the angel of mercy, the devil of petty resentments. We've all got something to serve. Everyone's got their measures, their needs, their fears, their places to be. So they all ride. We're all coming along on this one.

Bring the masses unto me. The American highway is broad and forgiving. Let them ride.

"One more bad day is all it's going to take," a colleague said to me. He was one of the nicer bus drivers, never had a bad word for anyone. But, like the rest of us, he was being ground to a pulp. His spirit was breaking. I think he speaks for all of us at this point. And not just bus drivers. All of us. One more bad day.

I drive the bus, day after day, and I see things—crazy things, brutal things, prophetic things, hilarious things; things so sad you can't believe it—but I can't stitch it all up. Everything swirls together. The narrative does not cohere. It begins where it ends and it ends where it begins. It's all the same day. Groundhog day.

Or maybe it's an infinite stretch of separate but identical moments, and it turns inward on itself like a serpent swallowing its own tail. What a hellish idea. All I know is that, for a bus driver, one day feels like an eternity and yet a single year passes like an eye blink. There is nothing to hold on to. Time is out of joint. How did this happen to us? Perhaps nobody is to blame for it. In that case, there are no heroes, and certainly no villains.

Except for Doyle Claggart. Fuck that guy.

Who I am

Not to gloat but, on paper, my cultural résumé is fairly sophisticated. College educated, well-read, travel abroad, not afraid of foreign movies, etc. You know, a real citizen of the world.

That said, I would like to offer some different bona fides which, say what you will, I do not consider contradictory: Whenever I have to blow my nose, I plug one nostril with my index finger and fire a string of snot into the street. My favorite place to piss is off the end of a porch at sunset. Growing up in a small rural town on the Olympic Peninsula, I was reared among an extended family of Croatian immigrants who fished and logged for a living, who drank Rainier beer out of cans and drove Ford pickups that were bashed in from sideswiping trees.

My jobs have included running skiff on a commercial fishing boat, pumping gas, shoveling shit, picking gypsum in Omak, and butchering salmon in Dutch Harbor. I lost my virginity by walking a wooded trail behind my house to visit a sweet girl who lived in a double-wide trailer and whose mother drove my school bus. My favorite smell is turpentine, and I think farting is hilarious. These are my class credentials. Class credentials are important.

Fast-forward again, to a list of symptoms I jotted down on my cell phone: I am afraid I will not see something that's there, like a kid in the street, or see something that's not there, like a rhinoceros crossing the road.

The familiar suddenly seems unfamiliar, and it scares me horribly. Everything is either completely surreal or painfully way too real. I quite suddenly don't know where I am on a route I've driven hundreds of times. I fret that I'm going to see green lights as red and red lights as green. I trust my mind and perceptions less and less.

I can't think, and simple tasks seem extremely difficult and fraught with risk and danger.

I stop at a train track, check both ways, proceed, and then immediately wonder whether I've actually stopped at the train track. Ditto for any number of routine basic tasks.

Most of my free time feels like a furlough from prison. Sometimes everything is moving way too fast.

My awareness that these are symptoms of stress and anxiety does nothing to alleviate the authenticity of their effect on me.

No matter how much I care and how hard I try, I am failing at fairly easy tasks.

I have never been prone to headaches, but now get them regularly. Like, all the time. When I lie down to sleep, my body literally vibrates, as though I'm receiving a mild electric shock. I am becoming reactive and quick to anger.

I feel vulnerable and ashamed that I can't handle this, but I'm also afraid that if I continue trying to handle it, I will go insane, and extinguish my humanity completely.

I'm afraid I'm losing myself and everything I care about and becoming a trapped work automaton in a cruel and unusual system, and that I won't recognize the point at which that happens, if it hasn't already.

One day at work feels like two, or three, or forever. I fear aggression and violence and bad things happening on my bus. Actually, not just on my bus. Everywhere.

I am disengaged, absent-minded and hypervigilant all at once. I'm second guessing every move I make, which leads to crippling self-doubt and often panic.

It feels like there is zero time and zero space to address any of this, and instead I am perpetually being shot out of a cannon into an endlessly recurring work week.

New symptoms include shortness of breath, shallow panting, rapid pulse and a tightness in my chest …

I'm having horrible nightmares, totally apocalyptic. I'm

afraid I'll relapse and die.

F. Scott Fitzgerald famously pointed out that the true test of a first-rate intelligence is the ability to hold two opposing ideas in one's head at the same time without becoming dysfunctional.

I am not a first-rate intelligence.

"You might want to think about quitting your fucking job." This is exactly what my doctor said to me after my umpteenth visit to her office for work-related health issues.

She's a kind and soft-spoken person, my doctor, definitely not prone to cursing, much less haranguing me, so I knew she was being dead serious at this moment.

She ticked off a litany of ailments. My blood pressure, which has always been on the normal to low-normal side, had risen steadily since I'd started the job, and was now approaching the lower thresholds of pharmaceutical intervention. My cholesterol was way up, as was my weight. Both shoulders hurt continuously, alternating between a dull ache and a sharp pain that sliced like a piano wire under the scapula. I found it almost impossible to get comfortable in bed. My whole body buzzed and hummed like a refrigerator on the fritz.

The arches of my feet were permanently cramped. I'd thrown my back out, twice, badly, which precipitated a week in bed both times. Not once but twice I'd been pulled off work and sent to the emergency room for kidney stones.

My psych eval revealed a descent from mild anxiety and depression into complex PTSD and borderline suicidal ideation, and it was becoming increasingly difficult for me to find pleasure in even the most reliable enjoyments of ordinary life.

In short, she said, I was a wreck.

I walk into Ops at midnight, having completed yet another twelve-hour day driving the express bus to hell. On my final run of the night, I pick up three skinheads.

They stomped in unison to the back of the bus and sprawled themselves on the back seats. One of the dudes opened a butterfly knife and started picking dramatically at his fingernails.

Occasionally, the three of them would erupt into barks of mirthless laughter, their eyes darting to monitor my reaction in my rearview mirror.

Stop after stop my bus empties of passengers until it's just me and the skins. The streets along the 11th Avenue corridor are dark and mostly empty. A block before I hit the end of the line, the automated system announces that all passengers must deboard, this is the final stop. Don't forget to collect your belongings, including bikes. Thank you for riding the Cosmodemonic Unified Northwest Transit's express line. *Las puertas abren a la derecha. Gracias, hasta la vista.*

I drift the bus onto the platform and hit the button to open the right-side doors. The punks don't budge. They sit with their pale white heads tilted together in a pantomime of plotting. I picked up the intercom.

"Gentlemen," I say. "This is the end of the line. This bus is going out of service. Everyone needs to get off."

Nothing.

"Hey, guys," I say, more sternly. "I'm going back to the garage. Time to get off the bus."

One of the dudes looks up. "Just a minute," he says.

Fuck. Here we go. "Listen," I say slowly. "You gotta get off this bus. I'm not kidding." I consider threatening them with a call to security but quickly nix the idea.

At this time of night, security would show up half an hour later to find me beaten to a pulp and covered in piss, lying in the aisle of a gently idling bus. I don't particularly like my options in this scenario.

"Who's gonna make us, motherfucker?" the same guy shouts at me. His bosom droogie runs the tip of his knife against the plastic on the back of the seat facing him. The scratching sound makes my teeth hurt.

I take a deep breath. "Why you gotta be like that?" I say into the intercom. "I don't want any trouble. I just want to go home."

I've got no play here, and I'm scared. I reach down and unlatch my seat belt. I think about bolting out of my driver's side door. I mean, fuck this noise. Drivers around the country are getting assaulted, even killed, and I'm not particularly in the mood to test the odds.

As scared as I am, though, I'm even more frightened of the consequences of fleeing the bus. I am captain of the ship! Time to man up! So I resign myself to the impending violence, fantasizing about the exorbitant lawsuit I will file against the Company. This offers a modicum of relief.

I hear a chuckle flutter up from the back of the bus. I glance into the rearview mirror again, just in time to see the skinheads rise as a group and begin making their way toward me, very slowly and very deliberately, choreographed for maximum effect.

They pass the first pair of open exit doors and continue up the aisle, slapping each seat as they pass it, lips curled into vicious grins, eyes glaring up under tilted brows. Here we go, I think, shifting in my seat.

As they come to the next pair of open doors they stop and stand in a staggered phalanx, glaring at me. Then, one by one, they dart off the bus. The last guy to exit lets out a guttural howl.

I shut the doors as quickly as I can. I can feel my heartbeat in my eyeballs.

Disengaging the emergency brake, I get the bus into gear. I step on my left turn signal indicator and glance up into my side-view mirror to merge back into traffic. A rattling crash makes me jump in my seat.

I look to my right. One of the skinheads is now pressed up

against the bus, his face smeared hard into the Plexiglas, eyes bulging in a mockery of madness. He begins pounding with both fists against the door, screeching like a howler monkey.

If he moves to the front of the bus, I tell myself, run him over. Do not hesitate.

But he stops the pounding as suddenly as he started it—goes limp like a marionette with clipped strings. He tilts his head and looks at me, smiling clownishly, and then walks away on the platform. I pull into traffic and spin back toward the garage.

At the Ops counter I relay this story to Bernie. Most of the drivers like Bernie, but I find him off-putting and untrustworthy—just another middle-management axeman hiding behind a flimsy veneer of manufactured bonhomie.

"Yeah, yeah," Bernie keeps saying as I tell him about the incident. "Oh man, yeah," he says, "Wow, yep."

He has a big grin on his face, like I'm telling him a joke somebody just told me.

"Listen," I say, out of breath. "I'm not fucking kidding here. Somebody's going to get seriously hurt or killed on one of our buses. It's totally insane out there. I don't know if it's going to be a driver or a rider or what, but mark my words. It's not good. Somebody's going to die."

Bernie laughs. Ha ha ha. "Yeah, tell me about it," he says. I stare at him in disbelief. "Okay," he says, "you have a good night, buddy. See you tomorrow."

"Hey, Driver! Driver!" It's my final route of the day.

"Hey, Driver! How about turning up the heat?"

I glance into my rearview mirror. The lone woman who enters my bus wearing a hoodie and T-shirt is now stripped naked from the waist up. She's sitting on the very back seat, dead center in my line of sight, spread eagle, staring at me.

I pick up the receiver and press the talk button. "Ma'am, how about you try putting your clothes back on first?"

My colleagues have accused me of being far too patient with problem passengers, but I don't see the point in being a dick. If someone's life has led them to a place where stripping on a bus makes intuitive and immediate sense, who am I to condemn? I drive the bus for the people.

And look, she's actually taking my suggestion—by ripping her T-shirt into a single long loop of cloth and bandaging her exposed boobs in a kind of post-apocalyptic Thunderdome bikini top. I tear my eyes from this scene just in time to notice a couple of people waiting at the next stop.

This is one of the dangers of bus driving. You become so mortified or enraptured by some extravagant scene of human weirdness that you motor yourself right into a light pole. One nanosecond of inattention and you're toast. It happens that fast.

I pull to the curb and swing open the front door. A pair of teenaged Mormon missionaries enter, both smiling that trademark smile.

"Hello, sir," they say in unison.

There is no more pleasant and polite and therefore desirable bus rider than a member of the Church of Jesus Christ of Latter-day Saints. I don't care how you feel about them knocking on your door; they are good folk. As these fresh-faced young men make their way past me in their identical blue suits, Brother This and Brother That, I glance again into the rearview mirror, just in time to see the woman on the back seat haul the makeshift bikini off her tits and place it around her head like a sweatband.

Seated now, I watch as the faces of the Mormon boys drain of blood, until they come to resemble the chiseled statuary at Stonehenge, lips pinched and eyes blank in what I imagine to be the spiritual erasure of carnal shock. I am far more of a dirtbag than a prude, but suddenly I'm thinking that these poor boys shouldn't be exposed to this sort of thing. Love the sinner, hate the sin.

They don't teach you these things in training. I pick up the receiver again. "Ma'am, please cover yourself." But she no longer hears me. She's moved on to spreading crumpled wads of paper to each side of her on the empty bench seat. She's now inspecting these documents with the intensity of an accountant during peak tax season, nodding her head to some exotic internal rhythm.

And this is another thing you figure out quickly as a new bus driver: When to let go. I have engaged, challenged, insulted, and argued with passengers, and it's never brought me anything but grief. I leave the woman to her papers, topless or not. The Mormon kids are on their own.

Unless a situation rises to the level of actual physical danger or codified legal intervention, I've learned to leave it alone. No blood, no foul.

The late, great Cement Bob was an old-timer at the recovery club where Clare and I first got sober. He was a real hero to me—a child of the Great Depression and a Korean War veteran whose first day in combat included a shelling that wiped out half his regiment. Cement Bob might have been a grade-school dropout, but he was one of the smartest guys I've ever met.

I doubt he'd read more than five books in his entire life. His wisdom was lifted from the ground up. Cement Bob told stories about himself that would make Satan blush. And he told them laughing, with a joy that was infectious. I loved the man. He also scared me a little bit, because he'd mapped a thorny path to personal freedom that I knew I would eventually have to navigate, and I knew I didn't have the guts for it, not now and maybe never.

One day outside the recovery club, Cement Bob overheard me bitching about my job. He started laughing.

"You know," he said, "I used to be miserable about every job I ever had. Hated going to work. Hated having to go to work. Hated getting up at the crack of dawn. And then, one morning I woke up and immediately thought to myself, 'I might not go in today.' It was like God's voice in my head. And I realized right there that this is the choice I have every goddamn day of my life.

I can quit anytime I want. Nobody's holding a pistol to my head. From there on out, every day I got up for work I'd think, 'Maybe I won't go in today,' and then I'd laugh, put on my clothes and go to work."

Cement Bob chuckled, tapping his bald head. "This is the only prison we're in," he said. "You're as free as you wanna be."

"Yeah, but who's gonna pay my bills?" I said. Cement Bob just started cracking up. He actually bent over and slapped his knee, hooting and giggling.

"Ah," he wheezed. "You're alright kid! Keep comin' back."

"So," my therapist said as I sat down, "how was your week?"

"Clare and I got into a fight," I said, looking out her window at the river winding along the banks of the park. "Again. It got pretty gnarly. For the entire drive here I was trying to figure out ways to not tell you, and I couldn't make any of them work. So there it is."

"Why wouldn't you tell me?" she asked, gently. "Or why didn't you want to tell me?" I felt a hollow space open up in the middle of my chest.

"Because it's embarrassing," I said. "Because it's embarrassing that after ten years of marriage, we still get trapped in these insane spirals that spin totally out of control, until I can't tell what's what, I can't tell up from down, but I can't for the life of me let go of my, I don't know … my position, even though this little voice in my head is telling me that I'm wrong, and I'm sitting there watching her get hurt, I'm watching her cry, and I hate myself for it, but I feel so scared and alone, I can't stop, it's like she's running away from me and I'm desperately chasing her down, and the harder I chase, the worse it gets. And, plus, I don't want to show you any of this shit, because for some insane reason, I don't want to look bad in your eyes, which is stupid, I know, but I really do care what you think about me, and I suspect that the more vulnerable I get with you the more I reveal myself to be a total asshole."

"Okay," she said. "Why don't you tell me specifically what happened."

I shifted on the couch, squirming, sinking further into the cushions. I crossed my legs. "It was about sex, I guess," I said. "I mean, it started about sex, but it pretty quickly devolved into this battle royale. Just wholesale annihilation. I still can't wrap my head around it. I don't know how we got where we ended up, from point A to point B. I'd be hard-pressed to remember anything that was said, specifically, but I can tell you it wasn't good."

What actually happened was I'd asked in a hesitant tone if just maybe Clare might be interested in having sex. I'd sounded like a beggar, weakened by need and timid with lonesomeness. There'd been a pause, followed by a "sure," as though she were accepting another cup of coffee, which felt like charity, which felt like sorrow, or perhaps neither charity nor sorrow but vanquishment, and a familiar feeling boiled up in me.

I grew very calm, very precise.

"Are you even still attracted to me?" I asked. "I mean, we haven't had sex in almost a month."

I felt her stiffen beside me. "But who's counting," she said.

"That's not fair," I said.

"You're right, I'm sorry," she said. "But, really, do you have an idea of what would be enough? Do you have a number in mind?"

"Here we go," I said.

"I'm seriously asking," she said. "Apparently it's really important to you. I just want to know."

I took a deep breath. "Listen," I said, "all I know is that when we first got together, we couldn't get enough of each other. We fucked almost every day. I've never had so much sex in my life. Those first couple years were ridiculous. I don't know what's happened, but somehow things have completely run dry. It's like a desert, the exact opposite from the way things used to be. I'm not sure what I did wrong. Now I'm the only one who initiates anything, and it's like pulling teeth."

"Good lord," she said. "Pulling teeth. That sounds hideous."

"You know what I mean," I said. "Am I so repulsive as all that?"

"No," she said.

"Oh, well thank you for that rousing endorsement," I said. "I mean, don't be so enthusiastic."

From here, things just went from bad to worse.

An appetite of intolerable need opened up inside me. I watched as though from a distance as I employed a litigating cruelty that at last forced her to retaliate with an equal and opposite cruelty, a cruelty that miraculously justified all of my suspicions from the outset, *a priori*, suspicions named and those yet unnamed. Until finally I was satisfied I'd successfully uncovered the very verdict of loss I was looking for. And still we continued, we continued, we continued, we kept on until the battlefield was completely leveled, littered with shells and bodies and not a white flag to be seen.

My therapist listened as I dredged it all up. It was like trying to describe a movie in reverse.

"I just feel insane," I said. "We're doing so well, at least most of the time, and then something gets said and I go from zero to divorced in sixty seconds. The hilarious thing is, it's not even about sex. The sex is great. Clare says our broken pieces don't fit together so well sometimes. Or maybe they fit together too well. And that seems true to me. But it doesn't matter when we're in the middle of it. We get totally swept away. It's like every fight turns into a referendum on our whole relationship."

"Every marriage has intimacy issues," my therapist said. "It sounds like the two of you triggered some old traumas for sure."

"It feels like I'm possessed sometimes," I said. "But at the same time, I have … I don't know what to call it …"

"You have grievances," she said.

"Well, yeah," I said.

"And guilt," she added, "like it's all your fault."

"Of course," I said. "That's pretty much a constant."

ROAD
CLOSED

In one of the dreams, I'm carrying the sailboat over my shoulder. It has no real weight, and yet the burden of it is enormous. I am trudging around the neighborhood, alone in the dark, lugging this huge boat, and each house I pass features an elaborate Christmas display: gaudy colored lights strung on rooflines, inflatable plastic Santas anchored on strings, reindeer woven from copper wires, awful holiday songs crackling from hidden speakers. Families are milling around me, murmuring and pointing.

Finally, I stop in front of a dilapidated white house at the end of the street. The people have disappeared. A huge cross stands planted in the lawn, towering over me. Jesus is nailed to it. There is nothing mystical or godly about him, nothing dreamy; he is only a man, grotesquely real, made of flesh and bones. I can see the blood mixing with the sweat squeezed from his agony, the unbearable pull of muscles and tendons against gravity.

His head hangs limp on his neck, his long greasy hair falling about his face. I am terrified, but I approach. As I do, he raises his head, slowly, and looks into my eyes. An expression of total devastation. He opens his mouth. Nothing comes out. His lips start moving mutely.

I drop the boat to run but I am now inside the boat. The hull is empty, like the inside of a boxcar, and in fact the boat is rattling along, clacking, as though on rails. Clare is sitting across from me, her back against the wooden planks. She is drenched and shivering. My therapist is standing in the bow, dressed in vaguely Soviet military fatigues. There is a name tag pinned to her chest, but I can't read it.

"We need to reconnoiter the rim," she says. Clare looks at her and nods.

"The rim is the end of everything," Clare says.

"It's almost time," my therapist says, and at this a siren starts screaming in the distance. I get up in a panic and start running toward Clare, but I trip, and as I'm falling through infinite space I jolt awake.

My alarm for work is going off.

"I'm sorry," I said.

"I'm sorry, too," she said.

"That's not a proper amends, I know," I said. "But that's all I've got right now. I'm still sorting things out in my head. What I mean is that I'm sorry for my part, and when I figure out what that is, I'll be more specific. I suspect it's a lot. For now, the less I say the better. I feel like shit. Hurting you is the last thing I want."

Clare looked at me, a serious look, a look of empathy but not sympathy, which is why loving her is both inevitable and excruciating. "I know that," she said, a note of resignation in her voice. "It's not about that. It's never about that. It's about fear, and we're never going to sort that out for each other. I can't fix you and you can't fix me. That's why it's so hard."

"Yes it is," I said. "Hard," I said.

"We're codependent as fuck," she said, smiling.

"Yes we are," I said. "I'm sorry I'm so needy sometimes."

She smiled. "We all just want to be seen," she said.

"You don't think I see you?" I asked.

Clare didn't answer right away. She rarely answers right away, because, unlike me, she carefully considers the question as well as her answer, while I squirm, pinned and wriggling on the wall.

"I think you do see me," she said at last. "I also think, sometimes, you box me in by expectations, to such an extent that it doesn't really matter what comes out of my mouth, because no matter what, it'll fit into whatever it is you're anticipating. And that is crazy making," she said. "Sometimes, it feels like I'm suffocating."

"Oh my god," I said. "I really am my father, aren't I? I'm a fucking pathological narcissist with abandonment issues and a martyr complex!"

She laughed. "No," she said. "You're a human being and an alcoholic with unresolved wounds from childhood, and the coping strategies you learned to survive way back when no longer always suit the current situation. Welcome to the world, baby Jesus."

"Why are you even with me?" I said.

"Because I love you," she said. "And I believe in you. And because I choose to be here. I mean, isn't that obvious? The real question is why you don't trust that. It keeps coming up."

That stung, not because it was an unkind or untrue thing for her to say but because … well, because it revealed a vulnerability I had not accommodated yet, and that was terribly embarrassing to me; it made me want to fight back immediately, as though my life depended on it, and it was only the memory of last night that kept me from making a case for myself—or against myself. Perhaps the pain was serving its purpose.

"I have a lot of big sadness in here," I said, tapping my chest dramatically and smiling.

"I know," she said. "I'm sorry. I'm here for you. And there's nothing I can really do about that."

"Make it go away," I said.

"I can't," she said.

"I want to take all your sadness away," I said.

"You can't," she said. "It's got nothing to do with you."

I sighed. "So, what?" I said. "Welcome to the lonely hearts club?"

"Yeah," she said. "It's called existence."

"Do you remember our wedding vows?"

"Which part?" she said.

"I'd be fine without you, and you'd be fine without me."

"I do," she said.

"I think about those words a lot," I said. "We were so much smarter then."

"Oh, I don't think that's totally true," she said. "That first year, we were crazy."

"Still crazy after all these years," I said.

"Still hurt after all these years," she said, "and we keep walking through it."

"Two steps forward, one step back," I said. "That's how it feels to me. Why does that one step hurt so bad? Like, worse and worse."

"Pride," she said.

"Fuck pride," I said.

Clare laughed. "You don't fuck pride," she said. "Pride fucks you. That's part of our problem. We think we can outsmart ourselves, but we're not nearly as smart as we think we are. And it's not about smarts, anyhow. Remember? Self-knowledge availed us nothing."

"Yeah," I said, "I know. Other people might have blind spots, but at least I can see mine, right? So what's the answer?"

Clare looked at me. "You know the answer."

"God?" I said, a word that never sits comfortably in my mouth.

"Unfortunately," she said with a smile.

"Then I'm really screwed," I said.

"We're all screwed," she said. "Time to stop fighting it. Raise the white flag."

"Surrender, acceptance, rosemary, and thyme," I said.

"It's the only answer," she said.

"I should have surrendered last night," I said.

"Neither of us exactly excels at surrendering until we've fired every last cannon," Clare said.

"So how do you surrender before the battle?"

"Same answer," she said.

"Ah, fuck," I said. "Yeah, that seems right."

"I'm not trying to be right," she said. "I'm trying to be better."

"I can't tell the difference," I said.

The first time I laid eyes on Doyle Claggart was in the parking lot of Cosmodemonic Unified Northwest Transit. The bus drivers parking section at Cosmodemonic was daily filled up with gargantuan pick-ups—row after row of these shiny, jacked-up monster trucks, invariably backed in, flashing their steely grills like Jurassic beasts ready to pounce.

As I was pulling my VW bug into an open slot on the day in question, the biggest truck I'd ever seen rumbled within inches of me, whipped a sharp left and slowly started backing into an open space nearby. The truck was festooned with Trump stickers, American flags, Celtic runes and gothic-looking bow hunting decals. On the back window was a tag that read "Oregunian."

I got out. Over the top of my bug, I watched as the driver of the truck opened his door slowly and lumbered backward onto a corrugated step. Grunting, he jump-hopped to the ground. He was a little fella, red faced, beady eyed, his body oddly pear shaped, giving him the appearance of a Weeble-Wobble. He heaved his backpack up and around his shoulders, shooting his arms through the straps, and finally turned in my direction.

I gave him a tentative head nod. He just looked at me, affectless, incurious, with the cold appraisal of an exterminator considering a cockroach. "Mornin'," he mumbled. Then he turned and trudged his way to the main building.

Cosmodemonic Unified Northwest Transit was filled to bursting with guys like him—salty, unsmiling motherfuckers, hard as bolts, dangerous as rattlesnakes, Oregunian Proud Boys, aggrieved and armed white men forever pissed at the world—but for some reason, he was the one that really got my goat. I hated him immediately.

Swim or Die

I'm at my annual employee review. My supervisor is looking at me from across the table. Looking for a long time, not speaking. At last he sighs and says, "You don't care about any of this, do you?"

"No," I say.

He smiles. "Well," he says with a chuckle, "okay then."

He proceeds to tell me that I am an excellent employee. I have a superb safety record, only one accident, as well as outstanding customer service skills. Only two customer complaints in more than four years. That's almost unheard of. I am a real benefit to the organization.

"And your appearance is … well, satisfactory," he says.

I scratch the stubble on my chin and smile. "I'm okay with that," I say. He isn't such a bad guy, my supervisor, all things considered—he's literate and hangdoggish, traits that recommended him to me. But also, like me, he's a bit of a mook.

One time, when he was serving me a warning letter for too many unexcused absences after I was twice pulled off the bus for those kidney stones—just total administrative bullshit—he actually admitted that I was, in this instance, a victim of bureaucratic error. In short, he confessed that I was being screwed by the system.

"So this is bullshit?" I said.

"Yeah," he said, holding out the letter for me to sign—a letter that would officially place me on a six-month probation. "I know it's kind of a Nuremberg defense," he added, "but I'm just doing my job here."

I stared at him. "Wow, that's an amazing thing to say, man," I said.

"Yeah, I know," he said. "It's just one of those things."

"But if it's just one of those things, why do it?" I asked.

"Look," he said. "It's no big deal. Just sign the letter, behave yourself for six months, and this all goes away like it never happened. Everybody gets put on letter at some point. It's just kinda standard operating procedure. Consider it a rite of passage," he joked.

"Yeah, but what happens if I screw up during the probation period?" I asked. "For instance, what if there's another mistake and I get screwed again? What then?"

"Well," he said, "then you get put on another letter for a nine-month probation, that's your second letter, and then after that there's another letter, that one's for a year probation, and then there's further corrective actions taken, like a suspension or some such, and then, with one more offense, you run the risk of termination, barring union intervention, of course."

"Jesus," I said. "Here. Give it here."

I signed the letter.

Because the magnificent henchman of this mechanism, the lapdogs of power, were the supervisors, whose putative purpose was to serve drivers, but whose real function was to police us like professional hall monitors—death by a thousand paper cuts.

Try as I might, I couldn't help but find supervisors almost invariably repellent. Sure, there was a handful of good eggs among them, but the great majority were nothing but wannabe cops—these sadistic micromanagers operating with delusions of hospitable grandeur who seemed to derive joy from power-tripping on drivers, often over the most picayune details.

They gave off the general stink of having failed the local police force's psychological exam, now relegated to a life of militant-lite.

These are the scariest people in any organization: the frustrated, second-career psychopaths. Supervisors at Cosmodemonic played the good cop/bad cop routine to perfection. They would buddy up to you, cracking jokes and reminiscing about their bygone years of driving the bus, and then they'd suddenly snap-to, eyeing you like the piece of shit they obviously thought you were, or berating you about some pointless misdemeanor like parking too close to the curb or leaving your hazards on.

In their defense, I suppose they themselves were in an untenable position, sandwiched like bad tuna between the cold, calculating demands of the administration at the top, and the contempt of the drivers from below. They were packing material, insulating the bosses from drivers while also making sure we children stayed in line.

Just like everybody at Cosmodemonic Unified Northwest Transit, they were driven by fear, anxiety, and paranoia. It can't be easy. It can't be easy to be a supervisor. It can't be easy to be a cop.

But also: Fuck you, it was your choice to become a cop. I mean, really?

CHIP ON SHOULDER

Another time, after I'd nicked a stop sign with my mirror during a sharp turn, my supervisor made a road call to inspect the damage. He and I stood outside the bus, looking at the mirror. "I don't really see anything serious," he said.

There was definitely a notch taken out of the plastic casing around the mirror. It wasn't much, but it was certainly visible. I pointed to it. "I think that might be me," I said.

He stood up on his tiptoes and looked at it for a second. "Well," he said. "Maybe … I'll take a picture of it, check the video, and get back to you."

"Sounds good to me," I said. I didn't care one way or the other. It wasn't a fireable offense, not even close, and I'd given up sweating about anything but keeping my passengers safe and avoiding vehicular homicide. That was stressful enough. All the rest of it was noise.

The next day at the station, as I was awaiting my depar-ture time, my supervisor went cruising past my open door. He seemed in a hurry to get somewhere.

But suddenly he stopped short, as though struck by revelation. He turned back and approached my door. "Yesterday never happened," he said.

"Excuse me?"

"Yesterday," he said. "That thing. It never happened."

"Cool," I said.

He gave me a thumbs up and kept moving.

Rewind: I was brought to life and yanked upright and given my kicks at the blurry intersection where rural white trash muddling meets upstart bourgeois respectability.

One side of my family, my mother's side, were gut-it-out country types: women who stayed home and raised a brood of children, and men who earned their hard living on the land, in the water and up trees in the Pacific Northwest—as fishermen, loggers, carpenters, mill workers.

My father's side of the family, Norwegian immigrants, entered this nation clad in plaid and bootstrapped by the Washington timber industry, and yet they aspired to, and for the most part achieved, a standard of living that wavered hazily between the heat of middle-class attainment and the humid chuckle of upper-crust entitlement. Racism was rampant on both sides of the family, as was a fierce loyalty to place.

The working life and family fealty were paramount; everything else, including matters of the spirit, was merely pastime.

From as early as I can remember, I feared that I was a fraud among these stolid, stoical people. I was neither the one nor the other—too heady and swishily romantic to be a proper mountain man, and too ill-born and uncharming to win friends and influence the people who might pave the path to my professional success.

When I was around my mother's kin, I suspected they thought I was a little pussy—just this scrawny, geeky, dreamy kid who read too much and had trouble finding his way home from his own backyard.

And when I was in the company of my father's family, with its prominently displayed bone china and brown liquor in chipped crystal decanters, I struggled in vain to interpret the languages of high finance and sexual hijinks, feeling that I was, and would forever be, an imposter mired in the chaotic flux of childish things.

Other things they don't teach you in training:

That in the eleventh hour of your sixth straight day of twelve hour shifts, you will stop at a red light and your bus will start drifting backward. You will pump the air brakes to no avail. Panic will set in. You will flip the emergency brake and consider bailing from the vehicle, until you realize you are only hallucinating. Nothing is moving.

You have spent so many hours propelling yourself forward without a break that this sudden halting of movement fools your brain into manufacturing a reverse zoom shot, as the world pulls away from you in slow motion. Even when you're not going forward, you go forward.

It is said that sharks keep swimming in their sleep, lest they die. There's an analogy here worthy of Karl Marx, but I can't for the life of me figure it out right now.

A hard stop on a bus traveling a mere 15 miles an hour generates enough raw momentum to throw a grown adult across space with such uncanny speed and centripetal violence that they seem less to fly than to vanish altogether.

I learned this the hard way. Within days of starting training, they put us behind the wheel of an actual bus—I imagine with the same general philosophy that compels certain parents to toss their toddler into the deep end of the pool.

Swim, or die.

I was driving down the road. The rest of my classmates were seated behind me, and my trainer stood casually in the aisle, holding the pole and chatting.

It's hard to express how scared I was those first days of training—actually, the whole first year of driving. Are you kidding me? Wheeling a 40-foot metal rectangle with the turning radius of a frigate down streets full of traffic? With people aboard? Give me a break.

I am prone to panic. Always have been. It's a disposition I inherited from my father, a child of the Cuban Missile Crisis and Cold War fallout shelters whose anxious mind automatically jumped to the most disastrous potential consequence in every situation. I suffered perpetual whiplash throughout my childhood, the result of my father slamming on the car brakes to avoid another phantom disaster unfolding in his peripheral vision.

And so, therefore, when that bicyclist pulled up beside me during my training run, seemingly out of thin air, my reptilian brain fired a flare into my tender limbic system and I jumped on that brake so hard my knee popped.

As though in a dream, I watched my trainer sail past my right shoulder and plaster himself against the windshield. Splat. I'm still amazed the glass didn't shatter, and I'm even more amazed I wasn't terminated on the spot. I figured my career was over. Stay off the road, kid. You're a menace.

Go back to picking nits on a newspaper.

But I should be so lucky. They kept me. Cosmodemonic needed drivers. Mistakes happen.

I never made a sudden stop like that again. I'd learned my lesson, just as I've learned every lesson in life—the hard way, through shame, and usually at someone else's expense.

As I pulled into the station, I saw another bus sitting in my bay. It was five minutes until the next departure time and I had a vehicle full of passengers, most of them already standing up to deboard.

Not sure what to do in such a case, I pulled a little tighter to the curb, set the parking brake, flipped the hazards and waited. The natives were getting restless. A couple of riders started pushing aggressively against the exit doors.

"Hey, let us off the bus!" somebody hollered.

"I gotta catch the 41!" somebody else shouted.

"This is bullshit! I gotta make my transfer!"

I picked up the receiver and triggered the intercom.

"Folks," I said, "I've got another bus laying over in my designated bay, and I'm not sure what's going on, so we're just gonna have to wait for it to depart and I'll drop you off as fast as I can. Shouldn't be but a second … um … thanks for your patience."

"Fuck that! Lemme off this bus!" Somebody started pounding harder on the rear exit, setting off the alarm in a constant staccato. Beep beep beep beeeeeeeeeep.

The bus parked in my bay wasn't showing the slightest sign of moving any time soon. The thing wasn't even running. The clamor on the bus was growing riotous.

I considered my options and finally made an executive decision, despite the fact that I was still on nine-month probation. I picked up the intercom again. "Okay, folks," I said. "I'm going to let you off here. Be really careful. Please watch your step as you get off the bus."

I lowered the chassis and checked my side-view mirrors, and then threw open the doors. The passengers poured off in clumps, pushing and shoving each other, a couple of them mumbling "thank you" or, inversely, "asshole." I watched as they ran to make their various connections.

I picked up the receiver again and called Ops, letting them know someone was laying over in my bay. Within a matter of seconds, I saw one of the drivers run out of the lounge, waving apologetically to me as she hopped aboard. She started the thing up and drove away.

I pulled into my designated bay and shut the bus down. I got out of the seat and moved toward the door to enjoy what was left of my five-minute layover.

Doyle Claggart was standing directly in front of me, arms folded. Expressionless. I pushed open the door and faced him. He was effectively blocking my way.

"Where'd you come from?" I said.

"That wasn't a good move," he said. "Dangerous."

"Excuse me?" I said.

"You shouldn't deboard riders unless you're at your bay," he said. "It's a lawsuit waiting to happen."

"There was somebody in my bay, and I had a busload of people needing to make transfers," I said. "The clock was ticking. I made sure it was safe and took the initiative … and, anyway, where were you five minutes ago?"

"Watching," he said.

"You were watching?" I said. "Instead of helping? While I was having a near mutiny on my bus?"

Claggert smirked. "It's not my job to tell you how to do your job," he said.

"Apparently it is," I said.

He didn't respond.

"So what is your job, then?" I asked.

"Same as yours," he said. "Ensuring the safety and security of our passengers."

"Ironic," I said. I glared at him and then looked away. "Anything else, Doyle?"

When I looked back for an answer, he was already walking away.

When people ask me what it's like to drive a bus, here's one of the things I tell them: I have worked a million jobs. I have scrubbed out butcher shops and mopped bakeries, bagged groceries and jerked espresso for smug college students. I have been a smug college student, paying my tuition through landscaping jobs and fast food gigs. I have picked baby's breath in the arid fields of eastern Washington and thinned apples in the Wenatchee Valley.

I ran the skiff on my grandfather's commercial fishing boat in the San Juan Islands and gutted salmon on processing barges on the Bering Sea.

I've worked in a bookstore and stocked shelves at night for a bougie food co-op in Seattle.

For some twenty years, I was a reporter, critic, and editor at various independent newspapers, turning reality into palatable lies on an endless deadline. And for every job mentioned here, there were likely half a dozen more that I no longer remember, nor care to.

And yet for all that—for all the toil and poverty, the exhaustion and boredom, the long hours and looming deadlines, the steep corporate learning curves and bullshit office politics, for all the blood, sweat, and bitter tears—for all that, bus driving is hands down the most difficult job I've ever had.

It levies a tax that is insupportable and ultimately unpayable, draining every account you possess, without recourse: physical, emotional, psychological, sexual, spiritual.

It pushes you to the frazzled limits of your humanity. It gobbles your life and spits out time plus movement.

Zero Hour

pull my express bus into the downtown station. Early Saturday morning, late spring, clear outside but cold, crispy.

I have a brief layover, so I engage the parking brake and step outside to stretch my body. I move a few feet away from the bus to hit my vape.

There's a guy standing nearby on the sidewalk, leaning against the wall—a tall fellow, greasy hair, missing two teeth right in front.

"How's it going, brother?" I say.

He looks at me and grimaces. "Meh," he says.

"Bad day?"

"Yeah," he says. "You could say that."

"I'm sorry."

"Yeah," he says. "I think I found somebody's dump site."

At first I figure he's talking about a trash pile outside one of the tent cities in town, then I wonder if perhaps he's fingering a drug stash. But I quickly flush both thoughts, because, actually, I know exactly what he's talking about.

"You mean, like, a body?"

He offers me a dark look and nods, once. "Yeah," he says.

"Jesus."

"It looks to be pretty old," he says. "Been there a long time."

"You should call that in, man," I say. "It can be an anonymous call, right? I mean, somebody might be looking for the guy."

"Or gal," he adds.

"Right. Either way."

He glances off to the east for a moment, ruminating. "I don't know," he says. "Maybe. Maybe. It's a fucked up situation either way."

"Okay," I say. "Well, I gotta run. Good luck, man. I'd think about that anonymous call."

He shrugs. "Yeah," he says, distractedly, hefting his duffel bag up off the pavement. "I don't know."

He lumbers off toward the intersection.

I step onto the bus, hop in the seat, belt up and ding the trolley bell, letting folks know we're about to leave. I close the doors, disengage the parking brake, punch the beast in gear and check my mirrors.

Directly across from me on the opposite sidewalk I watch a woman in a wheelchair motor past three teenage kids in an alcove smoking drugs off a tiny slab of tin foil.

I signal and pull into traffic.

I myself have sat in that alcove and I have smoked all the drugs. I was a blackout alcoholic and then, later, an opium addict, for the better part of three decades. I would like to say that I was of the functional variety, a debonair drunk and a gentleman junkie, maintaining a reasonable facsimile of respectability, but there is no such thing as functional addiction. Yes, you may—unlike the kids in the alcove—keep your job, hold onto a relationship, avoid sleeping outdoors, generally fool everyone around you—but not really.

Because the thing that is dying is not indicated by the things you lose. It is inside you. You lose yourself.

Hitting bottom wasn't about having the worst thing I could imagine finally happen to me. It wasn't about going as low as I could go. I'd gone so low so many times that I'd dug a tunnel right through eternity. After a while I'd just ball myself up like a pill bug and roll back and forth through that endless tunnel, to heaven and hell and back again.

The idea of bottoming out became meaningless. I couldn't give a fuck. Decked out like some junkie friar in the rags of my own disbelief, I made my daily pilgrimage through the wormhole of time. It was all the same to me. I was seeking the fetal truth of no faith, trying to get back to a place I'd never been, some nostalgic recollection of a life never actually lived.

Oblivion was a theory I teased out with the postulate of my inaction, testing death against the carnality of being. Down implies up, and I'd given up completely on the whole notion of upward mobility, betterment, becoming, blossoming. Progress of any sort struck me as a monstrous farce.

Everything simply moved around me, and dragged me with it. The needle on my moral compass had been plucked out—I used it to shoot up. I shot the works. Shoot the moon, baby, and resurrect the dead day. Disbelief was my religion. Despair owned me. I had the momentum of no momentum.

The bottom I hit was not a place, nor was it a situation. There were no loud crashes, no flying shrapnel. No—my bottom wasn't about winding up in a place I decidedly did not belong. It was about running out of time. My bottom was the bottom of the hourglass: Zero Hour.

So I gave up the ghost. I threw in the towel. And yet my physical form remained, a corporeal reality clinging to me with its hungers intact, yammering in a filthy alcove in the pitch-black dawn.

"Fuck these homeless kids," bus drivers say. "Fuck these meth heads. Fuck these bums."

"You know," I say, "that used to be me. I used to be strung out. It's true. In fact, you might have driven me around back then. And look at me now."

"Bullshit," they say, but then they look at me funny.

The irony of this is not lost on me. I've traded the time of no time for the no time of time. Same difference, quoth the raven.

I think a lot about Travis Bickle. I get migraines. I pray for a big rain.

Even before I became a bus driver, some of the worst moments of my life involved buses.

The first incident—my original bus trauma, you might call it—happened my senior year in high school. Normally I'd drive myself and my girlfriend to school, along with assorted friends from the neighborhood, but on the day in question it was snowing. Like, a lot—a rare occurrence for the Key Peninsula, but there it was, a real blizzard.

A good foot-and-a-half of snow was already banked against the front door by the time I woke up in the morning. I knew my little blue Toyota wasn't going to cut it. My girlfriend Rachel's family lived a half mile from our house, so I called her and told her she better catch the bus today.

I'll save you a seat, I said. Kisses.

The bus ride from our neck of the woods—a tip of land pressing out into the Puget Sound—to our high school was long and circuitous, ending with a stretch of travel along a bit of rural highway before arriving at campus. The whole trip that day was a slog. It must have been a nightmare for the driver, but none of us noticed. We gazed out the window, dreaming, as the bus chugged and fishtailed around town. When we finally merged onto the highway, things slowed even more, to a mere crawl. Traffic was being forced into the right lane, and at this point I took notice.

I was sitting on the left side of the bus, near the window, with Rachel on my right. Things got very, very quiet. The bus rumbled gently forward. I craned my neck and saw this gorgeous red-orange glow flashing in the big front windshield, snowflakes threading their way ever forward as though being birthed by a supernova before bursting and immediately disappearing in the swish of the wipers. A sensation of gliding through deep space. The glow enveloped us like a living thing, we were swallowed up in light.

"Holy shit," I heard the kid in front of us gasp. His nose was pressed against the window. I looked. I'm looking now, into my memory, and here's what I see: A Lincoln Town Car, its entire top sheared clean off, while in the driver's seat sits a large man with his head nearly severed from his neck, as paramedics swarm the car. His body is ramrod straight, spasming, as though frozen in an effort to leap from the car.

Time stops. I see every detail.

And then time starts again, palpably slamming back into gear. Everything speeds up. The whole bus leans hard to the left, as kids jump out of their seats to gawk out the window like they're rushing the stage at a concert.

"What?" Rachel says. "What is it?"

She rises from her seat to look over me and out the window, but I put my hand on her chest and push her back into the seat, hard.

"Don't look," I say. My voice stopped her dead. She stared at me. I looked straight ahead. She took my hand.

I don't remember a thing about the entire following week.

I lived in Oaxaca for a year. This was four women before Clare ago, three women before I finally stopped drinking for good.

Jill and I had rented an apartment just a few blocks from the zócalo. We had nothing but money and time on our hands. Oaxaca is a place that gets into your pores. It will meet you halfway, wherever you are, providing an abundance of joy or, in equal measure, a corrosive dose of death, depending on your orientation. I was stuck halfway between.

In one of our several abortive attempts to resuscitate a dying relationship, we took a trip down to San Cristobal de las Casas. We spent most of the morning before we caught the bus running errands, including me sneaking off to score some Valium for the long ride over the mountains.

As we were approaching the entrance to the villa on the sidewalk, our hands loaded with bags, a rickety city bus came careening down the busy cobbled street, coughing black exhaust as it approached the intersection in front of our place.

There were three kids horsing around on the sidewalk across from us, probably twelve- or thirteen-year-olds. As the bus spun right around the corner, the driver passed too tight against the side of the tienda, literally smearing one of the kids against the wall. I'll never forget the sound of his friends screaming his name.

As folks rushed to the scene, I watched the bus continue down the street.

When that relationship ended, I was devastated in a way I'd never quite experienced before. We cut our stay in Mexico short and flew home, without really mentioning what was going on. We were both exhausted and homesick, or at least that's what we told each other.

In Seattle, we stayed with a friend for a week, pretending to carry on, pretending to regain our footing, again without any definite plans. She decided one day to fly home to the Midwest to visit her family for a few days.

She never came back.

It was a brutal severance, and I don't blame her one bit. I was a real burnt-out case. I couldn't tell today from tomorrow from yesterday. I had a head full of disaster fantasies curated into romance by dope.

I became an emotional zombie. I couldn't even conjure enough energy to feel self-pity, typically one of my strongest suits. I floated through existence, flattened, a scrap of paper blown around by the weak breezes that send dust bunnies to rest under couches. I had a small chunk of money, so I rented a studio apartment, got a job filing grants for an environmental organization, and I merely existed.

I didn't actively avoid the company of friends. There was no effort in my banishment. It just was. I drank, but there was no passion behind it.

I rode the bus everywhere, sitting in the seat, staring out the window, watching the fog of my breath make blots against the glass. I became one of those peculiar men who watches the scenery pass by, not moving, not reading a book, just looking. I was 33, the age of Christ crucified, on my way to Golgotha.

Every evening after work and a couple drinks at the pub around the corner, I'd hop the bus home. And every evening, like clockwork, she'd get on the bus two stops later—yes, this raven-haired art student from the university, dressed all in black, emanating waves of fuck-off that I found delectable. She carried a cello in a black cloth case. She'd set the instrument on the seat beside her and rode with her right arm draped around it. I fell in love with her, this gorgeous cliché, this figment of my delirium.

Every cell in my body yearned for her, reaching out—not for sex, not for love, not even for a kiss, but simply for this grievous angel to smile at me, demurely, knowingly, as in my vision she straddles a three-legged stool, her black gown flowing around her legs, and plays a passage from Bartok's cello concerto in B minor, for me alone, after which I expire in a romantic solitary death, the shoddy movie of my life redeemed before the credits roll. The end.

She became my obsession, and the bus became the theater of the greatest loneliness I'd ever experienced in my life, playing itself out to the last quivering note. She never once looked at me, and I never caught her eye. Likely I gave off a stink of desperation, detectable even half a bus away.

Or, more likely, she had no cause to notice me. Either way, I never broached the subject with her. I was content to suffer in silence, my love unconsummated; in fact, nothing else would do. I could feel the cocoon being knit around me.

One evening as I was gazing at the back of her head, I felt a wetness on my cheek. I reached up and wiped it away.

Not too many nights later, I found myself once again at the bar around the corner from work, sitting in front of my third shot of whiskey. It was getting time to catch my bus—if I was going to see her, that is—but then this cute butch lesbian sat down beside me and we started talking.

Word by word she goaded me out of myself. Back and forth

we went. The time to catch my bus passed, and still we kept talking.

Every now and then she'd throw a shoulder into me, gently. I opened up a bit about the reality of my life and, hearing the words coming out of my mouth, I all at once realized just how dire things had gotten.

"Yo, buddy," she said. "Are you, like, okay?"

I grabbed my shot glass by the rim and twisted it back and forth against the bar. "I just realized that I haven't actually physically touched another human being in, like, a year and a half," I said.

She was silent for a moment. Then she pushed herself back from the bar, slid off her stool, took a step back and squared up to face me. "C'mere," she said, holding out her arms.

I obeyed. I stood in front of her.

"No," she said, cupping her hands inward. "C'mere, dumb ass."

I took a step toward her. She wrapped me in a massive bear hug. Her body odor filled my nostrils. She squeezed harder, dropping her head against my shoulder. Every possible point of contact was achieved.

I put my arms around her and hugged back. My legs went gooey. An embryonic warmth surged upward from the deepest part of me. Inside-out and outside-in became indistinguishable. There was nothing at all erotic about it, this big lesbian bear hug, and yet it was an incredibly sensual experience. I doubt Lazarus had a more stunning resurrection.

Finally we unclasped. She slugged me on the shoulder with the side of her fist. "How was that?" she asked. "Feel better?"

"That was … amazing," I said. "I had no idea how much I needed that."

"Yeah," she said. "Hugs are pretty cool."

"Thank you," I said. "I mean, seriously. Thank you."

"Ah," she said, "think nothing of it. Any time. Happy to help."

I woke up the next morning. Made a pot of coffee, poured

myself a cup. Put on some sweatpants and clumped downstairs and outside my apartment for a smoke. As I lit the cigarette, I said aloud to myself, "I'm all better now."

The words came without a thought. Yet the moment I said it, it became true. I felt my life open up again—not as a new, better life, free of pain and suffering, but as a regular old life.

I was once again free. Free to feel, free to fail.

It was my therapist who pointed out the irony of my becoming a bus driver after a fairly significant history of bus-related traumas. It took me off guard. "That's mighty Freudian of you," I said. "I thought we'd done away with old Sigmund."

"Just an observation," she said. "I didn't mean anything by it."

"And women," I said.

She frowned for a moment, and then nodded. "Yes, women," she said.

"Women and buses," I said. "Women and buses and heartbreak and death. It sounds like a John Prine song."

She smiled. I doubted she knew who John Prine was, but it didn't matter. I wanted to keep talking.

"I was in this disastrous long-distance relationship back in college," I started. "Real Syd and Nancy stuff, we just tore each other apart. But we couldn't seem to stay away from each other, either. Around and around and around. Talk about losing your fucking innocence. I mean, I think we were both insane, I know I was, but I felt drawn into this impossible riddle that I had to solve no matter how crazy it made me. I couldn't let it go. Anyhow, we broke up about five thousand times, and this one time, early on, I was literally halfway through a visit with her when I just left in the middle of the night during a fight. I felt horrible, just totally desperate, and I didn't really want to leave, but I didn't see any other option at the moment. It felt like I was possessed. So I stomped to the Greyhound station in the dark and caught a midnight bus and rode that fuckin' thing from San Francisco to

Seattle. There is nothing lonelier than an 18-hour bus trip up the I-5 corridor with a broken heart and a head full of crazy."

"Why crazy?" she asked. "It sounds like pretty standard young love to me. We're all full of unsorted big feelings in our early twenties. Lots of people's first or second relationships can be pretty tumultuous."

I thought about that for a second.

"I like it when I tell you something about myself that seems really fucked up to me, and you tell me it's not unusual. I'm, I don't know, honestly grateful for that kind of information, I guess is what I'm saying. What I don't understand is that, on the one hand, I have all this anxious attachment, as you call it, and then on the other hand I have this amazing talent for burning things to the ground."

"Those aren't mutually exclusive responses, necessarily," she said with a smile. "We all have lots of parts."

"I'm terrified I'm a pathological narcissist," I said.

"A pathological narcissist wouldn't wonder about that," she said.

"Still," I said.

"Possessing narcissistic traits doesn't mean you're a full-blown narcissist," she said. "The incidence of narcissistic personalities is actually pretty rare."

"I'm all I think about most of the time," I said. "Which is funny for a person that doesn't seem to think that much of himself."

"You really feel that way?"

"No," I said, "not really. I'm just talking crap. But I honestly have no idea what it means to love oneself. Love yourself? What does that even mean? All this love-yourself shit these days kind of makes my ass pucker."

"What sort of things do you do to self-soothe, then?"

"Self-soothe? I don't know. I know what I used to do, but that doesn't really work anymore. Drinking is sort of off the table from here on out. I don't know what I do these days. Meditate, I guess, sometimes. Masturbate."

"Why don't you try giving yourself a hug," she said.

"You're kidding, right?"

She raised her eyebrows and shrugged.

"Okay, what the hell," I said. I sat up on the couch and wrapped my arms around myself.

"How does that feel?" my therapist asked.

"Better, I guess," I said. "It's nothing dramatic, but I feel a little calmer, I think. It's nice."

"Dramatic is an expectation," she said. "Very few things change all at once. It's about gestures and habits. It's about a process. Dramatic isn't realistic, or even necessarily desirable."

"I get that," I said. "Not the journey, but the destination."

"Sure," she said. "Something like that."

"I just thought of another bus story," I said.

Clare and I got married on the cheap. We rented the local grange hall for a couple hundred bucks, enlisted friends to provide music and help with the decorations, volunteered someone with an internet-acquired license to perform the ceremony, and asked guests to bring homemade items for a potluck dinner during the reception.

Not only did this pleasantly demolish everyone's expectations, but it kept our family members busy and off our backs. Everyone enjoyed themselves. It was a lovely day.

We also forbid anyone to buy wedding gifts, but a friend, unbeknownst to us, set out a donation bucket near the entrance to the hall and we came away with a big chunk of cash.

Two days later we flew to Mexico City, on what I hesitate even now to call a honeymoon—not because it was awful, but because it was so perfect. It felt less like a celebration than a confirmation. Travel, in general, seems to be a real litmus test for new relationships. More often than not, it's a deal-breaker, as the lovebirds discover that whatever simpatico they've established in familiar surroundings translates very poorly abroad—needs and desires get jumbled up in transit, passions decommissioned, treaties broken, and suddenly you're sitting across from a very annoying stranger about to throw a guidebook at your head.

Not Clare and I. We were like Eve and Adam in the Garden of Eden before the Tree of Knowledge became a significant bonding issue—full of innocent, wide-eyed wonder. One day, we decided to visit the pyramids at Teotihuacan. We hopped a bus—a bus named Teotihuacan, no less—and took our seats.

I'd been to the pyramids before, so I was thrilled for Clare to see them. My recollection was that it was a quick trip, about thirty minutes or so, but as the bus rattled down unfamiliar streets, stopping here and there to pick up riders, I began to get antsy.

"This doesn't seem right," I said.

"Why not?" Clare said, looking out the window. "Seems right to me. This is amazing."

The trip took more than an hour and a half, because, rather than getting on the express, we'd boarded the regular old city bus instead. We'd inadvertently evicted ourselves as tourists, joining instead the everyday flow of life on the outskirts of Mexico City. That this bus went to the pyramids was merely incidental. Buy the ticket, take the ride.

The bus wound through neighborhood after neighborhood, picking up and dropping off passengers, motoring on Mexican time, bumping down the road until at last our bones settled securely into our flesh, and time took on the carefree, shifting dimensions of a dream. Clare and I sat silently, gazing out at the passing scenery.

By the time we rolled up on the pyramids, it felt as though we'd been prepared—properly prepared to behold these ancient monuments, not as something worthy of a postcard, but as a living part of the landscape, the past incorporated into the present, mysterious and ordinary all at once.

"So that's a good bus memory," she said, smiling. "Not traumatic at all."

"I'm not sure why I told you that whole story," I said.

"Do you do that a lot?"

"What?" I said.

"Question why you tell somebody something," she said.

"Yeah, all the time," I said. "I walk away from most conversations wondering what the fuck was that all about anyway? I'll start talking breathlessly, as though it's the most important thing in the world, and then afterward I immediately wonder if I've just exposed myself as a blithering idiot. I feel like Scheherazade with a time bomb shoved up my ass."

Samsara

Bus drivers, like taxi drivers, are society's great crank philosophers. We have an opinion on everything. We see a fuck-ton of fucked-up shit, and we have a fuck-load of time to think about the shit we see—although thinking might be the wrong term.

Thinking, even shallow thinking, implies some level of processing and sorting, and bus drivers don't have time for that nonsense. Our brain activity is almost entirely absorbed by the constant vigilance required of driving, and when you combine this with the repetitive trauma we experience in the unceasing act of navigating this broken social scene, there is very little room left for a deep dive into existential or epistemological considerations.

We are, instead, brute ontologists. We are bunk sociologists. We sweep things briskly into broad categories, the easier to sort them. Cause and effect get collapsed and hammered flat, the one subsuming the other in a monolithic pancake of tyrannical reckonings.

People are idiots. The homeless suck. The kids have no manners, they need a good whuppin'. Fuck the poor. Fuck the rich. Fuck the administration. Fuck the libtards. Exterminate the brutes.

Most people either don't understand or can't stomach the language we use to express our reactive thoughts, or rather our non-thoughts, and so we routinely express them to each other in a round chorale of incessant complaints.

We are grievance artists, and we sing to each other, loudly, in a minor key. An annihilating lullaby, a torch song that anneals and annexes our own psychic pain. This creates a massively reductive echo chamber, and it's a fantastic risk to step outside this choir and try out a different tune, in a new key—to offer an alternative take on anything. Soldiers on the battlefield cannot afford dissension within their ranks. It's a question of life or death, baby.

Ours is not to reason why, ours is but to do or die. Toe the line, shitbird.

Mind you, in no way am I saying, nor do I even secretly believe, that most bus drivers are stupid. That would be ridiculous. We aren't any dumber than your average American. But we are losers. "Good morning, losers," one of my colleagues was fond of saying, adding, "I mean, we must have failed at something to be here. We're all two screws short of a good chair."

So we swallow and digest and eventually come to resemble and replicate the bigotry leveled at the working class to which most of us have been relegated since well before birth.

No, bus drivers are not stupid—but most of us secretly suspect we must be in some disastrous way, because we've obviously blown it at the game of life. Nobody grows up wanting to be a bus driver; it's a job for Lego people and high school dropouts.

Yes, we've failed, so here we are. And because of this suspicion, and because it's as deeply unbearable to confront as a mortal curse, we tend to punch down, blaming someone or something else for the frustrations of our plight, typically a target selected from some demographic positioned a notch or two lower on the social ladder—someone to scapegoat and excoriate for the condition of our indecipherable internment in an economic system we continue to believe in and worship like a religion, all evidence of its own apocalyptic failings to the contrary. Livin' the dream—even if it's someone else's dream.

Or nightmare.

Yes, I jettisoned a 25-career year in journalism to become a bus driver. I couldn't sit in an office any more, I couldn't attend one more pointless planning meeting, I couldn't engage with one more reactionary jackass who'd discovered politics at the crossroads where disenfranchisement and fear shake hands with ideology and homicidal anger. Call it a midlife crisis: I wanted to get back to my hereditary roots, which are grounded in tangible, physical blue-collar labor.

That the work I chose might also be a form of public service was definitely a plus. I needed a shock to the system, and I wanted to do some good. I needed to scare myself, and perhaps to prove something—even if all I proved, in the end, was that my lifelong ability to wrap bad decisions in the fraudulent gilt of virtue remains irrevocably intact.

I will drive the bus for the people, I told my friends, most of whom received this information with a touching combination of bemusement, support, and bafflement.

But all of that is bullshit, actually.

The truth is I'd been looking to jump ship on the newspaper gig for years, but a combination of cowardice and comfort prevented me from committing myself to a lateral move that would pay the same salary I was now making with a minimum of effort. The truth is that a dear friend of mine was training as a bus driver and, knowing I was unhappily employed, he urged me to apply, with a refrain I would hear over and over and over and over again: The benefits are great!

So with the helium-headed swoon of a kid perched on a high dive, I pushed that icky feeling aside and stepped from the secure platform of my former life, free-falling into a pool I could only hope was just deep enough that I didn't hit bottom and shatter to pieces.

It started as an ache in my lower back. Adjusting my seat, I pumped air into the lower lumbar cushion and drove on. Back problems aren't new to me. I figured I could push through the final two hours of my day, after which I would go home, pop a couple Tylenol, do some YouTube yoga, take a hot bubble bath and kick it on the couch until bed.

The ache, however, soon sprouted tentacles. It spiraled outward from my sciatic nerve and began to squeeze my midsection like a boa constrictor, grabbing my ribs and compressing them inward until the warm ache combined with a sharp, stinging stab into my guts.

At some point, the pain cut loose from all moorings, becoming a generalized agony that was impossible to isolate in any one place. Things began to happen that I'd only read about. Sweat beaded on my forehead. I moaned involuntarily. A surge of vomit snaked into my throat.

And yet I drove on. There is no weakness in bus driving! My peripheral vision narrowed to a tight tunnel, and I had difficulty depressing the gas and brake pedals. The slightest movement of my right leg sent a thunderbolt of excruciating hurt through my entire body. *My appendix is about to burst,* I thought to myself with alarm.

And then I thought, with the defiance of a dying man: *I am not going to die while driving this bus. Je refuse!*

At the next scheduled stop, I picked up the receiver and beeped Ops. "You guys have got to get me off this bus," I said, noting in a crevice of my brain that, despite the reality of my circumstances, I was still attempting to sound convincingly sick.

"I can't drive this thing anymore," I added breathlessly. "I'm really in pain here."

"Can you make it to the station?"

No fucking way, I thought. "Yeah," I said. "I can do that."

I have no idea how I made it to the station, or from there home. It's all a big blur. From my living room floor, I called a friend, asking for a lift to the hospital. I had her drop me at the door of the emergency room like a gunshot victim.

I vaguely recall pacing the waiting room floor, shivering and moaning exactly like one of those emergency room people you watch out of the corner of your eye, wondering what the hell could be wrong.

The nurse found me on all fours, retching onto the linoleum.

"Ah, yes," she said. "I'd know kidney stones anywhere." She

helped me up, her hand wrapped gently into the crook of my arm. She led me through the magic curtains into that place where pain is washed away forever. One hopes, one prays.

In a hospital gown, my bare ass crinkling against the paper, I lay back in the bed and gazed at the wonderful sterility of the scene surrounding me—a blindingly bright geometric diorama celebrating the best of what our Enlightenment has to offer. Machines that breathe for you. Tubes that feed you. Syringes that deliver drugs that bring deep sighs. All of it administered by human beings who have taken an oath first and foremost to not hurt me, ever.

"There you go," the nurse said, inserting the needle into my arm. "You're almost there," she said. She patted my leg.

Almost instantaneously, there appeared through the curtains at the foot of my hospital bed a vision of such celestial beauty and benevolence that I shivered. My head fell back on the pillow.

She sailed toward me, wafted by a heavenly breeze, her face seeming lit from below by a gauzy Hollywood light. She was very pregnant, her blue-green cotton scrubs stretched to bursting. At last she bent over me and offered a smile of such reassurance that I no longer cared whether I lived or died.

"Kidney stones, eh?" she whispered.

I grunted and rolled my eyes.

"Yeah," she said. "Had 'em. I'd rather give birth any day. Worst pain I've ever had."

I almost started crying. "Thank you," I croaked.

"Let's get you feeling a little better," she said, poking a syringe into my IV and gently pushing the plunger. "There," she said. I felt a tickle of unbelievable pleasure start at the tippy-top of my head before it flowed downward in a spreading embrace of pure bliss.

Dilaudid. The Haagen-Dazs of painkillers, my drug dealer once said. I closed my eyes and let go.

The silicone stent that was inserted into my urethra after kidney stone surgery ran from the back of my bladder to the very tip of my dick. Its job was to prop open the urinary tract, ensur-ing easier passage for the jagged little asteroids of calcium that resulted from laser-blasting the big stone lodged in my ureter.

The surgeon had also been forced to go in manually and grab one of the stones with some kind of snaky bionic device mounted with a microscopic camera on the end—I imagined one of those claw machines at the state fair where you drop down with a joystick and try to haul in a stuffed animal from a pile of stuffed animals. Fun! Prizes! Step right up!

Two trips to the emergency room, followed by a week off for the surgery itself, had completely tapped out my sick time, so I was forced to drive the bus with that stent inside me. Forced—only the working poor know what this word really means. No, nobody is holding a gun to your head, and you are free to call out sick. And free to starve.

So you crunch the numbers, look at your mortgage, calcu-late your medical bills, calibrate the rising cost of living, and you realize that, once again, you can either work sick, or heal up and go broke.

Like most people, I opted for the former, once again proving in a very personal and convincing manner the Buddhist concept of samsara—the notion that short-term solutions, poorly chosen in a panic, only lead to greater destruction in the long term.

The real issue was peeing. The stent did its job with extraor-dinary efficiency—such efficiency, in fact, that it permanently wedged open the sphincter involved in shutting off the flow of urine back into the system.

What this means in praxis is that, the moment your flow stops, you receive what feels like a slow-motion heavyweight punch to the kidneys as urine backwashes into your guts.

The surgeon had warned me about this, but there was no preparing me for the first time I took a leak after surgery. As the last dribble of piss left my dick, a hot cannonball of pain pushed my innards against my pelvic floor.

It wasn't as nasty and sharp as the pain of passing the stones themselves, but it was just bad enough that I lived in abject fear of pissing that entire week. I had to stand at the urinal with one hand braced against the wall, lest I double over upon impact.

A couple of my colleagues mentioned offhandedly that maybe I should file for federal medical leave—the motto among drivers being "always cover your ass," 'cuz the company sure as hell won't—but nobody from administration or middle management at Cosmodemonic approached me about this, as was their legal duty. I would only learn all this later, after the damage had been done.

The human resources department was a running joke among drivers; there were times when it was unclear that anyone was staffing the department at all. So, stupidly, I played it as it laid, and figured I'd scrape by, as usual, through a combination of grit and belt-tightening. Goodbye Netflix, hello Top Ramen!

The stent itself was moderately uncomfortable. It was just there, reminding me of itself, like a bad urinary tract infection. There wasn't a moment that whole week of driving the bus when I wasn't aware of something very foreign happening in my reproductive region.

And here's the kicker: After I was hired and before I even entered training, that friend of mine was terminated. Coming back inbound at night on his first rural run to the mountains and back, he hit the Blue River off-ramp at freeway speed, not realizing that the exit cuts quick and hard to the right.

Instead of slamming on the brakes, that ballsy son-of-a-bitch power slid a forty-foot city bus into the gravel without flipping it or seriously injuring any of his passengers. It was the stuff of legend. The video footage of his wipeout became a staple of new-recruit training—a cautionary tale for the lead-footed.

And just like that, my one connection to the job was severed like a tendon. One more warning sign I failed to see.

A War of One

Clare and I would escape to the coast whenever we got the chance. Back in the long ago, when we first got into recovery and it seemed we had nothing but time on our hands, the two of us were relatively free to indulge our hippie wanderlust. It was simply a matter of scraping together enough money to get where we wanted to go. We'd bust up to Seattle for a week, and we did a lot of camping with no set return date.

It was great. Clare especially was a real fan of spontaneous road trips—"bugging out," she called it. She loved simply jumping in the car at the drop of a hat and going. It didn't really matter where we went. The going and the being someplace else was the main point.

All that changed after I became a bus driver. Time, at least for me, had become a precious commodity, monetized and measured and militarized down to the nanosecond, and wrenching ourselves free from the daily grind became a very calculated and strenuous affair, requiring an enormous flexing of willpower on my part, not to mention an emotional letting go that I found difficult, if not impossible, to achieve.

The job had gotten into my head. The job had tapped into my innate anxiety and transformed it from amorphous to acute. I couldn't relax—not that I'd been all that great at it to begin with. But now I could scarcely jump the ruts of my own routine.

The coast was a compromise to all that, and it was difficult for me to decide whether that qualified it, ipso facto, as a small victory or, instead, as a concession to failure. But no matter. It was a short enough drive—less than an hour, really—that we could justify even an overnight trip, something down and dirty.

And speaking of dirty, Clare and I both loved cheap motels, the more ramshackle and weird the better. There was something about a dive motel that got Clare pretty worked up. Hot and bothered. I tried not to question this too much, not because I didn't want to forfeit my chances of getting laid, but because I'd learned the hard way that indulging my darkest fantasies about a partner's sexual history was a pointless exercise in self-laceration, not to mention wildly hypocritical.

"Ooh, this is funky," Clare said, walking in and setting her backpack onto the linoleum floor.

The front door opened directly into the bedroom, which was dominated by a king-size mattress standing ridiculously high on its frame. Clare had found the place online for cheap, one of her many talents, and I liked it immediately. After the bedroom came the tiny kitchen, which spilled down a couple steps into a small living room festooned with faux-nautical decor and mismatched furniture that gave the whole place the ambiance of a slapped-together surfer's shack in Santa Cruz.

The apartment was part of a complex built directly into a hill that sloped precipitously down to the shoreline. I doubted a single beam in that place was plumb. Definitely not earthquake-proof, I figured, but right up our alley.

"I love it," I said. "Nice work."

"Thank you very much," Clare said, making her way through the place, inspecting things. The bathroom right off the kitchen was as tiny as a ship's shitter, just a metal shower stall and a toilet that Clare used without shutting the door, pee-ing loudly with her chin cupped in both hands. I opened the refrigerator.

"Hey, complimentary butter and half a jar of salsa," I said as she pulled her pants back up.

"Score," she said, peering into the mirror over the sink. She was picking something out of her teeth.

"What would you like to do first?" I asked.

"I'm good with whatever," Clare said.

"Maybe a walk to the beach?"

"Sure," Clare said, shrugging. I felt a lump in my throat. I was already thinking about time, breaking things down into dis-

tinct and manageable increments, into chunks of time, pieces of
time, discrete blocks of time to be filled and boxes of time to be
checked off and therefore finished with, first this and then that,
in a finite succession of disconnected activities and recordable
experiences that should happen and therefore would happen and
then will have had-happened-already before ticking time slipped
through my fingers and disappeared, in fact disappeared before it
arrived, and I was sucked back into time without end, which was
work time, which was death.

I had asked a question that was entirely insincere—no,
frankly dishonest—because what I had really wanted was for
Clare to free me from all this ache, free me without request, to
make me present, to kill time once and for all. I wanted her to
fuck me, but I didn't want to ask for it. I didn't want to ask for
it because I was scared. It was not a refusal that I feared. It was
something much worse.

"You know," I said, "fuck that. I don't want to go to the beach
right now."

Clare looked at me. "Well, okay then," she said, a note of
bemusement in her voice. She looked genuinely curious.

"Come here," I said. I reached down and took her right hand
into mine. I led her back into the bedroom.

"Take off your shoes," I said.

She smiled and slipped her shoes off, heel to toe, first one
and then the other. I grabbed the bottom of her T-shirt.

"Arms over your head," I said.

She reached into the air without speaking. I pulled her shirt
up and over her head, slowly, catching her hair in the bunched
fabric. She tilted her head slightly forward and I got it off. With
a hand on each shoulder I spun her around. I unclasped her bra
and threw it onto the bed. I turned her back around. She stood
in front of me, unmoving, her arms at her side.

I tucked the thumb of each hand into the waistband of her
sweats and felt the heat coming off her. I lowered myself to my
knees, taking her pants and her panties with me. I heard her

gasp, and I realized how long it had been since I had actually undressed my wife.

Afterward, we indeed took that walk down the hill to the beach. It was a good walk, it was a good beach, we were good people, we held hands. The day was cool and overcast, but Clare and I were wrapped in warmth, sultry and generous of feeling, padding along the sand on rubbery legs, enjoying the immeasurably satisfying give of the alluvium under our feet, the earth a sponge that absorbed just enough and no more.

We walked and walked. The crashing and churning of the Pacific was a cottony metronome that underscored everything, like a suspicion of eternity. Hint of eternity? Promise of eternity? What more can be said about the ocean? There it was, big to shrink you small, wide to squeeze you narrow, the far horizon a dreamy mist where your brain fell off the edge and disappeared.

Is there anywhere else for us to be, really, we little animals, than standing on the edge of the ocean? Everything else is vanity.

"I don't want to go home yet," I said, squeezing Clare's hand. "I'm totally not ready. I could use another couple weeks of this. Or months."

"It's easy enough getting out here," she said. "Just takes a little planning. You know I'm always game to get out of town. Just say the word."

"Word," I said. We kept walking, to our left the roaring ocean, to our right a dune that rose into a sedgy hill topped by rows of beach houses and motels.

"I have a plan," I said. "We quit our jobs, sell the house, cash out our savings, fix up the sailboat which, obviously, nobody is coming back for, and we sail the seven seas."

"That sounds lovely," she said. "Say when."

I laughed. "It's pretty to think so, isn't it?" I said. Yeah, pretty unlikely, I thought. Dream as I might, plan as I may, I understood in some half-revealed corner of my mind that I was the one who lacked the courage of it all, which kept it merely a dream—of flight, of escape, of destruction. Clare didn't lack the courage, and I secretly resented her for that. So the dream itself became a part of the trap I felt myself in, and for which I struggled not to blame her.

The illogic of all this didn't matter for shit, because the struggle taking place inside me was beyond the reach of reason; it was primordial and absolute. I saw no middle ground between wanting to blow up the world and wanting to make my final exit. It was all or nothing: go postal and light out for the territories, or suffer like a schlub in silent desperation, which was the source of my guilt and anxiety.

"Jesus," I said. "I'm really glad I'm in therapy."

Clare grinned. "Yeah, me too," she said. "It's a good thing. For anyone. I'm proud of you."

"I wish it worked faster," I said. "I want to be fixed."

"Wish in one hand," Clare said. "We don't get fixed. We just keep moving forward with more and more clarity, or at least that's the hope. There's no great popping sound when your head finally comes out of your ass."

"So it's just my head slowly coming out of my ass," I said.

"Something like that," she said.

"Do you think I'm changing?" I asked. "Like, can you tell any difference?"

She nodded. "Yeah, I can," she said.

"It doesn't feel like it," I said. "Sometimes it feels worse. Like one step forward, fifteen steps back."

"That's normal, I think," she said.

"What is normal, anyway?"

"Fuck if I know," she said.

"Should we get something to eat?" I said.

"Sounds like a plan," she said.

The overwhelming sense that I am a bad actor in the wrong

movie has never really left me.

During my teens I learned to hide this discomfort, covering my fear and anxiety with a soluble mixture of charm and wounded pride that looked, to most people, like confidence.

In high school, I was popular in a nebulous sort of way, able to make friends with a broad spectrum of kids from different walks of life, the stoners and the brains, the lesser jocks and greater geeks, though never with the truly "in" kids—those fabulous winners who walked and talked a patois of privilege I was too abashed to imitate.

In my fevered imagination, all these rich gorgeous winners were forever fucking each other at posh weekend orgies staged when their parents went away on ski trips in Aspen, all of them laughing at me behind my back.

And so I established myself as the high-achieving straight guy, the situational chameleon who could switch colors according to a canny interior logic that analyzed each scene to see what it needed from its secondary players, its character actors.

My antennae for social protocol, along with my ability to read people and project myself into their needs and desires, grew acute, though my talent for accommodation never quite quelled the distinct feeling that I could and would be called out as a fraud at any moment—a single hostile word reducing my cheap charade to a horror show of exposure and humiliation.

In this way, my mind became the center of the universe. But it was a center that never held.

I lived inside an elaborate fantasy world that I mistook for reality. I could see though everything, or so I believed, and nothing I scripted in my head held up to the glaring finality of death.

In every truth I discerned its inherent undoing, its negative reality, and I was perpetually overtaken by a nausea that spiraled into despair.

Life was a joke—a tale told by an idiot, full of sound and fury, and its stupidity only confirmed my unwillingness to enter it with anything approaching faith. Nihilism bit at my heels.

Thoughts of suicide were a constant companion—but suicide as an empty threat, an imaginary friend whose hand I held in the dark.

I was way too much of a coward to actually off myself. I lacked the courage of my convictions.

If I felt any hope at all, it was only in my superhuman ability to figure out life's great puzzle, which kept revealing itself as a maddening maze full of dead ends and no exit. And that, I suspected, might be the only point of it all. The point of no point. Circles within circles.

I discovered books. In books, I could commune with like minds and feed off their salty existential despair. The bad boys of literature, those poetic motes of fading consciousness.

The conclusion I drew from all this reading was perhaps the greatest misfire of my life: I decided I wanted to be a writer. With my abundant talent and withering perspective, I would participate in the spiritual unveiling of the world, ripping off the mask and tearing down the curtains, if only to distinguish myself as worthy of your attention. The better to earn your love. The better to ease the pain.

If I brought my mind to some palpable fruition on the page, knitting my lonely chaos into the fancy lace of poetry, I might be allowed through the door.

I never questioned why I wanted inside. Never mind that the door led into yet another room with yet another door opening into nothing.

And then my mother got sick, and she never stopped being sick—she just got sicker and sicker until, during my final two years of high school, she became an invalid, undergoing chemotherapy and taking longer and longer trips to the hospital in between stays at home, during which she sat in a darkened bedroom, intermittently choking on her own spit and nodding off on the cocktail of drugs that withered her spirit while failing to kill the thing that was killing her.

An exuberance of white blood cells amassed themselves on her upper spinal column in a mute progression of a mysterious illness that turned her existence into a horrible biological imperative—a pyrrhic striving against an irreconcilable force, to beat on like a piece of waterlogged driftwood on the swells of an ocean vast and inconceivable as mortality itself.

For some reason, her illness filled me with shame. It was a shame I hid deep within, masking it with a furious show of responsibility that, in my mind, was synonymous with rectitude.

I was the achiever, the man-child of suffering, vigorously moving forward in a world that met me halfway with sympathy, and congratulations for my capacity to overcome a tragedy.

I was a good student.

When my mother died, I was overcome by a fury I have never been able to shake.

It wasn't God I was mad at, and I wasn't mad at my mother for dying. The sort of psychology that might divine that I was angry about being abandoned by a person who just so happened to die was beyond my reckoning, since from the start I'd viewed life itself as a bad mistake. Death was only one more bit of pointlessness.

No, my anger was directed outward at a world that didn't recognize the futility of existence—a world that persisted in pretending everything was hunky-dory.

My existence, of course, wasn't futile. My existence was an act of defiance that held the burning ember of an important secret. I needed to believe this. Without it, I was nothing.

This secret created a tension in me that was brittle and terrifying. I decided that I was an atheist, which was tantamount to admitting I was a murderer of dreams.

Had I aired my lack of belief to you, it might, God forbid, have been reflected back at me and therefore confirmed. And that fear was shattering.

So I carried this burden, self-imposed and self-flagellating, through a life that increasingly resembled a kind of bloodless warfare.

I was at war with myself, but it was a war that was never properly declared. A cold war. A war of one. A war of no one.

What a mess.

"So listen, I want to preface what I'm about to say with an understanding that I'm not suicidal, because I'm not. I mean, I don't think I am. I don't have it in me to follow through with it. But anyway, I don't want anything I might say here to trigger an intervention or anything like that, mandatory reporting wise, because if that's what has to happen if I talk about it, I'll just stop now. Though, now that I think about it, it's probably already too late, right?"

"This is a safe space," my therapist said.

"Cool," I said. "Thanks. I've just been thinking about suicide more than usual, I guess, and I didn't want to not bring it up in therapy, of all places, because that would be dishonest, and if I'm not honest here, I'm pretty fucked, right? What would even be the point of it all? Anyway, I think it's stupid to pretend I don't think about it once in a while. I'm guessing all of us do. Seems to me to be an entirely normal response to being a human being on this planet. It's not like this is an unmitigated joy ride or any-thing. Especially now."

"The numbers are certainly going up," she said.

"And oddly enough, I just read that they're going up in my age bracket fastest," I said. "That's not lost on me. Middle-aged white men offing themselves. Seems the patriarchy isn't really working out all that well for men either."

"A lot of people are feeling despair, yes," she said. "It's very sad."

I nodded stupidly. "Anyway, what I was thinking about the other day is this idea of suicide as being a cry for help. Like someone who's lost all hope and has been backed so far into a corner that they feel all alone with no other recourse than to kill themselves. They just want the pain to end. If we call it a cry for help, that's just us, right? It sort of lets us off the hook. Because we can see the options where they didn't see any at all, at least in retrospect. If suicide wasn't such a taboo topic, if death didn't make us all so uncomfortable, maybe someone thinking about it could talk about their reasons instead of triggering alarm bells that send us all scurrying in a panic to stop it at all costs."

"I'm not sure I understand," she said. "There are all kinds of reasons someone might decide to commit suicide. Trauma. Abuse. Physical pain. Mental illness. It's a complex issue."

"But why do we pathologize it at all?" I said. "Isn't that part of the problem? I guess what I'm trying to say is, can we imagine a suicide that is not a cry for help? God, that sounds horrible, but I don't know how else to say what I mean."

"Go ahead," she said.

"What I was thinking about the other day was a perfectly rational suicide. Not as in, everybody should off themselves, I'm not saying that at all, but I'm thinking of a single person who took a calm, balanced look at the information, at the world and everything in it, and everything not in it, and then that particular person made a realistic assessment in the face of life versus death, and just said, 'Nope, I don't want to be here anymore.' And it wasn't an emotional decision, or at least it wasn't a decision made in haste and all full of a sense of revenge against existence or righting wrongs or any of that. It wasn't a statement on anything, and especially not a cry for help. It just was. Does that make sense?"

My therapist looked at me. "Are you by chance describing yourself?" she asked.

I started laughing. "Hoo boy," I said. "Touché, well played. This is why … Yes, I am describing myself. Exactly. And maybe Jim Jones."

"It's common that people who have decided to commit suicide experience a kind of calm," she said. "Almost a sense of relief, a singularity of purpose, as though a great problem has been cleared up. That sounds similar to the individual you describe. Which could mean the idea of rational versus irrational distinction is merely a matter of emotional displacement."

"I get that," I said, "and it makes sense. It does. But what I'm getting at is sort of, I don't know, a reversal of polarity. What I was thinking about was not what the suicide says about the person, but what it tells us about the causes that lead to a person deciding to commit suicide. To point away from the patient to the symptoms, and not to ignore the effect they have, but to take an honest and objective look at what those reasons tell us. I don't think the two things are mutually exclusive, symptoms versus causes, I guess you could call it, and it would be seriously unkind to argue that. But therapy, this therapeutic model we're participating in, seems distinctly ill-equipped to effect any serious change in systems that are frankly, well, deadly. Everything points back to the subject of therapy. You look out the window of the therapist's office and say, 'Jesus, it looks bad out there, doesn't it,' and the therapist immediately points the arrow back at you. Not for bad reasons, obviously, because a person has to find some sort of balance with the bullshit in this world to exist at all. It's just that the dynamic itself is pretty limited, isn't it. I mean, is it really a good thing to emotionally adjust yourself to a country plummeting into this fucking cheap Nazi Reich. Not to bring politics into it, but …"

"The factors in suicide are very complex and very personal," she said.

"And in some cases might be alleviated by one well-placed Molotov cocktail," I said.

She smiled. "Or get you shot in the process," she said.

"And so we've come full circle," I said, laughing. "I mean, are the factors all that complex, really? Alienation, isolation, disenfranchisement, loneliness, lack of meaning, lack of purpose. I don't think the Iroquois or the Yanamamo or the Fulani were running around offing themselves or committing mass spearings in huge numbers, were they? At least, not until they were introduced to the joys of capitalism, at the business end of a gun."

"You don't think people have always had problems?" she asked.

"I don't know, man," I said. "I tend toward idealism, certainly, mea culpa, but I'm not so sure I'm totally romanticizing some utopian past. Sure, Rousseau was an asshole. I don't think we can go back to our glorious tribal roots. That's ridiculous. But why is that argument always used to shoot down anybody who starts criticizing the way things are now. I find it highly suspect. It speaks to a fantastic lack of imagination. Because it sure the fuck looks to me like something has gone disastrously wrong over the past, say, two hundred years, at the least. Maybe since the Enlightenment. I don't think that's a political statement. It's way bigger than that. It's existential, even spiritual. It doesn't seem like anybody's having much of a good time lately. Does it to you?"

"That's a very broad assertion," she said. "I know plenty of people who would say they are pretty satisfied with their lives. Nothing's perfect, obviously. But ..."

"I'm sorry," I said. "I've steered this completely off course in about a thousand different directions. As is my tendency. I drive my wife crazy with this shit. Spitballing the apocalypse, she calls it."

"This is your time," my therapist said. She smiled at me, so kindly. "Nothing is off limits here."

Oh, yes, I thought: I can think of a few things that are definitely off limits.

"Thank you," I said. "As silly as I feel vomiting all that up, I also feel a huge sense of relief. I appreciate the way you push back against me. You always seem to know the right thing to say. I feel like you get me. I don't feel that way with a lot of people."

She smiled and said nothing, because she possessed a tact I almost entirely lack. Instinctively, I glanced at the small clock sitting on the window frame. Five minutes before the hour.

"I'm almost out of time," I said. It was odd that not once had she ended one of our sessions; it was always me who noticed time running out. "What would you like to talk about?" I asked.

"We didn't talk about work," she said.

"Still hate it," I said. "And I'm no longer interested in adjusting myself to it, at all. I'm merely surviving it. I've come to terms with that. I have a shit job, period. That in itself—just finally admitting that I've tried hard as I can to like it, or make it acceptable, and after all that I just totally loathe it—has provided a modicum of relief."

She nodded. Unlike Clare, she did not push back on my negative feelings about the job. I even got the sense, though my therapist never said it outright, that she found it perfectly reasonable that I was traumatized by being a bus driver.

I suspect this attitude partially revealed the educated snob in her, in that she found it unfortunate such an intelligent and well-read and charming and handsome man as myself was slaving away in the lumpenproletariat of the service industry, but I'd take it.

So she thought I was better than all that, cool; I didn't, but that didn't matter. I merely needed someone to genuinely wince and empathetically nod when I spoke of my terrible job and the toll it was taking on my body, my mind and my soul. That was enough to fill me with love.

"Anything else?" I said, making the same lame joke I made every time when we were out of time.

She grinned and shrugged, flipping her palms open on her lap. Her delicate hands. Her lap. This was the awkward time. Leaving was the most complicated thing I did in therapy. One part of me wanted to flee, to get the hell out of there as fast as I could and never, ever come back, while another part of me desired to stay forever, to plant myself like a parched orchid on her windowsill and never, ever leave.

This part of me—the bad part, the real part—wanted her something fierce. I longed to wrap her in my arms and hold her tight and, at the same time, I wanted to press myself flat as a piece of paper and disappear, an itemized receipt slipped through her mail slot.

Leaving was also, or therefore, the only totally dishonest thing I did with her, because it forced me into a stilted propriety that failed to address the intensities that had just taken place. It was anticlimactic, this scheduled departure, an anti-resolution that always left me feeling stupid and ashamed.

It was excruciating to pass so close to her as she held the door open for me, smiling. It was impossible for me to believe the idea of physical contact, the possibility of it, never crossed her mind, not because she desperately wanted me, but because she was human.

Sex is a channel that is constantly open, if not tuned directly into. Not only did that turn me on, but it woke me up to the potential threat I posed, the possibility of me, and so I slunk past her with every fiber in my being struggling to appear harmless and uninterested but convivial nonetheless, and the performance made me twitchy and clownish, a marionette on tangled strings.

I heaved myself up from her couch and patted my thighs. "Okay, then," I said. "Thank you."

She pulled her sweater primly across her chest, covering the neckline of her blouse, and rose from her chair. She walked to the door and pulled it open and stood beside it, smiling.

"See you next week," she said.

I stopped in front of her and watched myself hold out my right hand. She looked down at it and then took it into her hand.

"So formal," she said. We shook, and I let go almost immediately. I'd never touched her before.

"I'm nothing if not a gentleman," I said. I watched her eyes drop to the floor for a moment. She was grinning. "Bye," I said.

"Goodbye," she said.

As I walked past the front desk, the receptionist—a pretty young thing, college aged—turned from her computer screen to look at me. She had a big smile on her face, and her eyes telegraphed a familiarity, devious and wise, that immediately shot a bolt of postcoital guilt through my whole being. Thought crime! I couldn't have felt any more busted if she'd caught me stumbling and skipping from the office with one shoe in my hand, madly trying to tuck my shirt into my pants.

"Have a good one," she chirped.

"Will do, you too," I said, flashing her a smile that felt wolfish. I drove home with my heart hammering in my chest. Sitting in the car in the driveway, I called Clare at work. "I love you," I said.

"I love you, too," she said quietly. "What's up?"

"Nothing," I said. "Just wanted to tell you that."

"How was therapy?"

"It was therapy," I said.

She snorted. "Yeah, I get that. What are you going to do now?" she asked, distractedly. I could hear her clacking at her keyboard.

"Take a nap," I said.

"Sounds like a plan," she said. "I gotta run. Sorry. Love you," she said.

"Okay," I said. "I love you, too. See you tonight." Click.

Every Whore has His Price

It's a beautiful day, early summer, clear skies, perfectly warm with a nice breeze. I'm three months into my first year of driving the bus for the people. I pull into the station a bit early, giving me a solid 35 minutes for my meal break. Score! Of course, I've forgotten yet again to pack a lunch. I decide to pick up a gyro at the pita place across from the station.

Crossing the street back to the station with my sandwich, I notice a man lying on his back in the middle of the sidewalk. No shirt, no shoes, tattered blue jeans, big mountain-man beard, drool spilling from the side of his mouth. He isn't breathing. I look at the sandwich in my hand. Thirty minutes left.

"Fuck," I say aloud.

I bend over the body. "Sir! Sir, are you okay?"

No response.

I position myself in such a way that he could be my shadow projected onto the sidewalk, and I give his feet a solid kick. "Sir!"

Still nothing.

Now I'm scared. I grab my cell phone from my back pocket and dial emergency.

"Hey," I bark into the phone. "I'm outside the downtown station and there's a guy here ... a gentleman who appears to be not breathing."

The woman on the other end of the line informs me that the paramedics are already on their way, but in the meantime I will have to perform CPR.

"Um, okay," I say. "It's been a long time ..."

The woman instructs me to put my cell phone on speaker function and set it nearby on the sidewalk. She tells me she is going to walk me through the procedure for administering CPR. People continue to stroll past, seemingly oblivious to this situation.

I consider hanging up and walking away. Would anybody notice? My heart is hammering so hard in my chest I can feel my pulse in my fingertips.

I set down my sandwich, click the speaker function, set the phone next to the guy's head and take a deep breath.

"Okay," I say.

She walks me through the action of making sure his airway is clear. I tilt his head back gently, then find the space on his breast bone right between his nipples. I'm told to start pumping, hard, to the beat of "Staying Alive." I pump once, tentatively, and then again, a bit harder, feeling the sickening give of flesh against the human skeletal system, taut and rubbery.

Suddenly the guy heaves a huge breath and sits straight up. He starts coming at me, windmilling both arms.

I stumble backward and stand up. The paramedics are here. They move quickly. I looked at one of the EMTs.

"Can I go?" I ask. "Am I free to go?"

"Yep," he said. "Good work. We got it from here."

I snatch up my phone and grab my sandwich from the pavement. I put my head down and move in the direction of the driver's lounge. Now that it's over, I start shaking, really hard.

I survived training, despite my generalized anxiety and characteristic lack of confidence in operating heavy machinery.

I also made it relatively unscathed through the nine-month probationary period, which I promptly memorialized by scraping the back end of my bus across the sharp metal overhang of a shelter. There was this awful metallic sound, like a band saw cutting through galvanized tin, and my guts just hit the floor.

I stopped, pulled the parking brake and sat motionless in the seat for a good thirty seconds before deciding to inspect the damage. It was impressive. I'd gouged a jagged line into the top back end of the bus, poking a spider web of broken glass into the furthest left-side window.

That was a difficult call to make to Ops. I thought I was going to puke into the receiver.

And I have puked, literally, into my mouth, out of pure anxiety. I'm also not ashamed to admit that I've cried more than once, drivin' and cryin', drivin' and cryin', from anger, sadness, fear, heartbreak, exhaustion. Mostly exhaustion.

Trapped in the seat, you become as powerless over your own body as an infant. I've sneezed explosively into my mask and then driven for blocks with both hands on the wheel as a warm oyster of snot drips down my chin.

I've cut farts so thick and noxious, I considered filing a union grievance against myself. I've gained weight and developed a slouch.

Yes, I drive the bus for the people. It's a gesture of love, of yearning, of democracy at its finest. I am Eugene Debs with chronic hemorrhoids and a lead foot, Jesus Christ handing out half-fare discounts, Ralph Kramden on steroids cruising the late-capitalist carnival of shits and giggles, picking up and dropping off the people one by one.

"Have a good day. You take care now. Thanks for flying the friendly skies."

Another thing they don't teach you in training: That you will bear witness.

You will bear witness to things most people never see or can't understand or refuse to believe, because you will chug and twist and turn your bus into every corner of this metropolis, up into the South Hills and down past Felony Flats, out Roosevelt and up Thompson, and your obligatory vigilance will keep you wide open and painfully awake to the scene scrolling past.

The endless unbroken hours on the road and the daily repetition of familiar routes will expose you at last to truths that are hidden from the vast majority of your fellow citizens—truths that could never be captured by a mere glance, a flick of the eye-

ning news, a reliance on secondhand reports, trips to the grocery store, visits to the dog park.

I am the roving eye, the mobile raw nerve. I bear witness to an American empire in full collapse, a society gone rotten from the top down and from the inside out. I am here to testify to the murderous cruelty of your politics, your escalating genocide on the poor, your religion of cutting throats, your sadistic pieties, your vapid thoughts and prayers, your yard signs of compassion and your patent maneuvers of disregard.

You can't get there from here, they say, but I'll try to get you there anyway. I drive the bus. For the people.

More than once I've seen a rafter of wild turkeys use a crosswalk to cross the road, passing slowly in single file. I have stopped for deer at daybreak. I have seen little kids jump up and down waving to me from the sidewalk, so excited I thought they were going to fall over sideways, and I have absorbed the wonder of it all.

I have seen enough dead squirrels and squished cats and flattened raccoons to last a lifetime.

And I have seen too many bodies of young men sprawled face down, unmoving on the sidewalk, block after blighted block.

I have seen too many impossibly old people crawl out from tents propped by the side of the road.

I have felt and participated in the disparagement and hatred of the poor, the homeless, the drug addicted, and it has scared me.

I have borne witness to the seduction and perversion of the working classes by the voice of the enemy, and I have mourned that particular knife in the back.

I have listened to my fellow drivers joke about running their buses into a homeless encampment and taking out as many of those fuckers as they can.

Likewise I have watched my fellow drivers commit acts of kindness they'd be afraid to reveal to each other. "There's no room for weakness in bus driving," they say. Sure, sure.

I have finally understood the real reason Christ was crucified. Verily I say unto you, inasmuch as ye did it not to one of the least of these, ye did it not to me.

Yeah, fuck that. Grab the nail gun!

I have also, at last, come to comprehend Nietzsche's terror of the eternal return—the idea that, just maybe, you will be forced to live your life over and over again, unchanged, just as you're living it now.

Because the illusion of time is the prerequisite for the illusion of your obligation to trade it for money, the better to enjoy, or simply survive, what little of it remains afterward. Time is not something we are moving through; it is moving through us, like a fluid, and it is hardening into amber.

Don't believe me? Drive a bus for thirteen out of fourteen days for twelve hours a day in the middle of a pandemic in a country tilting toward a postmodern holocaust, and you'll see what I mean.

Time is made real by the very things you sacrifice to survive it. Sacrifice enough of it and it starts to hurt, and you will do anything to stop the ache: bitching, moaning, blaming the union, cursing the stuffed shirts, drinking, buying a bigger truck, stockpiling ammo. Even, ironically, volunteering to work more, because what else are you gonna do? Time is everything and it is nothing.

Driving the bus, you can't afford one nanosecond of inattention—not really. I've accidentally followed the thread of an interesting thought, and before I know it I've blown past three bus stops, almost run a red light and then turned off-route. Where the hell am I?

It happens that fast.

It often occurred to me while driving the bus that the term

"driving" is something of a misnomer. I'm not "driving" the bus. I'm steering it, which is almost invariably a reactive activity. I'm not making it go here and there at my will; I'm actually making a series of micro-adjustments to keep it from going off course, like a ship.

I'm not an agent of direction; I'm a machine of correction.

Is anybody driving this thing, really?

Competence meets flow is about as good as it gets as a bus driver. The rest of it is pretty much a low-grade nightmare. But after a couple of years, once you're comfortable hurtling through space with a cargo of unbuckled meat sticks, you do encounter those rare moments where the suffering dissipates into a nearly imperceptible ache, and you think: I'm kind of a badass.

There is nothing sexier than competence.

So you learn not to think. Or you learn to not think. You have no choice. And what this does to your brain is astonishing.

Because the brain can't not think—not technically. The question is whether it is imaginative thinking, daydreaming, or repetitive thinking, or thinking about repetitive thinking. I do a lot of that last thing.

I have spent an entire shift singing the same line from the last song I heard on the radio as I pulled into the parking lot at work.

I have repeated the same inane phrases in my head thousands of times: You lookin' at me? You lookin' at me? You lookin' at me?

And the truly odd thing is, throughout it all, with a bus full of strange and exotic people, these symptoms of brain-lock are nothing but manifestations of a deep loneliness run aground on the shores of what amounts to assembly line factory work in perpetual motion.

Bus driving is fucking lonely.

It can also be quite beautiful. Because as a bus driver you are in a unique position as a quasi-civil servant to touch lives that don't seem to receive much touch at all. Your loneliness reaches out like a heart tentacle to another's solitude. Eye contact is key. A smile. I love flirting with the old ladies. I relish shooting the shit with the vets. Even the kids are alright sometimes. I try to be kind. It's a world of small gestures. It's going to have to be from here on out. The consolation of small gestures. This is all going to get worse before it gets worse, and love is all we have.

At last the day arrived to have my stent removed. I was ushered into the surgeon's office and told to take a seat. An assistant asked me to pull my pants and underwear down around my knees. "I'm going to inject a topical numbing agent into the urethra," he said.

"I don't get knocked out for this?" I asked. "What are you going to inject me with?"

"Nope, no anesthesia necessary," he said. "Just a stream of lidocaine into your urethra, and then we remove the stent."

"Hoo-boy," I said. "Okay then. Knock yourselves out."

I couldn't bear the further indignity of watching him fiddle with my ding-dong, which had retreated to a nub of shrinking terror. As I looked away, I felt the assistant insert the plastic syringe into the tip of my dick, followed by an icy sensation of cold liquid streaming the wrong way. "Okey-doke," he said. "The surgeon should be with you in a few minutes."

"Sounds good," I said stupidly. I sat there for a good five, ten minutes before the surgeon, trailed by the assistant, entered the office. I don't tend to interfere with medical procedures, but this one had me concerned.

"Hey," I said. "I've been sitting here a while. You sure that lidocaine hasn't worn off?"

The surgeon smiled kindly. I'm sure he'd heard the same anxious question posed a thousand-and-one times by a thousand-and-one helpless men with their pants around their ankles and their junk in full retreat. "Don't worry," he said. "We've got a good thirty-minute window before it even starts to wear off."

He grabbed a plier-looking micro-forceps thingamajig from a metal tray and held it up, then tipped his glasses down onto his nose. "Feel free to watch," he said.

"Yeah, no," I said. "But thank you."

"Okay," he said. "So you're going to feel something like a pressure against your bladder, but there shouldn't be any pain," he said. I stared at the white wall opposite. I felt him pushing down on my crotch, and then a vague notion of the forceps going in. "Alright," he said gently, "now I'm going to get a death grip on this thing… okay, ready?"

I didn't say anything. I couldn't breathe.

"Here we go," he said.

The sensation of having that device yanked out of me permanently altered my understanding of the cosmos. There was no pain. There was something more urgent: an all-consuming cellular sensation of being turned inside-out, as though my guts and my reproductive organs were being dragged backward by a tractor beam through my urethra into a black hole of nothingness. It's a sensation that has no real comparison in real life, no analogy that remotely touches it, and therefore, for me, there was life before stent removal, and life after. The best I can say is that the phenomenon was at once medieval and futuristic, like the mechanistic exorcism of an invasive android infrastructure straight out of a Cronenberg movie, but administered by the Catholic church during the Inquisition. And, strange to say, I immediately had the desire to experience that feeling again, it was so alien and transformative.

"Jesus," I said.

"All done," the surgeon said. "You can breathe."

"Cool," I said. I glanced left and caught sight of the stainless steel pan that sat on a tray between me and the surgeon. Inside the pan was a long, skinny piece of jointed metallic fiber, about eight inches long, slightly moist, with a closed loop at each end. It looked like something out of the *X Files*.

"What the hell is that?" I asked.

"Oh, that?" the surgeon said. "That's the stent."

"Holy fuck!" I shouted. "That's what was in me? It looks like an extraterrestrial snake! No wonder it hurt so bad to pee! I can't believe I was driving the bus with that in me! I deserve a raise! I should be employee of the month!"

The surgeon patted my knee. "You can pull your pants back up now," he said, standing up from his chair.

A pair of golden girls are waiting at the curbside stop for my bus. One of them is wheeling a handcart. "Would you like the ramp?" I ask.

"Oh, no thanks," she says. "I only need it when I'm loaded up."

As her friend walks past, she gives me a sly look. "Better watch out for what she means by loaded up," she says.

"Uh oh," I say. I make the universal sign for knocking back a drink. She grins. "I think you two are trouble," I say.

"Oh, you have no idea," she says. They both laugh.

"Don't let me catch you drinking on the bus," I mock-scold them, wagging my finger in the air.

"You want us to save you a snort?" the cart lady asks deviously.

During the ride, the two of them talk nonstop, laughing, reminiscing, joking around, being saucy. They are hilarious, like a well-worn comedy routine, just perfect. It makes me immeasurably happy to listen to them go back and forth. When they deboard, they both stop and give me huge, mischievous smiles.

"Thanks for the ride, bub," the one with the cart says.

Late evening, mid-summer. I pull over to drop a passenger. Moving away from the curb, I check my mirrors and see that the bus is empty. It's been a rare good day, no complaints. I'm in an excellent mood. Every once in a while the magnitude of your responsibility gives you a magnificent sense of accomplishment. I am King Kong, the Big Dog, I tell myself. Full of exuberance, I start reciting my man Macbeth: "Tomorrow and tomorrow and tomorrow creeps in this petty pace from day to day to the last syllable of recorded time …" As I drive on, gaining momentum, the performance gains in theatricality and exuberance until, by the last line, I'm shouting it into the hollows of the whole bus.

"It is a tale told by an idiot, full of sound and fury signifying nothing …"

Ding!

The young woman had been behind me the whole time, on one of the bench seats right in my blind spot. Had I bothered to check the fish-eye mirror, I might have spotted her. I'm not even sure if it was her stop. Chances are she just wanted to get the hell off the bus before I moved on to Hamlet. I gawked at her dumbly as she scurried past with her head down and eyes averted. She hopped off the bus and started sprinting down the street.

"You take care now!" I shouted after her.

It's become my patent phrase. You take care now. It seems to suit the times. I said it to an elderly fellow once and he paused in the doorway and, without turning around, hollered back at me: "It does no good to take care! We all fall apart and die no matter what we do!"

I agree. But some of us fall apart and die quicker than others. Like bus drivers, for instance. The first time I sat in the drivers lounge at Cosmodemonic, just another nameless new recruit awaiting the first day of training, I couldn't believe my eyes. Had I mistakenly found my way into a hospital ward? These people were broken. They needed serious medical help. I recall watching one driver in particular make his way from the seating area to the men's bathroom, a distance of no more than twenty yards. I wasn't sure he was going to make it. Slump shouldered and head down, he shuffled in such a way that neither foot ever left the ground. It looked like he was performing a butoh dance. It was mesmerizing. It hurt just watching him, but I couldn't look away.

The only other place I'd seen a man move with such aggrieved and deliberate care was at a dive bar after last call. It chilled me to the bone, this driver's death march, and I swore then and there that I would never let the job do that to my body.

I'll put a bullet through my head first.

The long and complicated history of any one person's employment among the peasant classes is likely filled with such famous last words. I'd put a bullet through my head first. As in: I would rather die than work here another day. Kill me now. Don't let me become that guy. And then, of course, it happens. You re-up, you hold on, you accept the regression, the depression, the next bid for work. You become that guy. And yet, somehow, we trudge on, working class heroes, slouching like crippled beasts toward some wonderful savanna of the mind where, God willing, time will take a kinder toll and just maybe everything won't hurt so bad. We make bargains, place bets, dispense threats, exact promises from ourselves and quit a million times in our heads, all as a means of relieving the terrific stupidity of surviving one more day on the job. It's a strange form of pain management, like death on the installment plan.

And then, one day, you stand up from your chair in the drivers lounge only to find that your knees no longer work, and your sciatic nerve is sending sharp daggers of pain into both legs and, as you commence shuffling your sorry ass to the bathroom, you wonder if you can make it without buckling completely in half.

I was born to tilt at windmills.

Because, in the end, there is nothing quite so quixotic as driving the bus down a quiet street on a warm summer evening and suddenly seeing a knight in full armor—helmet, chain mail,

85

iron boots, broadsword, pointy goatee—clanging along down the sidewalk.

I didn't know what else to do, so I saluted him.

I walk into the driver's lounge, shaking from head to toe. I'm finally starting to get my breath back. There's one other driver in here with me, a guy named Sam who's always reading books on Buddhism. He looks at me. "How're you doing?" he asks.

"Dude," I say, shaking my head. "I think I just saved some guy's life."

He stares at me. "What? What happened?"

I tell him everything I can remember. "I mean, I'm not even sure I did anything," I say. "The paramedics got there pretty quick. I barely did jack."

"Yeah, whatever," he laughs. "But that's totally amazing, right?"

"I was scared shitless," I say. "I honestly just wanted to run away."

"Makes sense," he says. "You were all filled with adrenaline. But, seriously, that's amazing."

"Please don't tell anyone," I say. I feel an instinctive urge to deflect attention away from myself, especially this early into my tenure as a bus driver. Fly under the radar, the senior drivers say. Stay invisible.

Of course, Sam did say something to somebody, and it filtered up to administration. A few days later I was summoned to the office of the head of Operations. "We're making you employee of the month for September, for performing CPR on a customer," Jack said with a pinched grin. He looked very uncomfortable.

"Okay," I said.

"Congratulations," he said.

"Yeah, thanks," I said. "You know, I'm not even really sure the guy was a customer. He was lying on the sidewalk outside the station. I was at lunch. It just seemed like something anybody would do."

"Well, either way," he said, "what you did represents exactly the kind of driver we want here."

Jack explained that the award came with a hundred dollar bonus, a little hat pin, and the gift of a company sweater. That, and my face would be plastered on placards around the district.

"Okay?" I said. "Am I free to go?"

Jack looked at me, scarcely masking his disappointment in my apathy. "Well," he said. "The only thing left for you to do is accept the nomination."

"What happens if I don't accept it?"

"We give it to somebody else," he said.

I considered this for a moment. That's a hell of a clause, I thought, and there must be a good reason for it. Everything in me screamed to reject the nomination, while in a corner of my mind I worried about the tactical significance of appearing ungrateful. Then I thought about the hundred bucks.

"Yeah, okay," I said. "I accept."

Every whore has his price.

Early Sunday morning, standing outside, waiting out a time point, a big, agitated guy jumps off my bus and rushes up to me.

"Driver," he says, panting, "four people have been following me in cars all night and that blond lady on the bus is one of them!"

"Okay," I say. "And what would you like me to do about it?"

He pauses. "Take me back to the station, I guess."

"Yep," I reply, "that's exactly where this bus is going."

The guy shrugs, stares at me a second or two, then gets back on the bus.

Listen. Validate. Ask questions. Present open-ended options. Defuse.

Driving along on a Saturday morning, lost in thought. Suddenly a blood-curdling, bone-rattling scream splits the silence. "OH GOD HELP ME!"

I quickly pull the bus to the curb and pull the emergency brake. "Ma'am, are you okay?"

"Yeah, I'm okay," she answers, calm as can be. "I just ate too much sugar."

So Much for the Magna fucking Carta

Connie was a driver with a few years seniority on me. She was in the process of moving her way up the administrative ladder, training as a supervisor and also participating in the company's Diversity, Equity, and Inclusivity committee. At this point, she was still driving the bus full time, and therefore she was directly experiencing the turmoil and confusion everyone below her in seniority was suffering through. I found it easy to talk with Connie. She got me. We got each other.

"I'm dying," I said. "This is such bullshit."

We were standing in the hallway, near the entrance to the driver's lounge. Connie put her arm on my shoulder. Her deep blue eyes shimmered with tears and her lips curled in a sympathetic smile. "I'm sorry," she said.

"It's not your fault," I said. "I'm sorry to keep complaining, but this shit is just so outrageous. I've worked thirteen out of the past fourteen days, and I haven't had driven a shift under eleven hours. I can't even see straight anymore. I go home, shove food down my throat, watch TV for half an hour and then crawl into bed. My body is literally vibrating with anxiety."

Connie nodded. "Everybody's suffering right now," she said.

"Tell me about it," I said. I glanced through the hallway window into the lounge, where my fellow operators were variously slouched in chairs or hunched at the lunch tables, gazing blankly at their time cards. They looked like a devastated regiment of grunts awaiting yet another ambush.

"It looks like *One Flew Over the Cuckoo's Nest* in there," I said. Connie laughed.

"And then," I continued, "you finally make it to your weekend after a 65 hour week, and they cancel your day off. It's fucking sadistic."

"I think you should talk to Jack," she said. I looked at her. The last thing I wanted to do was talk to the director of operations. Kill him maybe, but talk to him? Forget it. He was the primary author of our misery. Fuck that guy.

"Why?" I said.

"You're smart and articulate," she said, uttering a refrain I'd been hearing my whole life and which always made me deeply, deeply uncomfortable—and not only because I found it completely untenable. I did not want the responsibility of being smart.

"I'm not smart," I said. "I'm a blithering idiot. What would I say?"

"Stop it," she said, punching my arm. "You'd tell him exactly what you're telling me, so he can hear directly from a driver what we're all going through right now. You'd be doing every one of us a favor."

"Why can't you do it?" I said.

She gave me a pained, knowing look that telegraphed waves of meaning while revealing nothing specific. Because you're a woman? Because you're a lesbian? Because the patriarchy? Because all these things? Yes. Indeed. I got that look a lot from the female drivers at Cosmodemonic, who were forced to swallow such a continuous toxic sludge of retrograde macho bullshit that half of them developed testicles by osmosis. It was a matter of survival. They broke into a male-dominated working class trade only to be shunted into a humid sauna of swinging dicks and swollen nutsacks, and it never failed to astonish me the extent to which the women had to mangle themselves to fit the mold.

This wasn't only a matter of gender under siege by the evil patriarchy; it was also a mechanistic outcome of an economic corporate ideology, and the ideology dominating Cosmodemonic—regardless of what the Pharisees in administration wanted you to believe—was aggressively het, bitterly individualistic, chronically unkind, and casually cruel. It was a force of absorption and erasure. So the women not only had to go along with the juvenile, sexist, homophobic, classist jokes that littered the drivers' lounge; they often became their most rabid and voluble purveyors. They maligned the homeless and slagged the poor with the rest of us miserable white dudes. They slapped their dicks on the table and compared length and girth side by side with their male counterparts, and they regularly came out on top. They bashed our LGBTQ population. They watched Fox News and regurgitated the fascist party line on abortion, immigration, the lesbian governor, gun rights, the evils of the pinko communist libtards, the stupid college kids standing up for Palestine. They turned themselves inside out to appear right side up. Or they just kept their mouths shut.

Or maybe that's just who they were. Maybe Cosmodemonic was where these right-wing butch chicks finally found a room of their own. Who am I to say? Bully for them. We all get to play our parts, and far be it from me to impugn that particular spot where anyone decides to reside on the emotional and political spectrum, vis-à-vis their complex class status. All I know is that, at Cosmodemonic Unified Northwest Transit, the pervasive sway of aggrieved and mindless hyper-masculinity was so anaerobic and unilateral as to create a mono-culture, one that tolerated zero expressions of otherness, lest you brand yourself a freak. You had to keep that shit under your hat.

One of our most outspoken Q-Anon quacks—a guy named Briggs who had a "Trump Train" sticker plastered on the back of his truck, and who walked around the lounge with a Bible in his hand—actually said to me in the hallway once, out loud, that lesbian and blacks in the administration at Cosmodemonic were currently targeting white men. I laughed in his face. "Are you kidding?" I said.

"It's true," he said, smiling.

"White men?" I said. "You mean, like eighty percent of bus drivers?"

He shrugged and gave me one of those Svengali brow-tilts conveying the weight of conspiratorial truths.

"Listen, dude," I said. "That's patently absurd, and you know it. But, granting your proposition, I only have one thing to say. White men are being targeted? Good! It's about fucking time. Bring it on. I hope you're first to go."

He laughed and slapped me on the back. "Snowflake," he said, and walked away.

"Jack's already heard plenty from me," Connie continued. "But I've been here a while. I don't think he fully understands how hard it's gotten for new drivers, with the pandemic and all, the work shortage, the hours. He said he's open to hearing from you."

"Wait, what?" I said. "You've already talked with him about this?"

"Don't worry," she said. "He's cool."

"Yeah, I'm not so sure about that," I said. "But whatever. I'll do it."

"Oh, good," she said. "Let me set it up and I'll get back to you."

I disliked Jack McNaught from the moment I set eyes on him, long before I ever learned he was head of operations at Cosmodemonic—basically, my direct boss, and second or third among the top brass. I'd never once seen the guy smile. He lumbered around the building like a prisoner on a life sentence, joyless, mirthless, doing his time.

Jack had the corner office near the Ops entrance, so every driver returning from work passed his window, and when he was in his office—which was rare—you'd see him sitting there like a lump behind his desk, grimacing, never once looking up and deigning to give a friendly nod. I took to flipping him off beneath the window sill, and muttering "asshole" under my breath. When you're a working-class stiff, it's the little things that get you through.

The fateful day arrived. Connie had done the paperwork to

get me pulled off my shift in order to have the meeting with Jack. She met me in the hallway and led me into his office, made the introductions and left with a gracious, hopeful smile on her face.

"Take a seat," Jack said, nodding to the chair across from his desk.

I sat down.

"So what's up?" he said. If ever I'd seen anybody caught in the act of painfully going through the motions of feigning a curiosity he resolutely did not feel, this was it. He actually looked like he was in physical pain, which encouraged me.

I hoped he was as deeply miserable as he appeared.

"Well," I said, trying to choose my words carefully. "You know, it's kinda rough out there. Actually, it's hell. We're working these ungodly hours … twelve, thirteen hour shifts … and the hours are all over the place … and then we get our days off force canceled all the time, so you just can't catch up on rest … and, you know, on top of that, it's really fuh … it's crazy out there. Just trying to keep masks on people is proving well-nigh impossible … It's like there's no relief. I'm a wreck …"

I stopped myself. What was I doing? This was class warfare at its worst. I knew better than to show my soft belly to a boss— especially a boss like this. Vulnerability was strictly verboten in these circumstances, but I'd immediately neutralized myself by playing the common kvetch with this litany of crude complaints.

I could see it in Jack's eyes: He would dispatch me with ease.

"I don't know," I said with a big sigh. "It all feels a bit like being thrown into the deep end of the pool right off the bat. All us new drivers on the mini board are barely treading water … I mean, I heard a lot in class about how this place cares so much about my health and safety, but I'm not so sure what's going on right now is very healthy, or very safe."

Jack flinched. He tapped his fingers on the desk, glanced for a moment out the window.

"Yeah," he said. He turned back toward me and grinned. "I started out here as a driver," he said, chuckling. "Graduated in a class of twelve. That first summer I think I only got four days off total. We were working regular fourteen hour days. It was something else. There was this one time …"

Jack proceeded to talk for the next twenty minutes, reminiscing about his early days of driving in fondly comical and faux-nostalgic terms that made bus driving sound like a crazy cartoon adventure for heroic wildmen, as well as a rite of passage into some kind of vaunted brotherhood of survival.

I didn't believe a word of it. In fact, I later heard that Jack only drove the bus for a couple years, during which he was an even more miserable fuck than he was now, and that he routinely called in sick for days at a time.

"And I can make you one promise," he said at last, wrapping up his pastoral soliloquy on driving in the glorious olden times. "I'm going to keep an open hiring policy in place. We're going to keep hiring drivers until we overcome this current shortage. In fact, I'm going to keep hiring drivers until there isn't enough work for all of them, and we call people off the mini board. No work available."

"That would be nice," I said.

"Just hang in there," he said. "If you can gut it out the first couple years, it gets better. You'll get some seniority under your belt and you'll get to choose better work. Bus driving is a really good job, compared to what's out there right now. It's a good career if you can hold on."

"Actually, that's not what I hear from senior drivers," I said. "They're just as miserable as they've ever been. People who have been here a long time keep saying it never gets better."

Jack frowned. "You know," he said. "You shouldn't believe everything you hear in the drivers' lounge. A lot of people just like to complain no matter what. It's contagious."

"Yeah," I said. "I get that, I guess. But what I've also noticed is that the only people who talk about what a great job driving the bus is are the people who no longer do it. And people who make way more money than I do. Isn't that kind of telling?"

Jack frowned. "Well," he said. "This job isn't for everybody." This job isn't for everybody. Translation: Go fuck yourself.

At other times, when people ask me what it's like to be a bus driver, I just tell them about Hank DiFranco.

Hank DiFranco was something of a personal hero to me. I wasn't the only driver who felt this way. Among a substantial subsection of drivers, the chronically disgruntled ones, Hank was considered a living legend, a man whose name was spoken aloud with a heady combination of reverence and fear. Reverence because Hank certifiably did not give a fuck, and everything about him spoke to this one salient fact of his work being. Fear because, when your cork finally popped and you yourself ran out of fucks to give, you might become Hank DiFranco. He was essentially a tragic figure. As with so many tragic figures, he was also a bit ridiculous. With his gray Trotsky beard and wire-rim spectacles, he looked like some rotund Soviet adjunct relegated to the mildewed records basement, awaiting a blow from behind with the assassin's ice pick. For all this, Hank had a tantalizing dignity about him, an aura of aggrieved Old World bookishness, grainy and a bit out of step with the times.

It occurs to me now that these observations would probably make Hank DiFranco very angry with me, which only further reveals the delicious schadenfreude of Hank DiFranco—like Charlie Chaplin stuck in the gears of the factory and doing his futile damnedest to maintain composure. The chuckle I got from Hank being Hank was the laugh one gets watching a man hit his thumb with a hammer and go into a wheezing rage before at last hurling the hammer across the room, only to have it bounce off the wall and smack him in the forehead. The irony of this, of course, is that the immense existential agony Hank DiFranco exhibited was the very same pain we were all experiencing. Hank mirrored and enlarged our predicament. And yet some impossible gulf yawned between Hank DiFranco and the rest of us bus drivers, perhaps similar to the gulf that separated Jesus from his disciples as they fled the crucifixion in terror.

Probably my favorite Hank DiFranco story is about that one time he stopped to check his employee mail slot before heading out to drive for the day. Seeing a large manilla envelope among his mail, Hank makes this extravagantly comic display of total surprise, putting his hands to his mouth. "Well, lookee here," he exclaims in the voice of a man stumbling upon his own surprise birthday party. "What, pray tell, could this be?"

It was rarely a good sign when you found a manilla envelope wedged into your mail slot. It usually signaled some sort of pestiferous bureaucratic bullshit—anything ranging from warnings about an outdated medical card to a customer complaint, which had to be signed promptly and returned to Ops, either with an admission of guilt or a challenge for further review.

Glancing first left and then right, Hank DiFranco bends down and retrieves the envelope, making an ostentatious show of slowly unwinding the string twisted around the cardboard nub holding the flap shut.

He extracts the single sheet of paper from the envelope and holds it aloft, shaking it vigorously, in the manner of a medieval herald preparing to read a proclamation from the king. Squinting, Hank reads the memo silently to himself, nodding and grunting with satisfaction.

"My goodness," he says aloud. "A customer complaint!"

And thereupon Hank DiFranco crumples the paper and hurls it into the recycling bin and walks away, in full view of everyone behind the desk in Operations.

"Fucking morons," he mumbles as he walks through the door to retrieve his bus.

One more bad day is all it's gonna take.

This story about Hank DiFranco is, of course, apocryphal and highly embellished, and yet completely believable and irrefutably true, because you don't know Hank DiFranco, and you'll just have to trust me on this one. As they say, you had to be there, but you didn't have to be there, because you know what I mean.

If Hank DiFranco had never existed, we would have invented him. Out of sheer necessity. Because Hank DiFranco was our aggrievement incarnate, Ted Kazinsky in a monkey suit, a walking and talking manifesto for working-class revolt, American style, all piss and vinegar and no real direction home. I'm telling you the truth.

But in order to fully understand the man and the myth, you need to hear about the most Hank DiFranco thing Hank DiFranco ever did. It was his coup de grâce, and it almost cooked his goose for good.

I submit that the middle finger salute remains the single most potent universal gesture in American society, and perhaps in the world at large.

A strategically flipped bird is capable of crossing all linguistic, ethnic and socioeconomic boundaries with an ease that is entirely out of proportion to its apocalyptic capacity to deliver a payload of such instantaneous judgment and corrosive dismissal that it has led grown men to outrageous acts of retaliation, up to and including murder.

The bird doesn't merely say "fuck you." It's way deeper than that. The bird says to its intended target that, yes, you have indeed exposed yourself as an incurable idiot existing somewhere beneath my contempt, and with this raised middle finger I now pass an eternal judgment on you that rivals the Old Testament omnipotence of vengeful Jehovah himself. Go fuck yourself.

So when Hank DiFranco—waiting in the station between runs, slouched in the driver's compartment of his bus—sighed dramatically and held up a bony middle finger to the rider yelling at him through the front windshield, he should have known he was exercising the nuclear option. He should have known he was unleashing his own personal Armageddon.

Hell hath no fury like a bus driver scorned. Yes, Frank should have known. But also, taking into account the self-immolating rage of Hank DiFranco, I seriously doubt he even considered the consequences of this decisive action, any more than a child contemplates the consequences of shoving a marble up his nose.

Should have, would have, could have. Because, let's face facts: It is practically impossible for even the most levelheaded bus driver to resist flipping people off on the regular. The outrages and indignities you suffer as the operator of an enormous vessel navigating the broken roads of a collapsing empire amid a population flirting with collective insanity and civil war are continuous, absurd, unnecessary, and psychosomatically untenable.

It's simply too much to ask—demanding that a lone individual toiling as a servant in the public sector perpetually stifle the all-too-human urge to retaliate against a compounding confrontation with despair, entitlement, and aggression is itself a form of obscenity. It violates the basic tenets of the Geneva Convention.

There were several times every day that I had to fight like hell just to not flip someone off, gripping the steering wheel in white-knuckled anguish—like Peter Sellers in *Dr. Strangelove* physically restraining his right arm from breaking into a Nazi salute. I can't do it; I must not do it; I can't not do it; and then, like Hank DiFranco, you might do it. Fuck. You.

The great irony, of course, and deeply telling in its own way, is the fact that the middle finger, held aloft with a wry smile, was how many of us drivers greeted each other in passing. With us it wasn't hail-fellow, well-met; no, we flipped each other the bird instead. By this, then, were we telling each other to fuck off? Well, yes and no.

It would take too much time here to fully parse the tangled psychological and political implications of this hallmark gesture of working-class love. Let it be said, simply, that the aggression contained in the standard acrimonious bird-flip is inverted and repackaged by the proletariat bird-flip, in such a way that the unspoken undercurrents of class warfare are satirized in a tragicomic gesture that says: Yes, hello, in some distant world we may become brothers and sisters in solidarity, free and self-actualized and in control of our destinies, but for now we're fucked, so fuck you, you asshole, I love you, I'll see you down the road …

It was, sadly, as intimate as we could get—this ephemeral airborne communion that hinted at the impotent nature of our dilemma.

Because of its prevalence, in fact, and largely due to the Hank DiFranco affair, the administration warned drivers that the middle finger absolutely would not be tolerated, even as a form of greeting, no matter what the circumstances. This at last revealed the desperate truth of it all. Admin was totally out of touch. They possessed not a jot of empathy, much less humor, toward the wage slaves they exploited on the one hand and policed on the other.

Then again, it's difficult to imagine the asshats running the show greeting each other with a middle finger. Why? Because they have no cause for it. They aren't fucked; they are the ones doing the fucking. Thanks to their fuckery, they are free to fully indulge the fruits of their power and express their devotion to each other by whatever means they choose—perhaps by sitting down together for a company lunch of vagina cooked in green sauce or the genitals of a newborn whipped into a rage plucked as it comes out of the maternal sex. Why tip their hand with a middle finger, so to speak?

No need. Their domination and oppression is an open secret.

But we bus drivers—like feudal peasants, like hunted-down revolutionaries, like all shat-on peoples everywhere, in all places at all times throughout history—we bus drivers became ingeniously adept at giving the middle finger to each other on the sly.

We pushed up the glasses on our nose with a middle finger. We scratched our face with a middle finger. We adjusted the side view mirrors with a middle finger. We steered the bus with two middle fingers wrapped around the wheel.

For those in the know, it was unmistakable, but it went

largely undetected by the militant twats watching us on cameras from behind the consoles of central command. Try as they might, they couldn't take the bird away from us, not really. That glorious fuck-you was our shibboleth and our battle cry.

It was a tangible gesture of false consciousness in active agony, trying to break free, signaling toward a new world it would never, ever reach. Fuck. You.

Needless to say, this was decisively not the meaning behind the middle finger Hank DiFranco raised in salute to the distinguished rider yelling at him through the windshield of his bus. Hank's bird was standard issue, delivered with a fillip of bored certitude. It could not be mistaken. Here was a man at wit's end. The point was made, clearly, and it was received and acted upon.

The expectation of receiving a customer complaint is a constant source of low-grade anxiety for most bus drivers. All it took, on our part, was a bit of unguarded grumpiness toward an inveterate tattletale and—viola!—that dreaded manilla envelope would show up in your mail slot several days or several weeks later, long after you'd forgotten about the incident.

Alas, this was one customer complaint Hank DiFranco could not crumple up and blithely toss in the shit can. It went straight to the top. Jack now wanted DiFranco's head on a pike.

Hank was immediately suspended from duty. Jack let it be known during his disciplinary hearing with Hank that he, Jack, would do everything within his power to make sure that he, Hank DiFranco, never drove a bus for Cosmodemonic Unified Northwest Transit again. I want you fired, Jack told him.

The fact that Jack himself first started out as a lowly bus driver in the system he now ran like a penny-ante Mussolini reveals the corrupting influence of class, cash, and power over time—a triple threat that seems to cast an irresistible spell, divorcing a man from his own history of toil and suffering, as well as all the circumstantial evidence contained therein, turning him into a hypocrite as well as a traitor to the reality of his own arbitrary ascension up the pyramid scheme of the great American capitalist system.

This was true especially at the Cosmodemonic Unified Northwest Transit, where middle-management slots were routinely filled by former drivers with zero administrative skills who now waxed nostalgic about the good old days of driving while routinely twisting the knife in our backs—not even aware of the glaring contradictions, not to mention villainy, contained in the act of escaping hell only to advocate for its glories to those still stuck there.

So much for the Magna fucking Carta.

Not to mention the fact that Jack, with his lingering air of spiritual defeat, was himself nothing more than a walking middle finger to everybody and everything at that place. In this regard, Hank and Jack were merely reflections of each other in the fun house mirror, mimetic twins trapped in a rivalry neither of them could comprehend, and separated only by the entrenched workings of caste politics, like Capulets and Montagues. Remove the power quotient, and they might be star-crossed lovers.

But it's a thin, thin line between love and loathing, isn't it?

Fuck you, I love you, I'll see you in hell.

So we drivers existed for days in a state of muttering anticipation, awaiting the institutional fate of Hank DiFranco. The union got involved, coming to Hank's rescue. I can't imagine this was an easy battle for either side.

Having shown its teeth, the administration likely perceived that, should Hank keep his job, the rank and file would see this victory as an unwritten precedent setter—meaning, of course, that every driver would automatically be allowed at least one middle finger without threat of termination.

We all knew what was at stake here, but mostly we feared losing a hero of Hank's tragic stature. Should Hank DiFranco get the ax, one of us would be forced by sheer necessity to step into his vacated role—if only to re-balance the scales that would be tipped to Cosmodemonic's advantage by the excommunication of an unregenerate malcontent. Every kingdom has its holy fool, and Hank was ours. Losing him was an inglorious proposition, and the consequences of this unnerved us.

As the gossip escalated and the uncertainty mounted, we drivers eyed each other with suspicion, anxious about an outcome that might force every one of us to show our coward's ass.

There is no room for weakness in bus driving.

The union prevailed. Hank DiFranco kept his job, and the rest of us were now free to shape the story into another mythopoeic anecdote that we fed into the master narrative like an anodyne against the eternal pain of being a bus driver in this kingdom of death.

It was a big relief to us, Hank being spared, but—in the weird calculus of disaster and its aftermath—it was also something of a letdown. Because the system didn't crash after all. The coup had failed, the revolution was stillborn. Hank didn't escalate the battle. It was all over, and nothing in the least had changed.

Another crisis would come along in due time—because the entire organization thrived on an endless series of crises, the better to keep its drivers destabilized and malleable, and the better to keep its inept bosses wrapped in the ersatz garb of troubleshooting experts to justify their bloated salaries.

Yes, the resolution of this particular crisis gave us the blues. The threat of Hank DiFranco had been neutralized. He had been neither elevated nor martyred. Yesterday never happened. Back to work.

Short of an act of violence, it was hard to imagine how Hank could possibly top giving a rider the middle finger. There were no more fucks left to give, quite literally. One more door was closed—slammed shut on the organic genius of the proletariat with its middle fingers raised in solidarity.

Chaos was contained. Order was restored. The machine chugged on, unscathed.

"Fuck the union," I later overheard Hank DiFranco say in conversation with a group of drivers. "The union has never done shit for me. To hell with it."

Of course, this was demonstrably untrue, not least so because his reinstatement would have been utterly impossible without vigorous intervention by the union.

And yet Hank's bitter words seem to contain a deeper truth that has been revealed to me over time at Cosmodemonic—a truth not just about Hank DiFranco, but a broader, more complicated truth about the state of the working class and, by extension, the madness that has seized us all—a madness that points toward a very nasty outcome in the near future, something much worse than the rise of a clownish tyrant like Donald Trump and the populist coup he inspired on January 6, 2021.

The truth is, the institutions that propose to protect Hank DiFranco from the institutions that screw Hank DiFranco have become one and the same, and their dynamic failure—a failure indistinguishable from malignancy, perhaps from evil itself—has given rise to a contagion of collective despair and nihilism, turning our politics into a barbaric form of cultural suicide.

There is nothing to hold onto. Everything is up in the air. It's somebody else's fault. Symptoms are mistaken for the disease itself. The disease is ignored, and then defended as health. Nothing is true, everything is permitted.

"What is truth?" Pilate asked Jesus. Well, let me show you … that political power grows out of the barrel of a gun.

So get a gun, or remain powerless.

Because, at its core, fascism is less a political designation than a spiritual orientation. The fascist orientation is rooted in unmitigated fear and festering resentment, and it abhors otherness and fluidity, on principle. What it requires is rigidity and constancy, the better to navigate a broken world it regards with withering pessimism—the better to identify and exterminate an enemy it cannot, ironically, exist without.

Yes, it might be true that Hank DiFranco, my hero, turned out to be just another apoplectic old white guy bitching about libtards, socialists, communists, and transgender bathrooms, but the fact that his politics shocked me says way more about me than it does about Hank DiFranco.

False consciousness implies consciousness, first and foremost, and Hank did not operate at the level of consciousness; he operated at the level of pure reptilian response. He was a nuclear reactor in full meltdown, and the glow he gave off was both glorious to behold and terrifying in its implications.

Hank DiFranco was not ideological; he was idiomatic, and his politics were perfectly logical after all. The bird he flew to the world was existential—an omnivorous, indiscriminate, all-encompassing symbol of negation contingent on his suffering a lifetime's worth of systemic betrayal.

There is no quick cure for this. If the legit angst boiling away in Hank DiFranco's soul was being manipulated by monolithic powers beyond his comprehension, much less his control, can any of us really claim immunity?

Maybe. But I doubt it.

Deny, Defend, Depose

It's an irrefutable fact of history that there is no surefire means of disbanding a mob once it starts crying for blood. You either give it the blood it wants, or you get rid of the mob with all due force.

The human soul is a perceptive and resilient instrument, an intangible but ever present internal barometer registering the movements of good versus evil. It is that quiet inner voice whispering in your ear that this is right, this is wrong. It is a force constantly at work in each of us, taking reliable readings of reality far beneath the realm of thought, of consciousness itself. I believe this. I can't not believe. Such faith is my concession to the divine principle.

This faith, however, says nothing about heaven or hell to me—about rewards in some fantasy afterworld. What it really says to me is that a human being who is caught in an untenable situation—like Hank DiFranco, like me, like you, even like Doyle Claggart—will shove down the best parts of himself in order to get by, ignoring that inner voice in the face of the world's cruel requirements for survival.

But the soul, no matter how stymied and strangled, needs to speak.

If you ignore it long enough, it starts to scream.

Call it this bus driver's crank theory on the human soul. Push that fucker down enough times, and eventually it will assert itself automatically and unexpectedly, and sometimes with disastrous results.

It seems to me we've gotten it all wrong. The opposite of love is not hate. That's ridiculous. The opposite of love is indifference. The opposite of hate is freedom. The reason we confuse love and hate is because we can't untangle death and desire from our terror of nothingness.

So, anyway, one day I found myself sitting in the human resources department. I was flanked by one of my union representatives, George Dingle, a lanky gay guy so full of piss and vinegar that he himself would later be targeted by the administration, put on paid administrative leave while he was investigated for undisclosed charges that, in the end, turned out to be a bunch of homophobic bullshit—but that's a whole 'nother story.

I liked George a lot. He was fierce and uncompromising in his support of bus drivers, and fearless in his confrontations with the powers that be at Cosmodemonic.

Across from us sat Percy McDougal, the interim head of HR. The department itself was in a total shambles. Incessant turnover, exacerbated by the ravages of the pandemic, had led many drivers to question whether the department housed any personnel at all.

Yet, here was Percy, seated blithely at the table, hands folded on the table before him.

"So here we are again," George said with a smirk.

Percy smiled that pure administrative smile perfected over the millennia by incompetent but protected middle-managers.

"It would appear so," he said. "So what are we dealing with today?"

"Well," George said, shuffling through his notes. "I'm assuming you've seen the paperwork I sent you. Have you had a chance to look at it?"

"I have, I have," he said. "Yes."

Apparently, nothing more was forthcoming from Percy, a gambit straight out of the Art of War—let your adversary make the first move, and assess. The two of them sat there silently, facing off, smiles frozen.

I felt myself receding from the field of conflict, an unnecessary adjunct in a battle I'd joined well past the midway point.

"Okay, well," George finally said, "if you've read the complaint, then what you should understand is that what we are dealing with is an issue of unfair discipline bordering on targeting and harassment. In fact, that's exactly what it looks like. This operator suffered a series of medical emergencies that escalated into surgery, and then received a verbal warning for too many occurrences of missing work, with the threat of being put on letter as a disciplinary measure."

Percy nodded.

"Okay," he said. He looked down at the papers sitting in front of him. He looked at me. "So let's hear your side of the story," he said, giving me a perfunctory nod.

"Well," I said. "I got kidney stones and had to go to the emergency room a couple of times. One of those times I had to be relieved of work, taken right off the bus, the pain was so bad. It sucked. I got referred to a surgeon, and went almost immediately in for surgery, like two days after my final trip to the emergency room."

"Okay," Percy said.

"I used up all my sick time, so I just figured I'd go without pay for the time that wasn't covered by paid leave," I said. "No big deal, right? I brought in a doctor's note after each visit, including one from my surgeon. I assumed I was covered. I'm pretty new here, so I really don't understand why all this is happening."

"Did you fill out an FMLA?" Percy asked.

"No," I said. "I literally did not know I qualified for one. I thought the doctor's notes would cover my absences. In fact, according to federal regulations as I understand them, they should have. Plus, I was in, like, excruciating pain for two straight weeks. I could barely see straight."

"Well," Percy said, "I'm not sure I'm seeing any problem here so far."

"Well, then I got COVID, not a week after my surgery," I said. "And that's when Doyle Claggart approached me with a verbal warning, telling me I was at risk of being put on a disciplinary letter. I mean, I don't get it. I'm just trying to do my job here, but you guys are making it awfully hard. I don't really see how a person has any control over getting sick. And then getting punished for it? Does that make any sense at all?"

"You needed to fill out an FMLA," he said. "That's the issue."

"He wasn't informed about an FMLA," George jumped in.

Percy looked at me. I shook my head. "Hmm," he said.

"Yeah," George said, hitting his stride. "It's legally on you guys to inform an employee of his rights whenever an ailment rises to the level of an ongoing medical condition. You're aware of that, right? That you were supposed to hand him the FMLA paperwork, so he could be protected? Instead, you're using this as an opportunity to discipline him, which looks a lot like targeting and harassment. You're trying to prevent workers from getting federally protected status. It's bullshit."

"Okay, whoa," Percy said, waving his hands as though warding off a bird attack. "Let's take a step back here."

"I mean," George said, "if there's been a change in policy recently, the union needs to be informed of it. Even if that policy violates federal regulations," he added with raised eyebrows.

"No, no," Percy said. "No change in policy. Don't get all worked up here. We're all in this together."

They went back and forth for a few minutes, arguing over policies and procedures, with George listing off a long history of macro- and micro-abuses inflicted by Cosmodemonic's management against its driver, and Percy, for his part, laughing it off nonchalantly, shaking his head as though it were all a benign misunderstanding.

I felt myself recede yet further into the background, a mere pawn in something much, much larger than myself.

Finally, Percy turned to me.

"Listen," he said. "Let's do it this way. You get that FMLA paperwork filled out, turn it in to HR, and you'll be good as gold. I got your back. That sound like an acceptable solution?"

I looked at George. He shrugged. "Yeah," I said. "That works. I just want all this to go away."

"Perfect," Percy said, slapping his hands together. "Deal."

"This isn't over," George said.

"Yeah," Percy said. "I figured. It never is."

I went directly home from that meeting with HR and wrote a letter to my surgeon, all but begging him to fill out the FMLA paperwork for me, in a tone at once gracious and apologetic, thanking him in advance for his generous attention to this matter.

Truth be told, it was one of my finest pieces of writing ever, forged in a spirit of angst and desperation, up against a ticking clock.

I printed it out and folded it neatly into an envelope, along with the FMLA paperwork, and drove it directly to the urology center. I hand-delivered it to the receptionist.

By the time I got back home, I'd already received an email from my surgeon, thanking me for the kind letter and promising me that the paperwork would be filled out by tomorrow.

The next morning I drove to the center, retrieved the paperwork, and drove it directly to Cosmodemonic. I handed it in at Ops, and asked for a copy.

Two days later, a manilla envelope appeared in my mail slot at work, labeled confidential. I opened it.

My application to cover past occurrences by FMLA had been rejected, on the grounds that too much time had passed since the initial medical emergency. It was signed by one of Percy's underlings.

It was at this point that I ceased giving two fucks about my job. I wanted to burn the place down. Deny, defend, depose.

Bertis Dicks was one of those huge corn-fed motherfuckers born and bred so deep in the Midwest it might as well be the South—you know, those Kansas or Missouri farmer types who buckle their belts so low below their bellies that their pants look like they'd fit a five year old. Yep, Bertis Dicks was just another good old boy raised on dry weed and wet feed who'd somehow wandered too far from home and suddenly found himself on the

liberal Left Coast driving a bus full of weirdos for Cosmodemonic Unified Northwest Transit.

I liked Bertis immensely. Beneath his aw-shucks exterior
and off-color jokes, the guy had a heart as big as an express bus.
He was whip-smart and uncommonly kind, and he balanced
the failures in his life with a kind of cowpoke acceptance that I
envied. You know, my kind of loser.

Bertis was making a left-hand turn on a green light in a
60-foot articulated bus. Witnesses to the incident noted that the
pedestrian seemed distracted and didn't start crossing until well
after the bus commenced its turn.

Either way, Bertis spotted the guy, stopped his bus before
fully entering the crosswalk, and then sat there waiting for the
guy to get across the street. But instead of crossing, the pedestrian stopped short in the middle of the crosswalk, pulled out
his cell phone and started filming Bertis Dicks in this elaborate
pantomime—walking around the front of the bus, holding his
phone in the air, making a real show of it, like a journalist on the
scene. Bertis honked the horn a couple times, to no avail.

It was at this point that someone waiting in a car across the
street started filming the confrontation. What the video captures
is Bertis yelling out his driver's side window for the pedestrian to
get the fuck out of the way.

The pedestrian, for his part, continues skipping around the
front of the bus, TMZ style, making clown faces as he points the
phone at Bertis.

After a few seconds of this, the video shows Bertis Dicks
reaching down and unbuckling his seat belt. He stands up, opens
his door and hops off the bus, his big belly wobbling. He stomps
up to the guy. A brief struggle ensues: Bertis towering over the
pedestrian, the two of them locked in hand-to-hand combat.

Bertis finally wrests the cell phone from the guy and hurls it
into the street, after which he hops back on the bus and proceeds
to make his turn.

The video was posted to social media, local news outlets

picked it up, and the story ran on that evening's local news.

And that was all she wrote for Bertis Dicks. Cosmodemonic jumped into the fray lickety-split, giving the incident the old bullshit PR sheen: That his was not behavior indicative of most bus drivers, blah blah blah, we do not condone such responses, blah blah, action is being taken, blah blah, the incident is being reviewed, blah blah, goodbye Bertis, it's been real.

He was given his walking papers.

Of course, among us drivers, Bertis Dicks became an immediate legend—joining the ranks of Hank DiFranco and all the other antiheroes who came before us.

Whereas the company went out of its way to erase Dicks from institutional memory, we made damn sure he was solidly inserted into the growing narrative of driver lore, as another anecdotal example revealing the divide between what is and what can never be.

"Free Orville," I hollered regularly as I passed by the Ops counter, a fist raised in the air.

Weeks later, I met Bertis for lunch at a bar out in the industrial part of town.

"You know," he said, "it wasn't until I was canned that I realized how fucking miserable I was. I've never felt so free in my life. Thank God I got fired, really, because I might never have realized the hell I was in. It's the best thing that ever happened to me."

"I get that," I said. "You're kind of a hero to all of us, you know?"

"I mean, I shouldn't have done it," he said. "I lost my shit. I'm not proud of what I did. Obviously, it wasn't a good look for the company. And, you know, Jack said they didn't want to let me go. They had to, they said. It's all politics, man. But fuck them, you know? Ultimately, they're letting all these things boil over, they give us a bunch of lip service and do absolutely nothing, and then it all falls on the drivers whenever the slightest thing goes wrong. We catch all the hell, and then get blamed for it in the end. All the shit runs downhill at that place."

"I could be next," I said.

Bertis Dicks looked at me. "Dude, do not ignore your mental health," he said. "That's all I can say. Take care of yourself."

"Yeah," I said. "So what are you doing now?"

Bertis smiled.

"Driving Uber," he said.

I once told my therapist about an idea I had for an editorial cartoon. I asked her to picture a big fish tank, full of fish shit and dirty water—totally uncared for. At the top of the tank, on the surface of the water, a goldfish is floating, belly up. At the bottom of the tank are two other fish, both looking at their dead companion, their fins pointing in his direction.

One says to the other: "Ed just didn't show much vigor for self-care."

I thought it was hilarious.

My therapist didn't crack a smile.

Clare and I are lying together inside the sailboat. It's tight and mostly dark, close feeling, like a hall closet with its slatted swinging doors closed, yet somehow our king-sized bed fits perfectly. We hear distant gunshots, sporadic but grouped together, rapid dull thuds bursting intermittently from several different directions. Fire and return fire. The frequency of the gunshots increases.

A feeling of incredible hopelessness overwhelms me, all the more devastating because the source of this emotion, its cause, has long been expected, so the arrival of it feels like death come knocking.

"It's happening," Clare whispers.

I jump up and with zero transition I'm standing in a cavernous room suffused with flickering fluorescent light. It has the look of a county morgue right out of an SVU crime show, a very creepy tableau. I hear water dripping from somewhere.

The bed is gone. In its place, in the dead center of the room, there is now a rectangular marble slab. My therapist is lying upon it, face up, eyes closed, dressed in a gossamer-thin white silk dress, very Victorian looking. The dress ripples slowly, with the underwater undulations of a sea creature.

I can't tell if she is asleep or dead. For either possibility, I feel nothing in particular; I understand that these states of being are interchangeable here, temporary.

I approach the slab, or rather, I am drawn to it, pulled as though on a tractor beam. I feel fear, confusion, desire, excitement, sadness, dread. All at once.

I hold my hands above her body and let them hover, as though reading her energy field. The fabric of her dress rises from her body, and as I move my hands, the fabric moves, alive, drawn to me.

I look up, on the verge of tears, and Doyle Claggart is standing across from me. He's wearing a white shirt with a red necktie, but no pants. "You have objectified the transubstantial," he says with the finality of a judge.

I open my mouth, but nothing comes out.

"This is your third late," he says. "We're going to put you on letter."

"Fuck you, man," I say, but it comes out all garbled. I lunge across the slab to grab him by the tie, full of a sudden killing rage, ready to bash his head in, but as I reach out the tie flinches and slithers from my grasp like a snake, swinging around his neck and, as it does so, taking him with it. He disappears.

I look down at the slab, but all I see is darkness. Nothing. In a moment of terror, I am hoisted aloft, almost yanked, a sensation of reverse falling at incredible speed as everything zooms away from me.

This stops as suddenly as it began.

Now I am standing on a platform, some kind of crow's nest. I look down from a great height and see the rigging supporting me, the mast scraping the sky, stretching, stretching, stretching downward to the sailboat, far below, a mere bobbin on a midnight ocean spreading in every direction into landless infinity.

I woke from that one with a gasp, as though emerging from underwater choking for air. "What the actual fuck?" I whispered, pushing myself up to sit slumped on the side of the bed, head in hands.

Clare, who sleeps through practically everything, hadn't budged. I felt the nightmare receding from me, loosening its tentacled grip on my brain, but not quickly enough to go right back to sleep.

I got up and walked into the living room.

I had never used that word in my life, never heard it spoken by anyone, much less Doyle Claggart. Sitting on the couch, I finally chuckled.

I turned on the television to SportsCenter, a dream-cleaning practice of mine, and after a minute or two I started yawning.

I shut the TV off.

Getting down on my hands and knees, I pulled the dictionary from the bottom of the bookshelf. I flipped through, running my finger down the pages.

"I'll be goddamned," I said aloud. Transubstantial. It was a real word. I went back to bed, once again amazed at the cryptic transmissions of my own slumbering brain, and the gulag of my waking life.

I pull into the university station and throw open my doors. A gaggle of students trundles off the bus, and another load starts straggling on, including a long-haired surfer-lookin' kid on crutches with a brace wrapped around his left knee. I lower the bus to ease his entry.

"Thanks, bro," he says, and I tell him it's my pleasure.

I've got five minutes before the next departure. I unbuckle and step off the bus to smoke. It's stopped raining. The air is thick and swampy, with a hint of hot asphalt, like a wilted spinach salad dressed in kerosene and creosote. It's a good smell. I take a drag and scroll through the news feed on my cell phone.

The moment I step back onto the bus my nostrils are flooded with the acrid stench of burning wires. Blue smoke is pouring from the instrument panel. I look down the aisle and see that my bus is nearly at capacity.

"Hey," I say in a half-shout, my hands cupped around my mouth. "Everybody off the bus! We've got a fire!"

About half the passengers look up, uncomprehending, and about half of those that do look up immediately turn back to their cell phones. One or two of the students finally rise from their seats, shouldering their backpacks and scanning their fellow passengers with uncertainty, waiting for somebody else to make the first move.

I clap my hands together as loudly as I can.

"Listen up! Everybody needs to get off this bus!" I yell. "I've got an electrical fire on my hands! This thing is going out of commission … um, exit slowly and safely. Now!"

At this, most of the students finally stand up and begin filing slowly toward the exits, some of them in obvious annoyance, most of them exhibiting only the faintest concern for their immediate reality, like sleepwalkers interrupted.

"Thank you," I tell them. "I'll get you another bus here as soon as I can."

I suddenly realize that the bus is still idling, which seems like a bad thing, so I reach over the seat to shut it off, which seems like a good thing. I click the knob all the way to the left and hear the hydraulics on the doors wheeze as they whip shut.

Leaning against the seat cushion with both hands, I take a deep breath and sigh.

"Excuse me!"

I look at the front entrance of the bus. Nobody there.

"Excuse me!"

It strikes me as highly likely that I've breathed in too much of the toxic smoke and am now hallucinating. This realization sends a jolt of fear through me. I make a move to get off the bus when I hear the voice again. I glance up into my rearview mirror, scanning down the aisle. What I behold in the mirror is mind-bogglingly incongruent—a single human leg protruding at a perfect forty-five degree angle from the closed back door of the bus.

It hangs there, frozen, an abstract specimen captured exquisitely from the knee down. Apparently it is also a talking leg.

"Excuse me."

I push open the front door and peer down the length of the bus. Just past the articulated bend, at the very back exit, the kid on crutches stands pinioned in a state of arrested falling—leaning on both crutches, his right foot planted on the curb, his left leg cut off at the knee. He looks in my direction with a smile on his face, like Charlie Chaplin trapped in the gears of the machine. He raises his right hand from the crutch and waves meekly.

"Hi," he says.

"Oh, hell no," I say. "Jesus, I'm sorry!"

"No problem, bro," he says. The students surrounding him are laughing hysterically. "Maybe open the doors back up?"

I jump back onto the bus. My best idea is to start it up again. I flip the knob and hit the starter button, which immediately sends smoke pouring out of the instrument panel. The hydraulics hiss as the air pressure in the tanks builds up. The doors swing open, and then immediately snap shut again.

I hop off the bus in a panic. The kid is now stuck at an acute angle, having fallen forward and downward from his original position.

"Hold on!" I yell. "Brace yourself!"

"Okay," he says. "I'm good."

I push the lever forward two clicks, opening the doors all the way down the line, and step off the bus once again. A rather large crowd has gathered at this point. Most of the students are looking in my direction, smiling and giggling.

"I am so sorry," I say. "Are you okay?"

He nods. "All good, bro," he says. "No harm, no foul."

"Okay, cool," I say. "Well, I better call this broke bus in."

"Seems like an excellent idea," he says, smiling.

"Okay," I say. "Thanks." As I turn to get onto the bus and call Ops, the students start applauding.

It hadn't been a terrible day, all things considered. I'd spent a mere nine hours on the road, a rarity at Cosmodemonic, and the shift's asshole quotient had been pretty low, with only a blessed handful of irritations that left me feeling mildly chafed but relatively unscathed. Relatively is a relative word in bus driving, of course.

I was nonetheless exhausted. It had been a long, hard week, and as I stepped off my bus I felt a familiar tug in my spirit toward erasure. Real escape. Being done with work was never quite enough. I had to get it all out of my head somehow, and I was short on means.

Walking into Ops to sign in my bus and get the fuck out of there, I noticed a manilla envelope in my mail slot. This immediately set my blood boiling, sight unseen, but I also felt an itchy anticipation for whatever persnickety interoffice horseshit that envelope contained: I secretly wanted it to be terrible news, as bad as it could be, something really tasty, the better to rage and get this over with once and for all.

The slow boil of frog soup is such a miserable way to go; I craved murder, the bloodier the better. I wanted the big bang.

The customer complaint said that I had pulled away from my timepoint a full fifteen seconds early, leaving the customer stranded on the sidewalk. I actually remembered the incident, and I was guilty as charged. I had no real defense.

The guy had been strolling casually in the general direction of the bus stop. I'd rounded the corner, scanned the stop, saw nobody waiting, and decided to proceed on. I saw him raise his arms in my rearview mirror, and knew I'd fucked up. And I didn't care. Guilt or innocence had nothing to do with it anymore.

I thought about pulling a Hank DiFranco, crumpling up the complaint and sailing it over the counter in triumph, but suddenly my sense of humor was so demolished that I couldn't even summon the necessary outrage.

I put the complaint back in the envelope, spun the string around the nubbin and redeposited the thing in my mail slot. I didn't say a word to anyone. I was so drunk on anguish and self-pity I could barely push the door open. I leaned my shoulder into it heavily and slunk outside.

Fifteen seconds. Fifteen seconds. Fifteen seconds. Fifteen seconds.

Usually I couldn't get out of there fast enough, out and away and gone, bye bye, see ya, the music cranked on the car stereo, homeward bound, hallelujah, but on this particular day I simply sat in the Cosmodemonic employee parking lot with the key unturned in the ignition.

I didn't want to go home. I didn't want to see Clare. I didn't want to see anybody. I didn't want any more days off. Days off offered no relief. I didn't want solutions. I didn't want vacations. I didn't want a different job. I didn't want any job. I didn't want to escape. To where?

I didn't want to be free. Why? I didn't want to die, but I didn't want to live, either. I didn't want to be here any more. I couldn't cry. I couldn't scream. I couldn't move.

And then I found myself in the parking lot of the Alibi, a dive bar between work and home. I'd passed it a thousand times. Badfinger was blasting on my car stereo. I can't live, I can't give anymore … I couldn't remember how I got there. It might have been a dream.

But it wasn't a dream. It was realer than real, as really real as

118

real gets, real at last. I was completely calm. There was no fear. There was no confusion. A decision had been made—a decision liberated from the pinpricks of conscience and consequence.

I both knew and did not know what I was doing. Do you understand? Does a ghost concern itself with the pressures of time? Does time concern itself with the thirst of a ghost?

I walked inside—no, I sauntered through that door, confident, nearly reborn. I pulled up a stool at the bar. It felt for all the world like a homecoming. The smells were glorious. Music was playing. Gazing at the bottles arranged on shelves behind the bar, brown bottles, green bottles, translucent bottles, I ran my hands lovingly along the creviced hardwood and experienced a pang of sadness.

I pushed the sadness down. It wouldn't do. It had been twelve years, three months, and seventeen days since I'd had a drink, but who's counting? Seriously, who's counting?

Fifteen seconds. Fifteen seconds.

The bartender appeared before me in a baby blue Coors T-shirt and faded cutoffs, the whites of her pocket linings hanging like flags of surrender against her thighs. Her blond hair was pulled high and tight in a ponytail, and her face was tired and wise, keen to the struggle. She looked utterly prepared to accept me for whoever I was or might be, even if who I was wasn't all that great, just so long as I wasn't dangerous or too handsy or too loud, and I realized how much I'd missed that look on a woman's face—a woman who poured me liquor and simply let me pretend my fall mattered somehow. It was such a relief.

"Hey there," she said. "What can I getcha?"

"Whiskey," I said. "Please and thank you."

"Well okay?"

I scanned the bottles behind the bar again. "Jack is fine," I said.

"Coming right up," she said. I watched her bring a shot glass to the bar. I watched her turn and pull the booze from the shelf. I watched her pour. I watched her. I watched. She pulled a cardboard cocktail coaster from under the counter and flicked it in front of me like a blackjack dealer, then set the glass on it, dead center.

"Tab?" she said.

I shivered. I reached into my pocket and pulled out a twenty, set it on the bar. "Let's just do that for now," I said.

"Fair enough," she said, turning to look at the guy sitting two stools to my right—a desiccated piece of beef jerky in a cowboy shirt and trucker cap whose head seemed held up solely by his enormous Adam's apple. "Sam, you all good?"

I leaned in and stared at the whiskey, both hands cupped into my crotch. At the bottom of that shot glass sat my permission to finally tell the world exactly what I thought of it. There were some things I wanted to get off my chest. I wanted honest answers. I demanded them. This was my due.

Of course, none of the answers that might be provided would satisfy me in the slightest, but that didn't matter. I'd heard all the answers already, answers to why the terms were so hard, so stupid, so cruel, so inflexible. I was bloated with enough answers to fill every library on Earth. No more. I was no victim. My questions were rhetorical. I did not want recompense or reparations. I wanted revenge. I wanted to hear the world admit it was wrong. I wanted my death to mean something.

"Nothing is happening the way I pictured it," I said. "I've spent pretty much my whole life struggling like hell to stay free of all the standard traps they set for you. You know, life traps. Soul traps. Mostly, I was willing to pay the price for everything I rejected. I was willing to be a loser. Who wants to win this game, anyway? I never wanted the corporate career and the big house with a wife and two-point-five kids. The American nightmare, all that stuff, I'd rejected it by the time I was twelve years old."

My therapist said nothing.

"But now I look around and somehow the cage came slamming down on my head anyway," I continued. "Not all at once. It's way more insidious than that. It seems as if a series of free choices freely made led to some kind of compound error, and suddenly, here I am. I'm full of fear and anxiety all the time. I have a house, a wife, and a mortgage. It's so stupid. I'm totally strapped, too, stuck in a shit job. Living paycheck to paycheck. Treading water. One swift kick to the balls, and I'm toast. Game over. I feel like I'm stuck inside that Talking Heads song. 'Well, how did I get here?'"

"But you don't have kids," my therapist said.

"Yeah, thank God for that," I said. "Best decision I ever made. How people explain this dumpster fire to their kids is beyond me. I mean, sorry, I do love kids …"

"It's fine," she said. "Are you unhappily married?"

"No," I said. "Not at all. I love my wife to pieces. It's more like the cage is outside us, pressing in, and we're inside, still the same but not the same. We're being squeezed by all these pressures. That's the part I didn't understand before. I feel blindsided. Maybe I failed somehow. Or I'm just a chickenshit. I didn't have the courage of my own convictions."

"You could always look for a different job," she said.

I sighed. "Sure, I get it," I said. "Nobody's holding a gun to my head. I'm free to quit. Free to look for something that might make me happier. What does that mean, though, a better job? Happy or sad is just a matter of degrees. It's still work, and it's still their money for my diminishing time. It's house odds in Vegas. A gold-plated treadmill is still a treadmill. Part of me thinks, well, just stay at this job and suffer it out. Fuck it. The devil you know, right? Frankly, I don't have the energy for any of it anymore. I don't want to work at all. I've been working my whole life, and I'm done. I just don't see the point of it all. I know that's ridiculous, but there it is."

"If you could do whatever you want, what would you be doing?"

"Sitting at an outdoor cafe in Istanbul drinking espresso and counting my arm hairs," I said. "With a tattered copy of *Revolution Road* folded open face down on the table. Petting neighborhood cats. Watching the fall of Western Civilization from a pleasant distance."

"So why not make that happen?" she said, in all earnestness. I started laughing.

"What?" she said, cracking a smile. "What's funny?"

"I almost took a drink yesterday," I said. "I drove to a bar after work and sat in front of a shot of whiskey for damn near an hour. It was pretty stupid."

"That's concerning," she said. And her face showed it. Beholding her expression, the glibness was slapped right out of me. I found it hard to speak.

"Yeah, I guess it is pretty concerning," I said. "I think what stopped me was catching my reflection in the mirror behind the bar. I was still in uniform. My face was a blur, but I could see my hat and shirt. The minute the bartender walked into the back room, I left a twenty dollar bill on the bar and scurried out as fast as I could."

"What did Clare say?"

"What do you mean?"

"You didn't tell her?"

"Are you kidding?" I said. "She'd completely freak out. I might as well have gotten shitfaced drunk and crawled home on all fours for how upset she'd be. It would terrify her. She'd flip. I really do not have the bandwidth to deal with that right now. It's best she doesn't know. It's not like I took the drink, right? No blood, no foul."

"So you're protecting her?" my therapist said.

I stared at her. An avalanche of furious justifications tumbled through my brain—I don't need this shit, she won't understand, I'm under tremendous pressure, it's not a huge deal, I got this, I want to die—but she was one-hundred percent right. I'm an asshole, no doubt, but I hadn't ever lied to my wife, not really, and here I was about to lie, and it would be no less devastating for being a mere lie by omission.

Just like that, lickety-split, a darkness descended on me. Descended is the wrong word, though. Rather it swallowed me whole, this long-lost friend, this demon. I became a brand-new person inside it, transformed magically into the man who now lies to his wife. It was a hell I knew well. I'd spent most of my life there.

There was one and only one way out of it, and I didn't want to pay the price.

"I'm really angry at you right now," I said to my therapist.

She smiled. It wasn't a gotcha smile; it was a smile of compassion. "Of course you are," she said. "This is hard stuff. Getting honest is never easy. It's why open communication is so difficult, especially with couples. It can feel like a matter of life and death."

"In this case," I said, "it kind of is a matter of life and death. If I start keeping secrets, I'm fucked. I might as well start shooting heroin again. I can literally feel myself being pulled back to this terrible place I don't want to be."

She nodded. "So it seems like the choice is clear?"

"As day," I said.

FNG

When I first got into recovery, all beat to shit and buzzing with fear, it seemed to me that the old-timers at the club where I attended meetings were actively avoiding me. They weren't being particularly rude or anything. More like they evinced a complete lack of interest in my existence.

Obviously, this really hurt my feelings, which were already rubbed raw thanks to the withdrawals I was kicking my way through. But, more than anything, their disregard just confused me.

Was I being hazed? Was I doing something wrong? Was I the unlikable asshole I've always suspected myself to be?

One guy in particular, a Vietnam vet named Max, took to calling me "fucking new guy," or FNG for short. It wasn't until I collected my six-month clean coin that he at last called me by my given name. Max and I became pretty good friends after that.

Years later, I asked him about it.

"That's an old military thing," he said. "These new troops would arrive in the field, right off the helicopter fresh from boot camp, and we just took to calling them fucking new guys for a while. It wasn't because we were necessarily being assholes, though certainly we didn't give much of a fuck if that's how it came across. The thing was, you'd get close to someone there, get to know them, learn their name and where they're from and where they went to school and shit like that, how many brothers and sisters they had, girlfriends, et cetera, and the next day they get fucking killed. Just like that. Here today, gone tomorrow. Not getting to know them by name right off the bat was the way we protected ourselves. It was harsh, but it's survival. There's only so much grief a man can handle. There was a fucking war going on. People were dying left and right. War is hell, man. Easy come, easy go."

"Well," I said, "just to keep it real, can you still call me fucking new guy once in a while? You know, so I don't get too big for my britches and all?"

Max smiled. "Sure, fuckhead," he said. "I can do that."

A similar dynamic was in place at the Cosmodemonic Unified Northwest Transit, with a key difference.

Bus drivers, on the whole, are extremely wary and territorial creatures, often to the point of paranoia. Other people make us uncomfortable. In anthropological terms, we classify as hermetic, incestuous, and xenophobic.

We are reflexively suspicious of outsiders, which is anyone who isn't also a bus driver. As social beings, we mix almost exclusively with our own kind. We travel in groups. We go bowling and hunting together. We barbecue and go on cruises together. We often date and marry each other, and then, later, bring our children and even our grandchildren into the organization.

The borderline hostility we exhibit for every new class of drivers entering the system has little to do with whether those new drivers will survive their first year—though many of them, in fact, do not. What it took me a long time to realize is that what's at stake in this disregard for rookie drivers is a kind of subterranean test of solidarity that can only prove out over time.

It's an issue, ultimately, of trust: Will this new driver have my back when the shit hits the fan? Will he or she side with drivers as a group or, instead, start working his way up the ranks only to become another middle-management asshat? Is this fucking new guy one of us? Or is he a rat?

I finally sussed out this system of passive hazing by way of a situation that, at first, confused the hell out of me. Clancy was a newish driver, just a few classes ahead of mine on the seniority ladder.

The guy was a bit of a shitstick, I must admit. Long before he was out of his nine-month probationary period, Clancy took to arguing online with the more right-wing contingent among our fellow drivers—meaning, of course, the vast majority of us.

He wasn't particularly discerning about it, either. He'd take on anybody, any time, pushing back on the union's social media site any time another driver started grumbling about their predictable pet peeves: the meth heads, the homeless, the handicapped, the libtards who were ruining the city.

Of course, Clancy wasn't the only left-leaning driver—we were a silent minority—but the rancor he received shocked me. He was a universally despised figure, far as I could tell. I noticed that my fellow drivers immediately stopped speaking any time he strolled into the drivers lounge, while behind his back they talked mad shit. It was a real mean-girls act, total high school stuff.

Whereas most of us on opposite sides of the so-called political spectrum kept our rare debates on the humorous and stupid side, as a means of avoiding outright conflict and bad feelings, Clancy invariably got the silent treatment. Death stares. Turned up noses. Turned backs. Or else he got outright blasted.

Online in particular, where Clancy did the majority of his political grandstanding, he was the recipient of some of the most vile takedowns I'd seen on social media—called a coward and a weak man and a piece of shit by drivers.

I couldn't for the life of me figure out what was so different about Clancy for him to draw such venomous ire. It made me nervous. If one can talk about sides, I was, technically, on his side. I actually admired the guy, if just for his chutzpah, much as it also made me squirm.

Probably most infuriating to his fellow drivers, however, was Clancy's trenchant defense of Cosmodemonic's policies and procedures, especially those regarding the pandemic. Whenever a driver began bitching about this or that rule—say, the uniform code, or mandatory masking, or forced cancellations of days off—Clancy would jump in and point out the specific subsection of the employee contract explaining the policy in question, number and line, before adding a pointed little aside about how we were all just lucky to have such a great job with excellent pay and benefits, and maybe things would go better if we all actually quit complaining and just did our jobs and followed the rules, etc., etc.

This pushed his enemies over the edge. The rage leveled against him was palpable. It was hard to imagine such a contagion of hatred focused on a single person reaching a higher pique without breaking into mob violence.

For his part, Clancy took it all with uncommon aplomb. In fact, he thrived on the herd hostility he was inspiring. Sure, I grant that the guy had a serious case of oppositional defiant disorder—mea culpa—and, what's more, he was pretty fucking smug and goading about it all.

But, holy hell, did he really deserve this fervor of collective contempt?

It seemed like a classic scapegoat scenario. I'd seen it before, in school, in the workplace, in society at large. I started to worry for Clancy's safety. The guy was leading with his chin. I imagined a gang of drivers pulling him into a dark alley and delivering a real Goodfellas-style beatdown.

And then the rumors started flying. Whispers on the down-low had it that Clancy was now ratting out his fellow operators— turning us into Ops for such driving infractions like blowing a red light or passing up bus stops. Watch your back! He's a spy!

I didn't believe it for a second—it was just a logical amplification of the shit talk, I figured, perpetrated and perpetuated by certain gullible drivers already prone to grand conspiracy theories about everything under the sun: Trump actually won the election, Jewish space lasers are starting forest fires, Clancy is an undercover plant for Cosmodemonic. The journalist in me couldn't help but confront a couple of my colleagues about it.

"Wait, how do you actually know it was him?" I'd ask. The answer was always the same, delivered with a frown and a shrug. "Just trust me. I know things. I have my sources. So-and-so in security told such-and-who in supervision, who told me in private. And anyways, who else could it have been?"

Such a generic lack of solid evidence confirmed my suspicion that all this gossip swirling around Clancy was baseless. It was an instance of McCarthyism writ very small—some real Boris-and-Natasha bullshit reduced to the level of a single incestuous workplace.

He might have been a bit of a dick, but Clancy weren't no brown-nosin' tattletale. His enemies were overreaching. But I was missing the point, as usual.

In focusing on the alleged crime itself, I was ignoring the only evidence needed to convict. The man was the matter. Ad hominem fallacy, my ass, says the working class; character is destiny. This was an existential trial, adjudicated in the primordial court of public opinion: no facts necessary. Judge, jury, and executioner were one in the same entity: We, the People.

At the end of the day, it didn't matter one whit whether Clancy was reporting on his fellow drivers—I doubt that half the people accusing him even believed it themselves. What was really at stake in all this hurly-burly was the question of trust—or, more accurately, trustworthiness.

It was about a feeling, not a fact, and therefore you could accuse him of anything and it would stick. Didn't matter. Because nobody trusted the guy.

And nobody trusted the guy because bus drivers, as with most working-class folks, possess a hypersensitive and surprisingly accurate radar for dishonest outliers among the herd—liars and cheats who will betray you at the drop of a hat, simply in order to gain a foothold with the bosses, to rise among the ranks of middle management, where fear, anxiety, and a pervasive willingness to throw folks under the bus at precisely the right time are the eternal currency of professional advancement.

And I'll be damned if people weren't right about Clancy. Turns out all that fear and loathing my colleagues unleashed wasn't really about Clancy's politics after all. It wasn't about his holier-than-thou attitude, or his willingness to argue about anything under the sun, or even his infuriating imperviousness to the escalating epithets hurled at him nonstop.

Had that been the case, I might have received the Clancy treatment as well, joining him as a universally despised stooge hanging on the gallows of public opinion.

No—what was always and forever at stake in the Clancy Affair was the question of whether this man would stand shoulder to shoulder with his comrades against the system under which they slaved away—stand strong and long and proud, no questions asked regardless of the circumstances. In other words, it had been a matter of loyalty from the very start.

In this regard, Clancy at last revealed that he felt relatively little of this precious sentiment for his fellows—loyalty. He was not one of us. He was one of them.

Clancy began applying for every upwardly mobile position that came open at Cosmodemonic Unified National Transit: trainer, supervisor, dispatch, planner, whatever. He wanted to get out of the driver's seat and into that vaunted swivel chair, where he could spend his days rolling across plush carpet instead of potholed concrete. Clancy craved more power and more control and more money.

Eventually, he landed a position behind the counter in Operations, where he could now play little big cheese behind the system's switchboard, directing traffic. Crossing that counter was soul-death to us operators. He'd gone over to the dark side.

That had been the fear among my colleagues all along—that this traitorous fuckwit with the big mouth would wind up on the opposite side of the power divide, delegating to the very people he'd betrayed.

Solidarity is a strange thing. It can prove the source of our greatest joy, ratifying a sense of self in the very act of erasing it, by attaching us to something beyond the lonesome prison of the ego—a boon to the isolated, a validation to the seeker, a comfort to the lost.

I'm a Republican, I'm a Marxist, I am a grateful member of AA, I'm a Yankees fan, I hate the Patriots, Let's Go Brandon, etc., etc.

But solidarity can also, with lightning speed, become the source of our most horripilating nightmares, as any mob reveals. From the inside, near its smoldering core, solidarity is driven by an internal logic that is organic and reactive, moving with the choreographed immediacy of a herd of gazelles under attack by a pride of lions, when survival is all that matters.

Viewed from above, that movement can look counterintuitive and, in fact, insanely self-destructive. Are you, in fact, being driven toward a cliff? Are you being herded right into the jaws of another, more formidable enemy? Might that enemy be you?

Perhaps the analogy doesn't hold. It's tough to imagine what would constitute false consciousness for a herd of gazelle.

The point is, solidarity is often indistinguishable from the group's existential status as prey.

Working-class solidarity is a fragile and easily perverted dynamic—an amalgamated beast as prone to domestication and enslavement as to self-identification and liberty. It is always at once predator and prey, which regularly leads to a kind of self-cannibalization—a tragic devouring of its own limbs.

Labor is manipulated and exploited from above by the tactics of the wealthy, and poisoned from below by the false divisions of racism, sexism, classism, homophobia, nationalism, bunk patriotism—inspiring many of us, in our confusion, to punch down when we should be punching up.

To mix metaphors, then, the working class is a Frankenstein's monster that rarely identifies its real maker.

And yet working-class solidarity does exist, even when it is explicitly repudiated among its members by anti-union rhetoric or the shocking support of fascist con men posturing at the top of the political pyramid.

It reveals itself in fits and starts. It reveals itself when push comes to shove, and when inarticulate words are replaced by action. It speaks to a strangled love struggling against all odds to find its own voice. It speaks when you least expect it to speak, as a lonely croak in the midnight bog.

It speaks in a voice you can only truly hear when you listen with ears not clogged by dogma—when you learn to separate the crudeness of its croak from the purity of its suffering. When you focus solely on the anguished desire stuck in its throat. When you identify someone whose politics you abhor as yet a member of your oppressed class seeking a better world. When you identify the brilliance beneath the bullshit of identity politics.

I often say "they" when I talk about bus drivers, when what I should say is we. I am one of us. Despite it all, I've come to love bus drivers, deeply and unconditionally, regardless of their individual quirks and political leaning, which are, occasionally, rather abhorrent to me.

Bus drivers are weird, savage people, prone to disagreeability, dysfunction, disturbance, dyspepsia, delirium, derangement, and severely antisocial behaviors. But at bottom, they—we—are a badass bunch of warriors in this late-capitalist wasteland.

I stomped into the drivers' lounge at the downtown station. My last route had been a horror show. It felt as though I'd absorbed, by transit-authority osmosis, the entire psychic load of American pain in just under an hour's time. I desperately needed to talk about it.

And who should be in my path but Doyle Claggart—*mon semblable—mon frère!*—standing at the breakroom table, scrolling on his cell phone with his mouth hanging slightly open. He didn't look up.

"Hey, Claggart," I said, "let me ask you a question."

He gave me a barely perceptible grunt, not looking up from his phone. I felt the insult deeply, in my bones, which had the contrary effect of making me more eager to gain his attention. I hate this about myself.

"Listen, man," I say, "you've been a driver for a long time. I'm wondering how you handle it when you've had it up to here, you know? I mean, with people. With traffic. With everything. How do you handle it? What do you do when it's all just way too much, man?"

The faintest tickle of a smirk passed his lips. "I don't do anything," he said. "It's my job. I just deal with it."

It was, I admit, the perfect response—an expertly delivered brush off, modulated to maximum dismissal, not only vacated of empathy but so absent of recognition of me it may as well have been delivered with a backhanded slap. He may as well have called me a pussy.

The sting of it went to the bottom of my feet. I felt small.

"Alright, then," I said. "Thanks, man. I appreciate the advice," I added stupidly.

He turned away from me. I stood there idiotically, afraid to make a move for fear of revealing the humiliation I was suffering.

Finally, I backed out of the lounge, doing a sort of crab-walk to the door. Claggart never once looked at me. I was never really there.

I went into the furthest stall in the men's room and sat on the toilet, fighting back tears.

Between AIDS and Ebola

In many ways, training to be a bus driver was as good as it ever got. I've always been a stellar student. Classrooms and lecture halls agree with me. I like learning, and I like sitting on my ass. I can listen to people talk all day.

My training class at Cosmodemonic numbered nine people, men and women ranging in age from youngish to oldish, with me pushing the further end of that spectrum. For the first few weeks, we did a lot of listening and nodding, sitting in a chilly back room in the district's maintenance wing.

To get to the meeting room we'd stroll through the garage, keeping inside the yellow safety lines, passing all the buses we would soon be driving—these enormous passenger vehicles perched above concrete troughs, their innards exposed.

It looked more like an airplane hangar than an automotive garage, but the sounds and smells were oh-so-familiar to me from my college days working at a gas station: diesel fumes, chemical aerosols, rubber, grease, huffing and puffing hydraulics, the clang of metal hitting metal, and the high-pitched whir of air compressors tightening bolts, Lynyrd Skynyrd blasting on the radio.

We were each given name tags, pens, and packets, and then made to sit through a series of bullet-pointed presentations: about the dos and don'ts of customer service, about disabled accommodations, benefits, retirement, pensions, the union, scheduling, routes, traffic safety, rules and regulations, crimes and misdemeanors, the dangers of drinking and drugging, dealing with problem passengers, honoring diversity, equity and inclusion, company policy on personal conduct, self-care, health coverage, expectations, improvisions, diversion, revisions, controversion, liaisons, provisions, collusions, intrusions, effusions.

It was a lot to take in.

Between lectures we were taken out in buses for short drives,

at first only around the lot itself and, later, into remote neigh-
borhoods where we could practice away from the city's heavier
traffic. We learned to utilize the Smith System, a series of safe-
driving techniques developed in 1952 by a gentleman named
Harold Smith, who identified and troubleshot some of the most
common mistakes committed by everyday drivers.

Aside from the fact that the system was designed to in-
demnify corporations against the liability of employees driving
company vehicles, I thought the Smith System was pretty nifty.
It made good sense.

A cautious driver by nature, I found it easy to adopt the system's rules for safe driving. Aim high. Get the Big Picture. Keep
your eyes moving. Leave yourself an out. Make sure they see you.

I mean, if this isn't excellent advice for life in general, I don't
know what is.

Atop all the standard techno-administrative rigmarole,
recruits were fed a steady diet of corporate platitudes which,
of course, proved in the long run to be nothing but feel-good
horseshit.

You know the drill—it is the modus operandi of capitalist
brainwashing. The company cares about your safety. We care
about your health. We care about your continued success. We
care about the community. We're all one big family here. We are a
progressive and forward-thinking operation with everyone's best
interest at heart.

And you? You drive the bus for the people! You are the back-
bone of this operation. We love you to the moon and beyond!
Blah blah fucking blah.

Normally resistant to such Orwellian doublespeak, I nonetheless bought into this hyperbolic Cosmodemonic mind-meld,
with a willingness that surprises me to this day.

I drank the Kool-Aid, gulped it right down.

Apparently, my reckless and idealistic career change, increasingly revealing itself to be a Marxist midlife crisis, had also
saddled me with an abundance of false hopes—also known as

despair.

I desperately wanted to believe I had made the right move, for all the proper reasons. I wanted to believe that—as opposed to the endless evils perpetrated by private corporations—this quasi-governmental nonprofit public trust, funded primarily by taxpayer dollars and serving a perennial civic good, had every reason to stand on the very principles it evinced.

Like I said, I'm a romantic. Vulnerable to the con, I huddled up to their seductive carnival bark, all ears and appetite. And it went down like a shot of rotgut whiskey—hit my parched innards with a not unpleasant burning sensation, sending a jolting of toxic euphoria slithering through my system, while my higher brain commanded the sad voices in my head to shut up for a change.

It would all be okay. Or not.

One of the funniest moments of training came during a presentation on health and fitness by Marvin Lindberg, the director of human resources. Old Marvin was one of the most hapless men I'd ever beheld. He gave the impression of a hospital patient permanently emerging from anesthesia, trapped somewhere between sleep and stupor.

As Marvin strove to fill us in on the company's pandemic policy, his own protective mask kept slipping down below his chin, hanging from his face like a jockstrap. Every now and then poor Marv would reach up distractedly and drag the mask back over his mouth, holding it right below his flaring nostrils.

I could barely keep from bursting out laughing. It was high comedy at its finest. It was also, unfortunately, completely indicative of the generalized mission drift that revealed itself over the next several months of the early pandemic.

We new drivers were surrounded, clowns to the left and jokers to the right, but Marvin was both at once. I found over time that I could generate more sympathy for the pandemic deniers than overpaid stooges like him. At least the renegade right-wingers had some passion. Marvin Lindberg was just an inert lump of matter, a high-salaried placeholder siphoning a six-figure salary from the civic boondoggle of public transportation.

What I really objected to was not the incompetence he exuded, nor his own fumbling character, nor his lack of intellectual acuity.

No, what bothered me, intensely so, was the fact that here was yet another clueless middle-management asshat who couldn't seem to garner enough internal momentum to even pretend he cared about his job as the head of a department whose sole aim was to ensure the health and well-being of its employees in a massive public transportation concern funded by precious taxpayer dollars.

It was all a bad joke without a punch line.

Listen, I really do feel empathy for all of us, and the struggles we confront and the pain we evade, and the peace we seek. Beneath my harshest judgments there lurks a profound suspicion that, within the swirling meringue of this crazy existence, even the worst evils are somehow neutralized, and none of this matters beyond our blighted gestures of forgiveness and love, to the last syllable of recorded time.

Politics and punch lines aside, I do believe—I must believe—that every one of us is only looking to stitch ourselves back into the cosmic fold. We seek to return as prodigal souls to some fractured form of wholeness, a primordial connectedness and oneness of being, no matter how misguided our efforts—including, I suppose, those gutless twats in middle management.

All of this, however, comes with a serious caveat for me.

I get grouchy, and I lose my bearings. What really chaps my ass is the fundamental dishonesty exhibited by someone who knows a thing is glaringly broken and obviously wrong, and yet they persist in attaching themselves to it like a limpet, simply for lack of a better immediate option.

It's a matter of passion, and its absence. And imagination,

and the lack thereof.

You can't fix a problem until you identify it. There's really nothing worse than pretending there isn't a problem when there so obviously is, all because you want to gain and maintain a momentary foothold.

Stop pretending this is working!

Because, if you pretend long enough, and it pays off, you'll convince yourself that it's somehow right, and that the people who say it ain't right are wrong, and possibly criminal, and maybe even worthy of elimination.

At this point, the system you are participating in begins to look like an inevitable reality, unchangeable, inflexible and God-ordained, and therefore worthy of defending—if not to the death, then at least to someone else's.

Desire becomes belief in a vacuum of all real human needs. Sociopathy is cooked into the system itself. Human nature is locked in. No other options available.

Victims everywhere, and therefore no victims at all, only reflections of corpses receding to infinity. Only Marvin Lindberg, with his mask hanging off his chin like a poopy diaper.

And, honestly, at this moment, I can think of no better definition for evil in this world we've made.

And then this world actually ended—as the poet said, not with a bang but a whimper.

Of course, intimations of impending doom on multiple fronts has become the daily diet of modern life, so when I started catching snippets of news about a spreading viral outbreak, I noted it, put it in the hopper with my ever-expanding inventory of existential anxieties—filed between AIDS and Ebola—and let it go.

I figured it would recede, as usual, into the background, forgotten but not gone—buried, falsified, or simply replaced by a more immediate catastrophe. But this particular virus exhibited an unsettling tenacity. It continued to grow in urgency.

I'd become so accustomed to the soft apocalypse that the reality of an actual global event proved disconcerting—it felt surreal or, more accurately, hyperreal in a way that both confirmed and mocked my deepest fears. He who most embraces doom is doomed to flinch when it finally arrives. Prepping is impossible. The movies lie. No inoculation is available in these matters.

I was nervous. Actually, I was scared shitless.

I will never shake the otherworldly strangeness of witnessing the incomprehension on the faces of the professional basketball players when the Lakers game I was watching on television was unceremoniously called off.

The players were pulled off the court, followed by the evacuation of the fans in attendance. My mind could not compass this moment in its entirety, or wouldn't. It was too sloppy, too unmoderated.

New Yorkers who witnessed the towers falling in real time often say that it was like a scene from a movie—meaning, I think, that their usual reference points went spontaneously kaput, and their framing device reverted to a suspension of disbelief in the face of a massive special effect. I'm not equating the two events, but I understand. I get it.

And I'll make this blunt if damning confession: A significantly not-small part of me was secretly thrilled. Finally, I thought. Here we go. Let it all come down. I'm tired of the waiting. It's time. End this thing.

A new wave of wicked gallows humor unleashed itself on social media, addressing the perfect storm of pandemic-meets-fascist-ascension-meets-biosphere-collapse. One meme I encountered captured our current predicament perfectly:

Two big circles intersect. Inside the one circle is written "Apocalypse," and inside the other is written "Having to go to work." And inside the smaller bubble formed where the two big circles overlap is written: "You are here." We are here.

The pandemic was the truth of that awful knowledge rising

at last to the level of mass consciousness, and it isn't going away. We're not going back.

We are here.

I mean, nobody I know really believes we are participating in history anymore. If we actually believed it, we'd be running around blowing shit up, it's so hopelessly fucked out there.

But history has passed us by. The bad ideas have won out.

The fork in the road of Western Civilization has been jimmied up and sold for scrap.

This is simply the dustup. Now is the time to break free. Now is the time for death and metamorphosis. Now is the time of the assassins.

In the moment, however, everything just felt raw and confusing as fuck.

All us newbies at Cosmodemonic continued showing up for classes, appropriately masked and vigorously sanitized, while the organization scrambled like keystone cops to keep buses running, much less push a class of recruits through to graduation.

Ridership fell nearly to zero, with only the most indigent and unwell among us continuing to take public transportation around a town that was pulling up the drawbridge. Everything closed down. The streets were an empty movie set.

It was creepy, it was unsettling, it was oddly beautiful, it was surreptitiously thrilling. Admit it.

The majority of drivers at Cosmodemonic railed like hell against the company's new mandatory masking policy. The bulk of these drivers—no doubt goaded by the nonstop ejaculation of infantile angst on Fox News, which played in the breakroom like a double-good daily dose from Big Brother—seemed to fashion their rejection of pandemic policy as a kind of Boston Tea Party-level rebellion. That fake rebellion was fuelled by whack globalist conspiracies about deep state shenanigans engineered by liberal-gay-Jew pinko communist-socialist snowflakes seeking to destroy America.

What the actual upshot of such a conspiracy might be was anybody's guess. It didn't matter. I myself didn't care about their reasons for the antimaskery. We all gotta show cause, I guess.

What I objected to was the possibility that their patriotic refusal to wear a mildly uncomfortable cloth mask put me at mortal risk.

It all seemed very stupid. Stupid and deadly.

As if overnight, a handful of drivers became experts on the subjects of pathogens, epidemiology, science, medicine, and pharmacology.

One of them, a real chowderhead named Pete, informed me that, contrary to the hogwash they were reporting on television, nobody was actually dying of COVID. The number of infections was being blown way out of proportion, Pete said.

I asked him how he came by his information.

"I worked in the medical field for fifteen years before I became a bus driver," he told me, puffing his chest. "Trust me, I know how this stuff works. None of what they're telling you is true."

"Yikes, man," I said. "What exactly did you do in the medical field?"

"Plasma delivery," he said.

"So you were basically a taxi driver for blood?" I said.

"Yeah, whatever," he said. "I know things."

Another driver who claimed medical expertise on the Coronavirus reluctantly admitted upon questioning that she'd worked as a pharmacy assistant, while yet another driver/medical expert had been a part-time receptionist in a dental office. Mere proximity to authority, apparently, was enough to qualify you for the position of Surgeon General.

One of the senior drivers told me he'd dropped by the local hospital after work to ask how many beds were being occupied specifically by COVID-19 cases. They'd told him none, he said.

It was all a hoax, he said.

"Jesus, Larry," I said. "That's crazy, man. I was a reporter for twenty-five years, and I know that kind of information is pretty hard to come by, especially when it comes to medical stuff. So you seriously went to the hospital and checked into it for yourself?"

Larry shrugged. "I was in the neighborhood," he said.

"Yeah, the hospital isn't really in a neighborhood," I said. "There's nothing else even remotely close to it. But okay, you went to the hospital. So who told you they didn't have any COVID cases? Did you talk to the head of the hospital, or what?"

Larry shot me a look of irritation. "Jesus, I don't know," he grunted. "Fuck off, man."

But I'm getting ahead of myself. Let me wheel back on route.

From the moment the pandemic hit, it felt like someone had tripped the breakers at Cosmodemonic Unified Northwest Transit. Low-grade chaos, institutional confusion and ideological delusion ruled the day. The lights went out, figuratively speaking, and everybody was flailing in the dark, reaching for the switch to turn normal back on again—whatever that was.

A static system that functions on aggressive sameness and routine—calibrated anxiety and risk-aversion, compounded by zero imaginative faculties— was now plunged into completely unfamiliar territory.

Every asshat in administration was scrambling to minimize liability while maximizing output, all at the drivers' expense. The primary goal, it seemed, was to keep the ship on course, even if the ports were closing and riders were jumping overboard, figuratively speaking. Funding depended upon it.

Everything just got really, really weird. Classes were canceled and rescheduled, canceled again, rescheduled again. Messages were mixed, information muddled, competing promises made: Your jobs are secure, you might get laid off, we'll do everything we can, it's out of our hands.

It was unclear whether this was business as usual or, instead, the sign of an emergency situation requiring dramatic action that was continually being delayed a day or two.

Hurry up and wait—we're oiling up the guillotine!

Little did we know that status quo and emergency situations were not mutually exclusive conditions at Cosmodemonic Unified Northwest Transit. In fact, they were one and the same—a staggeringly successful strategy of perpetual crisis and eternally delayed solutions that trickles down in a steady flow of bullshit to the grunts on the ground, keeping them destabilized and nervously at arms, while the bosses remain unscathed, popping salted peanuts and giggling on their way out the door at four p.m. sharp every Friday afternoon—the whole weekend ahead, while Rome burns in the background.

It was the blind leading the naked, and yet—for all that— we somehow received decent training as bus drivers. I grudgingly hand that much to Cosmodemonic, though with little credit due to the cheesedicks lounging at the top of the organization: all they appeared to care about were efficiencies, numbers, flows, heads counted, lawsuits averted, costs cut, energies squeezed, seconds saved, bucks passed, casualties replaced.

Yet even in the most callous system, big or small doesn't matter, there will forever be people residing at the very bottom who toil away in good faith, doing their damndest to maintain some semblance of sanity and decency.

It's these folks, grinding away inside the soul-crushing chokepoints of any bureaucracy, who keep the world from falling into complete disrepair. Bless them all. They are American saints.

At Cosmodemonic, on-the-road training was the bailiwick of senior drivers, all of whom brought their hard-earned, hard-won experience and understanding to the game. They kept us new drivers in line and on point. They gave us the right stuff.

Sure, some of them were gruff, but to a person they worked hard to get us over the hump. They turned us into actual bus drivers.

And God help us with the rest.

Because it remains indubitably true that there's just no way to know what you don't already know, and you're only gonna know it by finding out the hard way. Working-class knowledge is acquired over time through the accumulation of embarrassments, indignities, bruises, and scabs—pun intended.

No matter how technically equipped we were to begin picking up real-live passengers, in the end we'd been seriously shortchanged on the time we spent practicing our routes, due in large part to the disruptions caused by the pandemic. There's no substitute for hands-on experience, especially for a bus driver.

This lack of repetition would prove highly problematic for me, especially in terms of keeping my bus on route.

To make up for lost time, the district sent us out in teams of two—not in buses, but in company cars—to familiarize ourselves with the routes we couldn't practice in full-sized buses. It was a shoddy solution, but it's what we got.

I was paired up with a younger guy named Jimmy Silvers. Jimmy had done a stint driving a logging truck, running short hauls up the river and back, but he'd found it lonely and dull. Plus, he'd hit a deer during one of his early morning trips, and after passing the mangled body lying on the side of the highway on his return trip, he'd lost heart. It still made him so sad he cried just telling me about it. The thing was just a baby, a fawn.

You never really know what it is that's going to finally do you in. A gob of spit in the face. A broken shoelace. A shot of whiskey. A dead deer.

We've all got our limits, and they will be met, eventually.

He was a good kid, Jimmy. I liked him a lot. He ended up not lasting long at Cosmodemonic—went out on COVID leave and never came back. He stopped returning phone calls, and that was all she wrote.

Like I said, smart kid.

The objective during training was for us to drive every route in the system at least once, preferably multiple times. We were told during these excursions to jot down in our route books any landmarks, tricky turns, hidden street signs or other on-route anomalies—anything to help us once we were cut loose on our own.

Jimmy and I compared notes to see which routes neither of us had done yet. We decided to kill time by doing the river run first—a three-hour round trip eastward on a narrow, winding rural highway. The route runs all the way to the mountain pass, where you finally turn around at the forest service ranger station and head back home.

This was the sweet stuff of life: getting paid to go for a leisurely ride in a company car, a white Ford Escort, sipping coffee and taking in the scenery as we steadily climbed in elevation toward the point where Western Oregon tilts and dips into the high desert.

"Dude, this isn't so bad, eh?" Jimmy said. He was driving, kicked back in the seat with his thumbs hooked to the bottom of the steering wheel.

"Nah, this is good," I said. I was looking out the window through the trees to the river beyond.

I'll admit it, I'm an awful passenger, no matter who's driving; I'm prone to jump scares and lots of nervous squirming in the seat. Jimmy had a lead foot. He started all his turns a millisecond too late, hugging the inside and then the outside lines of the curve in a woozy zig-zag motion that had me seasick in the seat.

"What's the rush, man," I joked. Jesus, I thought immediately, I sound exactly like my father. "Where's the fire, bro?" I added, trying to laugh it off.

Little did I know that not too far in the future, all the forests we were now passing would go up in a holocaust of flames, blanketing the entire western half of the state in a thick, deadly cloud of black smoke for the better part of a month.

Jimmy gave me a smirky sideways look. "Chill, dude," he said. "Don't you trust me? I'm a professional."

"I'm sorry," I said, shaking my head. "I'm a terrible passenger. I drive my wife crazy."

"I get it," he said. "It's cool."

We made it up to the ranger station, beyond which the highway climbed upward for a few more miles before plunging down again into the land of liberty. At the station's entrance there's a big wooden statue of Smokey the Bear, facing the highway, warning us not to burn the place down.

Jimmy and I participated in a sacred ritual, inaugurated by our ancestral bus driving kin in prehistoric times: We took selfies with Smokey.

During my photo shoot, I decided to stick out my tongue and licked Smokey's cheek.

"Jesus, dude!" Jimmy hollered in alarm. "What are you doing?"

"What?" I said. "Too much?"

"Nah, man," he said, shaking his head. "I don't care about your fuckin' bear kink. COVID!"

COVID!

It was a refrain I'd hear a thousand times in the months to come. Ironically, it always surprised me, this panicked reminder of the virus spreading across the planet like wildfire, killing millions and bringing life to a grinding halt.

COVID!

It gave me the fear. It wasn't like I was cavalier about the risk. I wasn't. Especially during the early phase of the pandemic, I was cautious as could be, almost to the point of hysteria. My obsessive-compulsive tendencies went into overdrive. I was the good soldier, the dutiful citizen, masked up everywhere I dared to travel, which was just about nowhere.

When I did venture out for the necessaries, I'd almost

invariably run into some unmasked Proud Boy stomping like a hayseed Nazi through the grocery store aisles, lips curled in a sneer and eyes on the hunt for confrontation, and I'd get furious. Those fuckers scared me. They were playing patriot games, or so they thought, trying to defend 'Murica the Beautiful and the Free, but for me the whole act stunk of something even more desperate than bunk patriotism.

Beneath their red-white-and-blue bullshit, I detected the corrosive nihilism of the mass shooter or the homegrown terrorist. These were men with nothing left to lose. They were the bad guys of the postapocalypse. They were stupid and dangerous.

I mean, if I was a liberal sheep being manipulated by a fake pandemic cooked up by some Jewish cabal of global elites in order to establish a New World Order that would rob us once and for all of our God-given liberties—whatever those might be anymore, beyond our right to own assault rifles and work ourselves to death at shit jobs—then these aggressively unmasked and heavily armed stooges represented a new breed of cholesterol storm trooper, their disenfranchisement and alienation being groomed toward vigilante violence against their fellow citizens, manipulated by right-wing politicians and their media outlets opening the spigots of primal fear and historic hatreds to seize every last bit of capital left and elevate themselves as our new feudal overlords.

In other words, an old game of class conflict was being wrapped in a brand-new postmodern garb, retrofitted for the particular derangements of late-capitalist Hobbesian collapse, digitized civil war, and rampant ecological devastation. Facts are flexible. History is bunk. Life is brutish, nasty, and short.

What is truth? That's what Pontius Pilate asked Jesus: What is truth? Not the truth—just truth.

And with that, everything snaps in half.

When we started hearing reports of convenience clerks getting shot and killed over mask disputes, I started to comprehend the fix we were in.

Anger Issues

"Men scare me," I said to my therapist.

"Why?" she asked.

"I don't know," I said. "There just seems to be this violence, or threat of violence, underwriting everything men do. It's like, what's waiting at the end of every male interaction is the potential of getting punched in the fucking face. It's always there, hiding. Lurking. I mean, me, I've faced violence my whole life. First from my father, then all the way through school, not so much in college but, yeah, still there in college, even with certain friends. I'm always a little afraid I'm going to get smacked at some point. It's a secret that's not very much of a secret with men. Like, we all know where any given conversation can go, so where is this one gonna go? I actually wonder if a huge part of my psychological development can be explained as a means of avoiding getting the shit beat out of me. It would explain a lot."

The look on her face—compassion, understanding—told me that this was one of those times I was meant to explore the issue further, without prompting.

"I honestly can't believe that just came out of my mouth," I said. "But there it is. I mean, it makes sense, when I think about it. It certainly hasn't been women who have hit me and beat me and screamed at me and called me a little faggot my whole life. I mean, sure, I have plenty of straight male friends. But in general I gravitate toward women. And not just for sex. I identify way more with women. I love women. And gay dudes, actually. I've always had a lot of gay friends, for some reason. I mean, whenever I'd break up with a girlfriend, all my straight friends would be like, 'Fuck that bitch, let's go out and get drunk and get you laid,' but my gay friends would be like, 'Aw, honey, why don't you come over and we'll order some pad thai and watch *Sleepless in Seattle*.' Pretty easy choice for me.

She was laughing.

"And I'm one of them," I said.

"One what?"

"Another violent man with unresolved anger issues," I said. "There's the rub, right?"

"Well, you don't run around hitting people, do you?" she asked.

"Not yet," I said.

Late afternoon. I was driving the inbound express. It was my sixth straight day of twelve hours plus on the extra board. At the Fred Meyer stop I triggered open the rear entrances and watched the riders trundle in like cattle.

I was about to close the doors and move on when I noticed a guy running across the parking lot toward my bus, hollering. I waited for him. He jumped through the doors at the last minute.

In my mirror I watched as he sat down and twisted sideways to look out the window like a man pursued. Scrawny dude, short, twitchy and sweaty, somewhere in his thirties, stringy nicotine hair, scabby. His legs bounced like pistons.

At the very next stop, he jumped up, bolted through the doors and hauled ass down the alley.

At the end of the line I dumped the last of my passengers and pulled a hard left into the station, where the express loops back around.

Ten minutes to kill. I took a piss, hit my vape, and scrolled on my phone for a minute. Then I hopped back into the seat, buckled up and said a quick prayer. I put the beast in gear and rolled down the road, back the way I just came.

My intercom beeped. I picked up the receiver. "Yeah, block 904, we just wanted to warn you that at your next platform you'll be picking up a rider who's wishing to exercise his Second Amendment right to bear arms. We're suggesting you let him on the bus and take him wherever he's going."

"Um, you're kidding, right?"

"We are not," Ops said. "We're recommending you pick him up."

Recommending. Right. Before I had time to formulate all the pertinent objections one might pose regarding such a request, I was at the stop.

I watched as the twitchy blond dude I'd previously deboarded on my inbound trip scurried back onto my bus. He took the exact seat he occupied not ten minutes prior.

But now there's a nine millimeter tucked into the waistband of his jeans, gangsta style. The pistol grip pushing into the belly of his T-shirt. He caught me looking at him in the mirror and gave a curt nod.

"'Sup, driver," he said. He swiped at his nose with the back of his wrist and looked out the window, eyes darting like Custer at Little Bighorn. High as a kite.

My heart rate shot through the roof. This is it, I said to myself. This is how I die.

But instead of simply stopping the bus and walking away from this pointless shitshow once and for all, as any eminently reasonable person might do, my brain short-circuited, defaulting to a characteristic mode of institutionalized panic. I lost the ability to do anything but follow orders.

So I drove on. But I wasn't driving well. At all. I was bumping curbs left and right, and braking too hard at every stop.

The intercom beeped again. I picked up the receiver and pressed the talkie button. "Yeah, block 904 … inbound, outbound, whatever the fuck I am …"

There was a pause. "Yes, block 904, we're just checking in to see if the passenger with the firearm has departed your bus yet."

"Are you serious right now?" I barked. "No, he hasn't left my bus yet. Jesus."

"Well, let's hope he departs soon," Ops replied.

"Yeah, let's hope so," I snarled, slamming the receiver into the cradle without waiting for Ops to clear the channel.

Over and out.

When I finally got back to the garage, I stomped into Ops, where I asked Bernie at the counter the following question: "Seeing as we're now letting our distinguished passengers exercise their Second Amendment rights by carrying firearms onto my bus, I'm just wondering—can I do the same thing tomorrow? I have a .38 that would fit nicely into my jacket pocket."

"Absolutely not" is the answer I received.

"Well, I'll be damned," I said. "Isn't that crazy? I thought this was America. I thought I had inalienable rights granted to me by God, the Constitution, the NRA, and Smith and Wesson! Not cool!"

I broke into the opening verses of the "Star-Spangled Banner." My patriotism was not well received. Bernie looked rather disappointed in me, which seriously hurt my feelings. My rendition trailed off into silence.

Turning to leave, I raised my fist in the air and chanted "USA! USA! USA!" all the way out the door.

DO NOT
TURN
RED

During another of my annual employee reviews, my supervisor informed me that my tone with administration was a tad, well, unprofessional. In all other categories, he said, I was an excellent bus driver. But the way I spoke to my superiors left something to be desired.

I tended to be a little testy, he said.

"You're talking about my blue cards, I suppose," I said. Blue cards were used by drivers to inform management of ongoing issues with buses and routes and the like.

He smiled. "You certainly could have handled that differently," he said.

"Maybe," I said. "But after filling out three blue cards about the shitty windshield wipers and getting no response, I decided to change it up a bit. Alter my tactics, as it were."

My final blue card had suggested, not unkindly, that every single person in the procurement wing of the administration should be required to drive on an unlit rural highway at night in the pouring rain, preferably in a 60-foot bus.

"Should that happen," I concluded the blue card, "the fleet would have new and improved windshield wipers within the week. Thank you for your sweetly faked attention."

Within days of receiving my blue card, it was "discovered" that Cosmodemonic Unified Northwest Transit had received a faulty batch of windshield wipers from its contracted supplier. This information was transmitted in language indicating that a minor miracle had occurred. New wipers would be arriving within the week, we were informed.

The claim, of course, was utter bullshit. I'd written my final blue card after being informed by a mechanic in maintenance that Cosmodemonic had been purchasing the cheapest wipers on the market, totally bottom of the barrel stuff, for years. It was policy.

"Those wipers are shit, and they know it, the cheap bastards," he said. "I wouldn't let my mother-in-law drive with them."

"I mean, it worked, right?" I said to my supervisor.

"You've got me there," he said, nodding. "I'm just suggesting you use a slightly more professional tone next time. Make it a safety issue instead. That's the magic word. Safety. It always triggers an immediate response."

"I did make it a safety issue," I replied. "Their safety. Ours doesn't really seem to matter."

"Well, anyway," he said.

A week before graduation, they gathered us in the meeting room in the maintenance wing. We were joined by one of our union reps. He pulled a stool into the middle of the room. He looked tired. Before he started speaking, he gave out a big sigh, running his fingers through his long, gray hair and offering us up one of those sad "what're ya gonna do" smiles that signals the imminent arrival of bad news.

"Well, you guys," he said, "we just came from a meeting with the administration. Look, I'm sorry, but it sounds like, with the pandemic and all the uncertainty about next year's budget, you're gonna get laid off."

A collective groan went up from the class. Someone whispered "shit," someone else muttered "that fuckin' blows, man."

I said nothing. This news struck me as neither good nor bad. My passion for the working life has always been tepid at best. My first thought was about state-funded unemployment, mingled with a vague sense of relief that, in the end, I might not have to become a bus driver at all.

Ten weeks of training had proven that driving a bus was, indeed, a rather unpleasant job. Would they take me back at the newspaper?

"So is that, like, for sure," Jimmy Silvers asked, "or what?"

"Looks like it," the rep said.

"When are we going to be let go?" Jimmy asked.

The union rep shrugged. "We haven't been given a date yet, but by the looks of it you'll probably officially be laid off sometime mid-month. The details are still being worked out. It's all kinda one big cluster-fuck."

Jimmy slapped the table. "Yo!" he said. "Wait a minute! Are you telling me that we're going to finish training, graduate, get cut loose on our own to drive the bus for what, a week or two, and then get fired?"

"Well," the rep said in the corrective tone of a kindergarten teacher, "laid off, actually. You'll be eligible for unemployment, of course."

"For how long?" Jimmy asked. "How long will the lay-off be for?"

"Who knows?" the rep said. "Nobody knows how long this

thing's gonna last. What I'd suggest is, get your unemployment lined up fast, kick back, and enjoy the summer. The union is already working on getting you guys hired back as soon as possible."

I actually believed the guy. He was an old-timer, and during his decades at Cosmodemonic he'd remained a bus driver the whole time, only climbing to the level of instructor and union steward.

What this indicated was that he was either a garden-variety loser, content to find his lot in life by default and stick there like a barnacle, or else he was actually firmly dedicated to the working class, loyal on principle.

Either way was fine with me.

Maybe it was a little of both. With us in the working class, it usually is.

Working stiff is not typically an identity one chooses right out of the gate. It's an identity chosen for you—like being a Mets fan—by forces largely out of your control. The designation might as well be God given, it's all so sticky and undemocratic.

I'm a working stiff. I was born a working stiff. I'll likely die a working stiff, ten years short on my mortgage and a defiant middle finger frozen in rigor mortis.

Turning such caste politics into a point of class pride is an act of resignation and acceptance, all at once, like snatching victory from the jaws of defeat. If the victory is pyrrhic, that's okay.

It's fine. It's good.

It's fine and good that you do all the real work in this world, and if it's bad that the people oppressing you are siphoning your surplus labor value in order to live their lives of pomp, pedophilia, and presidential pardons, it is bad to want to be one of them, because all that would really mean is some other poor sap getting shunted into your spot.

And that'll never happen anyway. There's no escape. It's fixed this way. They need you to stay exactly where you are, forever, so they can stay where they are, for as long as they can hold out.

That's why they don't call you a working flex. It's working stiff—dead, paralyzed, immobile, stuck in time, frozen in place.

So, like a good soldier, you surrender to being torn down, used up and shat out—not because you like it, but because, all things considered, it is right and good.

I was a total mess the day before my first official shift as a bus driver. I was assigned a 5:55 a.m. start time. I spent the entire evening poring over my route sheets, like a general on the brink of battle. I couldn't eat dinner. I couldn't sit still.

Before going to bed, I neatly folded my work clothes, setting them in a neat pile on the kitchen counter, like a kid before the first day of school. I set the coffee maker to brew at 4:15. I organized my backpack. I even polished my shoes.

All this nervous prep was almost pleasurable. The threat of failure in any given situation is a weird tonic for me—I expect failure, secretly crave it, while at the same time suspecting that, if things fall just so, this same situation might reveal me at to be a homespun genius, unfairly ignored up to this point but finally receiving my heroic due.

I checked my alarm at least a dozen times, kissed my wife goodnight, put my head on the pillow and proceeded to toss and turn until well after midnight.

Should I ever finally escape the wage-slave hell of Cosmodemonic Unified Northwest Transit and subsequently fall prey to that inbred psychological dynamic that salvages the least unsavory aspects of a job, wrapping them in the sepia glow of eternal nostalgia, I'm pretty sure the one consistently nice memory I'll carry to my grave is the brisk, bracing feeling of walking onto that massive lot in the predawn dark to prep out a bus for my day's work.

This was often, if not always, the best part of my shift—honestly, it was often the only thing I really liked about the whole miserable grind.

Bus drivers drop lots of *Groundhog Day* references—the movie, that is. The protagonist of that film played to narcissistic perfection by Bill Murray, keeps waking up trapped in the same exact day—a day that is infinitely repeated in every particular, save for his increasingly futile responses to it, which do nothing to halt the endless loop.

The movie perfectly construes a theoretical proposition that has forever haunted philosophers, the question of free will versus determinism—represented here less as a question than a nightmare collision of twisted and teasing fatalism. Try as he might, Bill can't escape the loop. And yet, for those first few moments after the alarm clock rings and before he starts once again suffering the slings and arrows of outrageous fortune, he does experience a fleeting sense of hope—a promise that, just maybe, this day won't suck like all the others.

Or rather, this day won't suck just like itself.

Ditto for a bus driver heading onto the lot to prep out his bus.

Drivers endlessly crack jokes about the repetitive nature of the job. You know, same shit, different day. Livin' the dream! Another day in paradise! Here we go again, stuck on the treadmill, spinning on the hamster wheel, trapped in the simulation.

And yet, no matter how crappy you may feel—and no matter how fucking awful yesterday might have been—you always experience a scintilla of hope as you trudge the lot to prep your bus for the day. Things might go well today. Just maybe I could have an okay shift this time around. Why not?

The daily renewal of working-class hope—an ancillary of amnesia—is a cheap but plentiful salve built into the malignant equation of punching the clock. It's a protective mechanism that temporarily prevents your spirit from melting away like a salted slug.

Or perhaps it's just a carrot-and-stick thing, another instance of corporate Stockholm Syndrome inflicted by the titans of industry.

Maybe it's all just one enormous con.

Or perhaps, in the final reckoning, nostalgia and memory are synonymous—not only inseparable but identical.

I recall reading Nietzsche's description of the phenomenon of dreaming: A man is awakened by a noise, but just prior to waking, his brain actually manufactures a credible story that not only ends with the noise waking him up, but explains to his dreaming mind the occasion and cause of that noise.

Anyone who has experienced this themselves will immediately recognize is as a credible description of the dream state. It is an astonishing thing—that the mind, moving faster than the speed of time, can manufacture an instantaneous narrative to explain a spontaneous jolt to its own perceptions.

But what if this describes our waking reality as well? What if everything we think we think, and everything we experience, is only a retroactive explanation propelling itself forward as truth? What a piece of magic!

This not only demolishes the neat dynamics of cause and effect, but it lays bare the idea that objective reality exists at all. I mean, we don't even really see anything until our brain projects a received transmission of the world back onto the optical nerve. It's not that things aren't there. It's just that they aren't there-there.

There is no direct, one-to-one correlation to the reality we apprehend. The stories we tell ourselves, in other words, don't even describe what happened or what is now happening; they are stabs in the dark at best, and maybe just excuses, maybe just apologies we make to ourselves.

And these excuses and apologies transport themselves in advance to swallow the present before it becomes the now, turning it into the past, prepackaged and tied up with a tidy bow.

And, therefore, if memory is nostalgia, and our awareness of the world is nothing more than an echo moving forward to devour its own object, how in the fuck can we escape this prison of time—no matter how miserable it makes us?

Could it be that the very misery we experience is only its own seduction to continue?

Why do I continue to go back to a job when, just a day or a week or a year ago, I swore I would never go back to it ever again?

Why do I get nostalgic about my own suffering?

Are nostalgia and memory in the service of something far bigger than our subjective perceptions?

Is this God's will?

Or am I in hell?

I can hear Cement Bob laughing.

What I do know is that on that first morning, I experienced something akin to religious awe as I walked across the pavement of the lot toward my 40-foot bus.

A hint of rose had crept into the dark sky, lighting up the clouds from below as the Earth's rotation spun the sun's aura into view on the distant horizon, way away over the mountains.

Everything on that lot was so massive and squared off and spread out—a Kubrickian panorama of geometrical precision arranged in vast space. Rows of buses sat lined up across the lot, Jurassic beasts rumbling to life one by one.

And here I was, a brand-new sad-happy human cog, trained and certified and suited up, ready to serve my time in this gargantuan enterprise of American industry.

At last! I was now part of a well-regulated system of quasi-governmental public service, participating in the great sprawling civic machinery of a city's lumbering infrastructure. It's corny, I know, but I'm a sucker for scope and scale.

My mind is fired up by abstract things integrated into reality over long spans of time, by covenant, by contract, by mysterious processes that dwarf the negligible wisp of my lone consciousness.

It is neither good nor bad, this feeling I feel. It says nothing about the moral or socioeconomic quality of the thing beheld. Its cost is irrelevant.

Rather, it is a sense of primordial wonder that sweeps over me whenever I first encounter these huge monuments and systems we have built: the Hoover Dam, the pyramids of Teotihuacan, the subways of New York.

You pull open the shuttered front door. Set your backpack down. Fumble in the dark for the starter dial. Turn it from off to night run. Flip the fast-idle switch. Turn on the aisle lights. Reach down and engage the air pressure.

The bus beeps and moans as the dashboard lights up like the cockpit of an airplane. You remind yourself that you are captain of your own ship.

You drive the bus for the people!

You wait for the orange "wait to start" light to blink off, then press the starter button. Watch the gauge needles swing into view, feel the testicular growl of the bus starting up.

With a startling hiss, the excess air pressure expels from the tanks, like a locomotive in motion.

Switch on the climate control. Turn the handle to open the front door. Reach above to switch on the check lights.

Step off the bus and execute your pre-trip walkabout: side-view mirrors intact, all lights beeping and flashing, bike rack functional, tire tread adequate, rims unbent, bolts secure and free of trailing rust.

No fluid leaking from the ass end.

Okay, back onto the bus.

Interior walk-through. Shut the front door. Make sure the needle on the fire extinguisher is in the green. Emergency road signs accounted for. Pull the cord and affirm that the dinger works. Fucking dinger. Ding ding. Ding ding ding.

Walk the inside of the bus, front to back, checking seats, making sure no festering corpses were left behind from the day before.

Okay. Settle back in the cockpit. Adjust your seat, tilt the steering wheel. Adjust all your mirrors. Make sure everything's just right. Honk the horn.

Now for the triple air-brake test: Pump them down to 90 pounds of pressure and hold the pedal to make sure pressure builds back up to around 120.

After this, pump the brakes like a madman until the red warning lights come on and the siren sounds. Roger that. Flip open the back doors to make sure the interlock brake is engaged. Buckle yourself in. Release the parking brake. Let the bus roll forward and then stomp the brake. Do it again, but engage the parking brake this time.

All good. Ready to rumble.

That first day I ran through my prep-out like a private in boot camp with an invisible drill sergeant barking orders over my shoulder. Here I was, in the shit at last. It was finally real. Keep it together, boy-o, and lean on your training like they warned you!

Of course, really real things immediately feel extremely surreal to me. I'm a Gen-X latchkey TV baby raised on suspended disbelief and cathode fantasies. When I suddenly find myself playing a starring role in an unfamiliar situation, I disassociate and de-realize.

How did I end up in this movie?

So I took a deep breath. In situations when the incipient threat of failure looms like a darkening storm cloud—in other words, for most of my life—I've come to rely on a form of Zen mantra that I've haphazardly pieced together and refined over the years, and now, before I put the bus into gear and began my deadhead to the station to commence my first day on route, I gave myself a little pep talk:

Listen, bro, what's the worst that can happen? I mean, in a couple decades you're going to be dead, and none of this will have mattered at all. Remember what Wittgenstein said. Dead is dead.

In fact, in the face of eternity and nothingness, this life of yours is just a comical little eyeblink. No one will remember you, much less care about you in a hundred years—if we even last that long, because it's not looking good—and here you are getting completely puckered up over driving a bus. You're already dead! Let it go! Laugh it off!

Now let's put on our game face, and go out to meet the mayhem.

Hooyah!

I wheeled the bus through the automated gate and off the lot. My whole body was buzzing. The streets were still lamplit and mostly traffic-free. I imagined I was at the helm of a big rattling spaceship, maybe the *Millennium Falcon*, heading to pick up a clutch of wanted rebels at Mos Eisley spaceport—a lone man in an empty vessel, ruggedly handsome if a little long in the tooth, battle-tested and attractively taciturn, even a bit sexy, now setting off on a heroic mission to save the frenzied citizens of this busted-up and besieged Republic, one castaway at a time.

Fear and exhilaration met and mingled, I was doomed and I was overjoyed, my head felt carbonated and my stomach was a warm oven of off-loaded adrenaline.

For no reason at all I started giggling, and then I let out a frenzied whoop that sounded locked-up and hollow inside the empty confines of the bus—the cry of a madman in his cell, free at last. He thinks.

What remains from those first days of driving the bus is a kaleidoscope of snippets and vague impressions, all of them floating free in narrative time: me missing bus stops, cut scene, me hitting curbs, cut scene, me blowing time points, cut scene, me weeping, cut scene, me approaching pale green traffic lights seized by the fear of God. Cut. Splice.

Especially prevalent in my mind is the lurking terror of going off route and not understanding how to get back on route. Going off route was indeed the grand mal of anxieties possessing me that whole first year of driving.

The potential of going astray in my bus—nay, the inevitability of it—reared up as tantamount to annihilation in my consciousness.

Going off route haunted my dreams and crippled my days. Fear owned me.

On the plus side, I did succeed in not killing anybody those first weeks of driving, or so it would appear. Perhaps the jury's still out. There's no statute of limitations on murder, right?

Because I lied a little bit—there is one incident from my first day on the job that I recall quite clearly. It occurred on my final run.

I was driving the Central route, one among a handful of notoriously crappy runs that wheels through the poorer, druggier parts of town. At its halfway point, that route crosses the Felony Flats intersection, a creepy-crawly nexus of bad behavior where the growing hordes of dispossessed among us vie for a tentative foothold in an uber-competitive free market of methamphetamines, fast food, social services, and camping space.

My bus-driving colleagues expressed almost universal loathing for Felony Flats, especially its denizens.

Certainly, nothing much good ever happened there. The place stank of failure. It was as close to a ghetto as we got: gray, industrial, littered with pawn shops and parole offices, all of it dominated by an auto salvage yard that cast a Mordor pall with its mountain of mangled cars looming over everything.

Passing through Felony Flats always involved some kind of psychic challenge that caused you to question the series of life choices that led you precisely to this place.

When I began driving for Cosmodemonic Unified Northwest Transit, the overwhelming attitude among bus drivers concerning issues of poverty, homelessness, and the lower classes in general, especially the drug addicted—especially the meth heads—greatly appalled me, to such an extent that I almost jumped ship that first year.

I wasn't sure I could stomach the rancor. The drivers lounge resounded with furious, withering tirades about the homeless.

I'm not talking about once in a while. I'm talking all the time. In fact, it's almost the only thing drivers talk about. The fucking homeless.

"Why is he even alive?" I once heard a driver wonder aloud about one of his, shall we say, less-than-fortunate riders.

Mind you, this was one of the tamer comments I might encounter any given day of the week, tempered at least by the timorous imposition of a question mark.

More often than not, comments by drivers inched shockingly close to the ultimate taboo, hinting at a Final Solution mentality—the verbalized desire to just get rid of these fuckers once and for all.

Exterminate the brutes!

The horror, the horror.

But here's the thing:

Regardless of my hardcore lefty leanings, and despite my spiritual inclinations toward love and equality, and snuggled somewhere beneath my moderately sophisticated sociopolitical understanding of the systemic roots of poverty and homelessness, and resting somewhere alongside my strong Marxist sympathies and, at the same time, well outside my general concern for the oppressed everywhere, and yet never once forgetting my suspicion that the scapegoating narratives targeting the homeless are leading us all into a very bloody mass reckoning—as surely as Hitler baited the Germans into the Holocaust, but on a far broader scale, meaning a wholesale genocide on the poor themselves—despite all this, I came over time to sympathize with the endless vitriol my colleagues expressed toward the people existing at the bottom of the social scale.

Because I experienced that anger and disgust myself. You can't not. Poverty is ugly. Poverty is dirty. Poverty is rude. Poverty hurts your head. It hurts your heart.

As a bus driver, the tangled consequences of poverty are in your face nonstop—physically, emotionally, spiritually—and minus the bearings of Gandhi, your compassion gets ground to dust.

Poverty, for a bus driver, is intimate and unavoidable, like herpes. You can't shake it. It is inconvenient and infuriating and emotionally disruptive. No one person has the emotional bandwidth to take it in without getting beat to shit.

Compassion fatigue, my therapist called it. That might as well be the defining characteristic of bus driving. Or, for that matter, any service worker stuck in his or her job and just trying to make a go of these days.

So, another cranky bus driver opinion: As politicians and business leaders continue to manipulate and exploit and play games with the exponentially increasing impoverished classes that they themselves engineer and perpetuate—and that they themselves desperately need in order to maintain their financial choke hold on us—it is the servant class, the bus drivers and fast food workers and convenience store clerks and coffee jerks, who swallow all their shit.

All of us in the service sector are forced to compensate for a horribly broken system, by embracing the human wreckage this grinder churns out like so much nonrecyclable trash.

And then, in turn, we are instructed, by the same people creating that wreckage, to blame the wreckage for the wreck.

Fuck the homeless?

Fuck the rich.

I picked up the woman in question in the Whiteside neighborhood. She was young, maybe mid-thirties, pretty, with long auburn hair, wearing jeans and a tattered Rancid T-shirt.

She plopped down in a seat near the front. We were alone together on the bus. I wheeled through the neighborhood, down past the Mission, onto the overpass to catch Roosevelt toward Felony Flats and points beyond.

Perched in her seat, the woman peered out the window, tapping her foot like a metronome against the floorboards.

Finally, she stood up and approached me. Grabbing the nearby handrail, she leaned in.

"Does this bus go up Cripple Creek Road?" she asked.

I had to think about it for a second. "Um, no, no I don't think so," I said. "No, it doesn't."

She looked out the windshield for a minute. "Well," she said. "I need to get to Cripple Creek. Can you take me to Cripple Creek?"

"Yeah, I can't really do that," I said. It was my first time trying to carry on any sort of conversation while driving the bus. It was surprisingly difficult.

"But you can," she said. "You can take me to Cripple Creek, can't you?"

The tone of her voice suggested that this was indeed a rhetorical question.

As calmly as I could, I said: "Ma'am, I can either let you off this bus, or you can sit down and ride. I can't talk to you and drive at the same time."

"But you are driving and talking at the same time," she said. "Are you going to take me to Cripple Creek?"

"Ma'am," I said, "you need to sit down right now. Please. I'm not asking again."

I heard her draw a deep breath. "If you don't take me to Cripple Creek, I'm going to get murdered," she said. "And that's on you," she added matter-of-factly.

"Excuse me?" I said.

"I'm being followed, and I am about to be murdered," she said. "And if I get killed, it will be your fault. So are you going to take me to Cripple Creek now?"

"Would you like me to call the police?" I asked.

"It's too late for that," she said.

"Well, this bus goes to Central and then it turns around and goes back the way it came," I said. "You're welcome to stay on the bus."

"Suit yourself," she said. She reached back and yanked the cord. Ding.

We were almost to Felony Flats. I pulled to the curb and stopped in front of the train tracks. I opened the front door. I didn't know what to say to her, so I opted for silence.

She stepped off the bus onto the sidewalk and stood looking at me.

"Goodbye," she said. "I hope you're happy."

"I'm not," I said.

She shrugged and began walking the way we'd just come.

I watched her in my side-view mirror for a moment before pulling away. She was walking briskly, not running, not fleeing, not pursued as far as I could tell, and I had the thought I've had a thousand times since this moment:

What in the fuck am I supposed to do here?

What if everything she told me was true, and I just epically failed in the worst way possible?

What if this radically unreasonable request for assistance is, in fact, the final desperate plea of a human being in real distress?

Have I misjudged someone's mental health?

Should I stop everything and help? What do I do here?

Maybe we're all murderers. Maybe we're all being pursued. Maybe death is the only thing on the menu anymore.

Or maybe help is on the way. Maybe someone will finally have the courage to veer off route and deliver us right where we need to be. But I don't think so.

I don't think this bus is going where we need it to go any more. We can't get there from here. The fare is too high and the dinger don't work no more.

We're off route.

Adapt or Die

The condemned man fools himself into believing that the cigarette and the blindfold means he's got just a little more time.

George Orwell marveled at the fact that a man being led to his execution took the time to avoid stepping into a mud puddle.

I wheeled my bus into the lot and parked it in the designated slot. Another bullshit day, another long shift finished. This was the lonely hour. I should have felt better, experienced some sense of relief, much less joy, at having survived another shift, but for some reason the minutes right after work, before I got in my car and drove home, they felt empty. I couldn't conjure any sense of celebration. I just felt worn down and depressed anymore.

I logged out of the bus's operations system, unbuckled and stood from my seat. Walking the aisles for my check-in, I scanned the floor for discarded or lost items, or any interior damage to the bus. I reached up and shut one of the cantilevered windows left open by a rider.

Reaching the back of the bus, I turned around. Something caught my eye.

I knew what it was immediately, maybe before I'd even seen it. A dime bag sitting on the floor beneath a seat. About the size of a postage stamp. Full of white powder. About the size of the universe.

There are cameras on the bus that record everything, inside and out. I was once told by a senior driver with an annoying habit of giving a thumbs-up every time he passed you that his best piece of advice for new operators was: "Act as though someone's always watching, because someone always is."

"Yeah," I told him. "I know. I can't give a fuck about that."

Now, however, I had the overwhelming sensation of being under surveillance, and it was terrible. I felt guilty as sin, as though I'd already hoovered up the dope and was getting ready to light the bus on fire. I inadvertently glanced at the flat black eye of the surveillance camera perched in the front corner of the bus.

I squatted down, tweezered the bag with my thumb and forefinger, and slipped it directly into my back pocket before quickly standing back up.

That night I dreamt I was breaking into the sailboat with a hammer. There I was, pounding on the outside of the cabin, violently, splinters flying everywhere. It was taking way too long, it wasn't working, this pounding, something was wrong. No progress was being made. I just kept hitting it and hitting it.

A tremendous sense of futility, as though, like Sysiphus, I would be there forever, pounding away. A feeling like suffocation, or running in quicksand.

Finally, I get inside. I'm seated at a table, in front of a huge pile of cocaine. A veritable mountain of cocaine. I've never seen so much cocaine. I'll never run out. I experience the thrill of a prospector striking gold at last. The arrival of no more wanting.

I put my face into the pile, but I can't get high. The more I snort, the more anxious I feel, a promise within reach denied, withheld.

I understand, with a horrible sinking feeling, that I have never been sober. I've never stopped. This whole thing has been a lie. Sobriety itself has been a fever dream, and now I'm waking up to something worse. Time compresses like an accordion. Hopelessness and grief seize me.

Just like that I'm driving the bus. It's full of people. They're all watching me. I'm barely in control of the bus, it's careening down the street, speeding through space, I'm full of cocaine and guilt. I take a quick left and immediately realize that I should have taken a right, and I'm in a sprawling metropolis, huge, a cinematic composite of New York City. There is a war going on. Bombs are exploding, people on the street are running with crazed fear, throwing themselves under my bus.

Cement Bob is standing beside me in the aisle, naked from the waist down. He has the hairless penis of an elephant. "You're dead," I tell him.

"I've never had it so good!" Bob shouts, gazing out the front windshield, smiling.

"Bob, you're not wearing any pants," I tell him.

"Speak for yourself," he says.

Buildings are collapsing in front of me in slow motion. The road unrolls like a ribbon, throwing people in the air. It seems to be pulling the bus along with it, faster and faster. "I'm really struggling here, Bob," I shout.

At this, his old man's face goes sad with disappointment. A sob erupts in my throat. "If you need help now, you've been drunk for a long time," Bob says rapidly. "I'm surprised but never shocked when one of us falls. It's what we … hey hey HEY … ."

The sailboat starts rocking madly. All the coke is falling off the table, and I'm scrambling to sweep it back together with my hands but they're covered in massive oven mitts. A sensation of abysmal loss swamps me and I start crying, crying with the despairing self-pity of a child watching his ice cream cone hit the hot pavement.

Clare was shaking me gently, her hand pressed against my shoulder. "Hey hey," she said. "Are you awake?"

"I'm good, I'm good," I said, breathlessly, feeling the dream—all of it—clinging to me like something alive. "Jesus, that was awful."

She rolled over to spoon me, both hands pressed against my side like a supplicant. "I'm right here," she said. "You're okay."

"I haven't had a relapse dream in a long time," I said. "Cement Bob was there."

"Aww, Cement Bob," she said. "Did you say hi to him for me? I miss that guy."

"He wasn't wearing any pants," I said. "Like Porky Pig or something. With this huge pecker hanging in the air … hey, I'm still sober, right?"

"As far as I know," Clare said.

ONE WAY ▶

Every single bloody time I walked into therapy I'd say to myself, recalling the previous week's session and every session before that: I'm very sick of listening to myself talk. Words, words, words. I'm a silly, self-preening, ridiculous fool of a man. Totally full of shit.

This time I'm going to be measured, focused and to the point. Let's do this!

"I've been thinking," I said to my therapist. "The truth is, I'm just not a viable candidate for survival. None of me wants this, whatever it is this might be. That's all there is to it. Honestly, I've had a pretty good run up to now, all things considered. I did whatever the hell I wanted for a long time, and it's not like I didn't suffer, but at least I was relatively free. Now it looks for all the world like I'm starting to pay the price for my past. Everything's coming due. It sucks, but boo-hoo, right? There's nothing special about me. A lot of people have it way worse than I do."

"Can you tell me which part is speaking now?" she asked.

"Well, certainly the part that says 'fuck it'" I said. "That part of me that wants to blow up everything, but it's also a part that asks me who the hell I think I am. It's a part that feels completely alone. It doesn't trust anything or anyone. It's the part of me that thinks this whole love and understanding thing is just a sick joke."

"So lots of parts," she said, smiling.

"Yeah, I'm full of 'em," I said. "They're a real pain in my ass."

"Do you really not feel loved?" she asked.

"I do," I said. "I do. But there's this … part of me, I guess … that's constantly chattering in my head, questioning the love I receive. I have this interior monologue. It's constantly looking for reasons to jump up and say, 'Aha, you see! It's not real!' There's a really smart, really critical judge in my head who's constantly on the lookout for the slightest sign that the people closest to me don't really love me, because they don't really know me. And worse, they don't want to really know me."

She nodded. "So there's some fear of abandonment," she said.

"A desire to be seen, and to be told you're okay. To be loved and understood."

"The problem is, this is all so very tenuous to me," I said. "I get what you're saying, I really do, but all this knowing doesn't mean jack-shit when I think I'm perceiving a particular tone in Clare's voice. A bitchy tone, a critical tone. I go on autopilot. The joker in my head gets way too loud. I mean, insane people don't know they're insane, right? I feel like that's how my emotions work."

"And how many times, in retrospect, have you mistaken her tone?"

"Almost every time," I said, laughing. "Usually I only realize it after about twenty-four hours of sheer hell."

"So can you short-circuit that by leaning into a different understanding?" she asked.

"I don't get what you're saying," I said.

"Well, instead of thinking she's being critical, or judgmental, maybe you could try to understand what she's saying, instead of how she's saying it," she said. "Everybody has a different love language."

"So you're asking me to lean into love?" I said.

"Lean into trust," she said. "Lean into trusting that the people around you really care about you."

I felt tears welling in my eyes. Was it really that simple? It sounded like a gussied-up version of the same bullshit I'd been hearing my whole life. Kiddo, you just need to change your perspective. Focus on the good stuff. While the world burns. I just wasn't built that way.

And yet, here I was, crying in front of my therapist. "Yeah," I said. "I can do that."

I was on day six of consecutive twelve-hour days, and day twelve out of thirteen. I'd been required to work on one of my scheduled days off—as the Conradian term had it, I'd been "force canceled"—and I was on the verge of a major freak-out. My nerves were shot.

I pulled into the station for a twenty-minute lunch break before my next run. As I sat watching my passengers file off the bus, I caught a glimpse of Doyle Claggart approaching from my left. He was slowly and deliberately strolling across the station pavement toward my driver-side window, which was cracked open.

I honestly thought he was on a humanitarian mission, coming to pull me off my work before I went postal.

Claggart leaned into my window, looked down at my side console, and noticed a stack of day passes wedged between a pair of control knobs, left there by the previous driver. I hadn't even noticed them until he spotted them. He picked up the passes and shook them in my face.

"What's this?" he asked.

"Well, Doyle," I said. "They look like day passes to me."

He shook his head disapprovingly.

"Never leave these in your window," he said.

"Um, okay," I said.

"… where somebody can nab them and start handing them out willy-nilly. Or selling them. Keep them in your pocket, or at the very least, away from the window."

Something in me snapped. Like Jekyll-and-Hyde snapped. I reached out, snatched the stack of day passes out of Doyle Claggart's fingers and flipped them right in his face. Claggart himself looked completely stunned, like the playground bully finally bopped in the nose by a wild roundhouse from the playground wimp.

In fact, for the first time since I'd had the misfortune of meeting him, he actually looked stupid and confused.

Claggart took a step back. He held up his hands in a gesture of whoa-daddy, cool it. But I wasn't done.

"Are you fucking kidding me?" I barked. "Day passes? You're gonna crawl up my ass about fucking day passes? We're out here getting slaughtered for fourteen hours a day, day after day, in the middle of a fucking plague, and you're worried about day passes? You should be kissing my ass! Every single driver driving in this godforsaken place is miserable and sick in the head right now. We've got our rear ends flapping in the breeze, completely unsupported, left to hang, and here you are tormenting me like a goddamn Pinkerton. This place is hell! It's completely inhumane! You should be ashamed of yourself! Sneaking up to my window to bust me for a measly stack of day passes? I mean, they taught us in training not to give a shit about fares! So what is it, Doyle? Do we worry about fares, or not worry about fares! Jesus Christ, I'm losing my mind here!"

"Okay, take it easy now," Claggart whispered, looking around at the drivers and riders now stopped in their tracks and gawking at us.

I was only vaguely aware of the scene I was making.

"Listen," he said calmly. "Why don't you get off the bus and come with me and we can talk."

I did what Claggart asked. He met me at the door as I stepped off the bus, gently grabbing my arm while I continued ranting. He led me like a mental patient toward the drivers lounge, obviously wanting to get me sequestered away from the public.

"I just don't get how you guys can watch us all die out here day after day and not do anything about it but keep grinding us to death," I continued, but I was winding down.

Embarrassment and contrition were starting to creep into my consciousness, along with a sinking suspicion that I'd probably just earned my own termination. Now I was fighting back tears—not for the potential loss of my job, but out of exhaustion and sorrow.

Claggart finally got me inside the building. We stopped in the hallway.

"I'm sorry," I said. "This isn't personal. I just can't take this shit. It's too much."

"Hey," he said. "Don't worry about it. That's what us supervisors are here for. You can talk to us."

"Yeah, I wasn't talking," I said. "I was pretty much yelling."

"It's okay," he said.

I looked at him. He was regaining control of the situation, and I sensed a subtle Machiavellian shift in the immediate atmosphere, a power play in the offing. I flinched a bit. "No," I said. "It's not okay. None of this is okay."

"Yeah," he said, "but do you feel better?"

And there it was: I'd been spontaneously pathologized. The content of my rant was irrelevant.

The content would be isolated, inverted, and neutralized into a mere expression of free-floating stress divorced from any discernible and potentially fixable cause. I was the lone gunman.

Do you feel better? Do you feel better now, honey? Did that help? Have you had your fun? Because we're here for you. We're not going to change a goddamn thing, but we will field your tantrums, up to a point, in the hopes that you will punch yourself out and get back to work asap. Because this is all about you, not us.

We are merely the steadfast defenders of business as usual, and our job is to fit you to it, by any means necessary, gently or with legitimate force, makes little difference to us in the end: to contort you, convince you, hypnotize you, brainwash you, shame you, blame you, celebrate you, divide you, dismiss you, demean you, absorb you, seduce you, reduce you, confuse you, amuse you, refuse you, accuse you, and recycle you, all in the hopes of maintaining a fitness sufficient to our needs, until that moment you are finally smashed to smithereens.

See? Isn't that easy? Don't you feel just a little better?

The people in charge don't actually think they're breaking your spirit. It's much more insidious than that. Because their own spirits were already broken long ago, they sincerely believe that what they are doing is helping you survive this reality—by setting standards, by enforcing unquestionable rules, by micromanaging and then disciplining you for any deviations from the norm. By dressing you up and dressing you down.

The goal is not to crush your spirit but absorb you entirely. Absorb your personality, your dreams, your energy, your time. Until you come to believe that, yes, this is indeed a family and it all makes sense, even if that sense is painful, even if you secretly hate it. So you hate it, but you stay, because you see no alternative, no real option. The world outside is so scary. There's no telling how you'd do out there on your own.

Adapt or die.

Budget projections were cited as the reason for the layoff. The pandemic was making everyone nervous. The board and administration were being proactive, or so it appeared—and for them, appearance was the only thing that mattered.

The fact that this was not a profit-driven corporation but a quasi-governmental entity predominantly supported by secure state and federal funding might suggest a different approach, one that did not slash over a quarter of its workforce in phantom anticipations of a crash, only to have it siphon yet more tax dollars sitting idle in unemployment.

But what did I know? Business is business, and Cosmodemonic Unified Northwest Transit was just following the corporate crowd—you know, cashing in on a huge opportunity presented by a global crisis. Of course, the organization would receive upwards of $40 million in COVID emergency funding—for operational costs, meaning, for the most part, worker wages—only half of which it would use before banking the rest, with drivers seeing little to none of it.

In fact, throughout the entire pandemic, those drivers who avoided the layoff continued to work without a contract, because the fuckwits at Cosmodemonic refused to negotiate on such things as a wage increase that barely matched the skyrocketing cost of living. Business as usual.

I knew none of this at the time. When the layoff date came, I dutifully turned in my uniform and my driving notes—which were promptly shredded, indicating that in fact they had no intention at all of bringing us back—and I walked away.

The whole process was weird, and kinda creepy in a dystopian sort of way. It felt like an evacuation during war time. Everything we handed in was dumped wonky-doodle into these huge cardboard boxes, with only the shoddiest attempt at inventorying the items returned.

It didn't seem to matter what you threw into the boxes—hats, jackets, jumpsuits, used condoms, dirty underwear, dead dogs, pornography, dog-eared copies of the Communist Manifesto, empty bottles, used syringes, cigarette butts, bitter tears. Your tax dollars at work!

They cashed out whatever sick pay and vacation time I had accrued, another indication of their true intentions regarding the layoff. We love you, we're sorry, we'll bring you back as soon as possible, but not really, now go fuck yourself.

I figured they were simply following the protocol required in such circumstances, rather than giving us the high hat. But they were indeed giving us the high hat. This job isn't for everyone—especially not you. Fuck. Off.

So I took my beefed-up final paycheck and headed for the hills. Nothing like throwing a little extra money at somebody to short-circuit their critical faculties.

"Hello, bus driver, how are you?"

I'm guessing she was 15, maybe 16. I picked her up regularly on one of the university routes, where student bungalows mix with low-income housing across from the school's resplendent football stadium, which stands like a fascist fortress against the general failure slowly swallowing everything in its midst.

"Well, hello," I said, in my best professional bus driver voice. "How are you?"

She stood just back from the driver's compartment, her hand on the handrail. "I'm great," she said. In her other hand she held a tattered shoebox. "I found a hurt bird outside the window," she said, raising the box up. "But my grandmother won't let me keep it in the apartment. I'm going to see if I can find somebody to take care of it. Do you know anybody that can take care of it?"

I shook my head. "I'm sorry, I don't," I said. I felt a surge of sadness. The bird was fucked, of course, but she didn't know that, and I wasn't going to tell her. "Maybe a vet? Maybe the raptor center? I don't know. But it's good of you to take care of it. I hope it works out."

"Yeah," she said, contemplatively, looking at the box in her hand. "Do you want it?"

I looked in my rearview mirror and caught her eyes. She gave me a tight grin as sadness and hope passed across her face. "Oh, I'm sorry," I said. "I can't. I've got hours left to go. But I sure hope you find somewhere to take it."

She shrugged, sighed and then revived, flashing me a look of pure determination. "I will," she said. "Thanks anyway."

I smiled at her. "You're a good person," I said.

She shrugged again. "Yeah," she said. "Anyway, I'm going to go find a seat. Have a good day. Thanks for the ride, bus driver."

Another time she had a kitten she'd rescued. I don't know where she was taking it. She was just taking it. Other animals followed. She'd sit in the seat and I'd watch her holding the portable kennel in her lap with the fenced door facing her, and she'd look at the animal with longing, talking to it quietly.

And it was always the same story: Grandma said I can't keep

it in the house, I'd better find somewhere else for it to be. These words were never delivered with rancor, only a kind of resignation, a shrug.

A portrait began to develop in my head, a partial understanding. Parents out of the picture, perhaps drugs involved, maybe death, but at any rate abandoned, given up, handed over, dutiful but reluctant custody assumed, poverty, generational trauma, perhaps child protective services involved, maybe grandma was a drinker herself, who knows? Maybe grandma was doing the best she could. And here was this child, this woman-child, standing on a precipice, trying to save every hurt thing she found. Every flightless bird. Every orphaned kitten.

I'd watch her jump off the bus at the station and go skipping to find other drivers. "Bob!" she'd holler, running up to the operator, or "Bill!" Always men. I'm no saint, and I try not to judge or guess motives, but I kept an eye on her.

There was nothing I could do, of course. I was powerless. My pity was useless, and I struggled against indulging it. For her part, she appeared unflappable, a dynamo of aggressive good cheer teetering into raw need, yet protected by an outer shell of fierce independence, a self-reliance that was maintained by an exertion of pure will—or so I thought.

I admired her. She refused the world its ugliness. It was a survival mechanism I did not have.

One evening she boarded my bus dragging a suitcase behind her. "Hi driver," she said, pulling the thing clunking up the steps.

"Hello," I said, glancing down at the suitcase. "Whatcha got there? A bag full of puppies?"

"No," she said. She shook her head. "Grandma kicked me out. She said I can't live with her anymore."

I looked at her. She wasn't making eye contact. "Jesus," I said. "I'm sorry."

She finally looked at me and cracked a smile. "It'll be okay," she said.

"Where are you going to stay?" I asked.

"Oh," she said. "I've got friends."

Over the next couple months she spent more and more time at the downtown bus station, wandering to and fro, taking different routes here and there. Her good cheer didn't dissipate, but it took on an edge, a slight darkness. The desperation that roiled beneath it slowly came to the surface.

The bus drivers she'd sought out began avoiding her. She became a topic of conversation in the drivers lounge, a curiosity at first, and then stories of her began to be wrapped into the general dismissal of the homeless around town.

If anyone felt sad for her, they smothered it.

She attached herself to some of the hood-rats who hang around the station—those kids of indeterminate age, busy, jittery, scabby, traveling in twos and threes, strung-out Romeos and self-mutilating Juliets who confront impending reality with an exotic façade of menace, preying on and protecting each other in equal measure, constructing a world unto themselves, maligned and fucked beyond hope.

Her hair got greasy and her skin went sallow. She began shuffling around in bedroom slippers and a bathrobe, and still she held that smile to the world, just a bit cracked now, not entirely convincing.

She started pulling around a little wagon, a Red Flyer, piled with bags and bottles and clothing, a kitten on a leash. Dark circles appeared beneath her eyes.

She got pregnant. Then she disappeared. I never saw her again. I think about her a lot.

Feast of the Vultures

And so I went home to Clare, jobless, purposeless, free, sequestered in a low-security house arrest of unstructured minutes and days, weeks and months.

We were told to shelter in place while the world unraveled. A severe and perhaps permanent disruption in the space-time continuum had occurred, precipitated by an infectious microorganism considered novel in its ability to unleash the fuckery of mass contagion.

We awaited the wages of plague. The pure products of everyday reality went sideways, and our already tenuous sociopolitical situation exploded into an evil, stupid circus.

There was also this sinking feeling that, no matter how bad it got right now, this was only the beginning. It was going to get a lot worse, and these would be remembered as the good old days—those days when we merely had a clownish con man running the show, and the nutjobs worshiping him had yet to heed the dog whistle of brown-shirted extermination.

Now, at least, I would finally have time to write that book I always wanted to write but could never quite find the time—you know, my great American novel. But I didn't.

I didn't even think about thinking about actually starting anything substantial. Time was too gooey. There was no endpoint, no final destination, and so there was no starting line, no place to grab a foothold in reality.

Life became an asylum without walls, a cell without bars. It was all the same day, full of identical minutes and ritual anxieties, sloth and frenzy, ups and downs, news bulletins, nits picked, toenails clipped, projects abandoned.

The hospitals filled up. There were panicked rushes on bizarre consumer products. Toilet paper! Buy all the toilet paper! The world may burn, but I will have a clean ass!

The President of the United States of America suggested

shooting up with bleach to avoid infection. Clerks in stores were shot for suggesting their customers wear a face mask. Kids were run down and beat to shit for protesting the murder of black men by fascist cops.

The sediment forever swirling at the bottom of our politics rose to the top once again. It was fantastic, psychedelic, terrifying, hilarious.

The lunatics took over the asylum. People who could barely read suddenly did their own research on subjects of staggering world importance. Morons became experts, and experts became irrelevant. Life online became the life for you.

Theaters closed. Tours were halted.

John Prine died. For a lot of people, including me, that finally made it real.

Weird how that works.

Yes, extroverts became introverts, and introverts became—well, introverts adjusted pretty well to it all. A lot of good people I know now express a queasy feeling of nostalgia for the COVID-19 shutdown—not for the damage it did and the lives it took, of course, but rather for the drastic ways it reduced the breakneck speed and ceaseless idiot clamor of modern life.

Everything quieted down for a while. Traffic evaporated. The air was cleaner. Our weekly mass shootings all but ceased. Work typically done in the office was done at home, with little discernible loss of productivity. Public life was reduced to necessity.

And all of us began to question this hellish treadmill we'd been on, the way we'd been busily building a rickety bridge to nowhere, predicated on power, administered by control, and adjudicated by ghouls and greedheads.

Armed fanatics, cut free from the brainless crush of labor, stormed the state capitol—my guess is less out of legit political angst than from a sudden realization that, without the job, there seemed to be little purpose to their lives.

The threat of endless quality time with the wife and kids reared up as an existential nightmare. They suddenly had feelings, and those feelings were murder.

The ruling classes teetered and trembled.

And then they clamped down on the fucker like a dog on a bone. The ruling class shored itself up. Millionaires became billionaires.

The vultures feasted.

I am exaggerating my response to the pandemic, of course. Yes, it scared the hell out of me. But I never feared the virus killing me, really.

What I feared was other people—that's always been my core fear, only here it was amplified and complicated, and I had to do a lot of so-called spiritual work around my issues of trust and faith and acceptance and, you know, everything. All of it. Just like a lot of us, I suppose.

So, yes, on the one hand, I had a pretty severe case of the apocalyptic humdrums—amorphous anxiety and heightened agitation mixed with mind-numbing boredom. The end of the world is, among other things, boring as hell—an assaultive sameness that declares itself in a perpetually compounding crisis of meaning squeezing itself to a pinpoint of dumb death. All whimper, no bang.

But the flip side of this was a perverse exhilaration at watching our massive house of cards finally start to collapse. The whole bing-bang-shebang felt inevitable. Beneath its flimsy veil, Western Civilization strikes me as little more than a protracted nightmare, lit up by occasional flares of accidental beauty and aestheticized brutality—a disaster in slow motion, a neon-lit death cult, a logocentric dead-end. We killed all the good stuff long ago. Look around. Prove me wrong.

And America is its most putrid recrudescence—this stupid,

noisy Las Vegas of the soul where human desire gets turned inside-out and infantilized in a gaudy cannibal dance of empty fetishes. American culture is the death rattle of the human spirit under attack. Fuck it. Let it come down.

Did I really want this lumbering beast patched up to hunt another day? Somewhere deep inside me resides this exquisite tension between rote survival and my so-called higher values. Fear and desire, desire and peace, peace and pain, pain and dreams of no pain.

That tension speaks, on the one hand, to the bourgeois comforts of the status quo and the appeals they hold out to my neurotic mind while, on the other hand, there is the realization that those very comforts are false and drenched in blood, purchased at the cost of existence itself. How many people have to die for my convenience? It's all so very stupid.

It's a question of ultimate values, I suppose, and the diminishing returns on what the Buddhists call samsara—those short-term fixes that bring us immediate relief but actually make everything way worse in the long run, further exacerbating our suffering. Like heroin. Like voting for the lesser of two evils.

There is nothing very special about me. I am a samsara junkie through and through. Uncomfortable as I was watching the social fabric get torn to shreds, that very discomfort presented a fantastic challenge to the truth of my politics, which behold history with fear and trembling. The revolution will never be the revolution I want. The fix will always be popsicle sticks.

Like everybody else, I was forced to question just about everything—reality, truth, my brain, my choices, my country, my life, life itself.

If I came up with an answer at all, it's that there is indeed a strange karma at work in the universe, a corrosive yet restorative cosmic justice that, in the end, balances all the scales. It's not nice, and it's not personal, and yet all of my joy and all of my suffering depends on my orientation toward that impersonality.

And the karma of the pandemic was a bitch. It pushed the

envelope big time. It pulled me inside the belly of the whale. I was brought forth, kicking and screaming, to confront a very banal but very real personal reckoning.

I was compelled, by dire necessity, to reverse the polarity of things believed: It was not that the pandemic equaled the end of the world, but that the end of the world equaled the pandemic. Not that Trump equaled the end of the world, but that the end of the world equaled Trump.

For me, this was as liberating as it was horrifying. It erased all distance between me and reality. Excuses and blame fled from my mind, as did any reassurance that I would be saved.

The kingdom of heaven is within, and it is small. Very small.

The universe will be fine without us. That awareness is the beginning of crawling out from under. You're dead already. Stop smiling at cops. Stop kowtowing to your boss.

Salvation is now or never.

We watched a lot of the *Great British Bake Off* on Netflix. Clare cooked up enough macarons to fill all the boulangeries of Paris. We did yoga together, via YouTube, with a Texan named Adriene, whose ass was a fantastic motivator for me. I downward dogged and baby cobra'd with great enthusiasm.

And still, Clare and I gained weight. What else was there to do but eat, sleep, watch television, fuck, and argue? We argued politics for sport, and then we argued politics not for sport but for keeps, often into a fifteenth round that found us battered and punch-drunk to the point of despair.

We let ourselves get pulled into some total whoppers that threatened the foundations of our marriage.

Shit got personal. History was contested. Cards were pulled. Feelings were hurt, and words were said that could never be unsaid. It wasn't good. For the first time, the specter of divorce reared its head.

Somehow, we pulled through, tattered and bruised, but

mostly intact. Maybe even stronger. That remains to be seen, I suppose. Time will tell.

The cliché seems to hold true, that the multiple obstacles to intimacy we confronted—imperfectly but honestly, with heart—made us, if not stronger, more durable, more flexible. Maybe that is the real definition of strength.

I knew in theory that marriage would prove to be hard work, but Jesus Christ, nobody knows what that means until you get there. If you could adequately prepare for struggle, it wouldn't be struggle. The rewards of overcoming are neither obvious nor immediate.

In fact, as far as I could tell, the rewards equal a kind of leveling-up into uncharted territory—a territory that looks absolutely nothing like what you might have expected when you first decided to give this thing a go.

The majority of work I did was dismantling my own habitual ideas about what a good marriage is supposed to look like, or once looked like to me in the long ago. This might sound suspiciously close to settling—to selling yourself out on a dour commitment with diminishing returns. But I discovered that the truth is quite the opposite.

The commitment to monogamy is fundamentally arbitrary in the grand scheme of things, and yet it is everything: No one person, no matter how perfect, can live up to all your hopes and dreams, and actually, those hopes and dreams are inspired by the false dawn of romance, which fades, as it must fade, being founded solely in novelty and the narcissistic thrill of discovery and conquest.

Any future discoveries must be rooted in friendship, and that's the tough part.

◇ BUMP ◇

What I had to overcome, I discovered, was my own fear of change, which is really just fear of death sublimated. If only everything would stay the same, if only nothing more was lost, nor gained, if only if only if only … Nobody can fix that shit for you—no amount of fucking, spouse swapping, drinking, pouting, blaming, bargaining. You're just mainlining time, shooting up hope.

So you walk side by side with a person who is only slightly less strange to you than most people, and you walk alone, on your own two feet, but you do it together, toward the same destination, wherever that might be—Calvary, Mecca, Nirvana, North Dakota.

The endpoint doesn't matter. What matters is that your circles intersect.

You are a team. That's not nothing.

It might be everything.

Thankfully, we built a clutch of super good friends we socialized with on a semi-regular basis throughout the entire pandemic— at first cautiously, all masked up and socially distant, and then with increasing intimacy. We weren't reckless. It was a pro-con, cost-benefits sort of deal.

We decided that among the members of our group we were willing to run the risk of cross contamination versus the benefits of actual human contact.

Clare, of course, pointed out that each of us hardly represented an isolated, fully sequestered unit; beyond our tight circle, each of us was courting possible exposure—at the store, or with perhaps one or two friends outside the circle—which meant there was always the possibility of introducing the virus to the group.

It wasn't a cynical assessment, suggestive of group betrayal. It was just a scientific fact, the realpolitik of the pandemic. Clare was being objective—one of her core strengths, and a gene I decisively lack.

We accepted that the exponential nature of contagion was nothing we could lock down to a probability of zero. And that was okay.

Without our "Quaranteam", as one of us dubbed it, we would have gone out of our gourds. The human being robbed of sufficient social contact tends to get weird. Like Jack Nicholson in *The Shining* kind of weird. Weird with a hatchet.

Even for the most ardent misanthrope, complete isolation is a dangerous game—it seems we kinda sorta gotta bounce off other people, if only to remind ourselves that too much bouncing leads to specific nausea.

Enjoying the sudden cessation of the great rat race is one thing; enduring a plague jail with no end in sight is a different story altogether.

Maybe it's true that ego is the prison of the soul. But you can't escape that prison, not while you're here on Earth, because the ego seems only to recognize itself in the reflected reality of its fellow inmates. Hell might be other people, but good luck finding a way out of that one. Better to find your proper cell block and start a book club. The best you can do is temper and adjust.

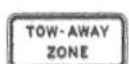

Clare and I, both on unemployment, were suddenly pulling in more money than we'd ever had, which was funny. Aside from eating out, our expenses dropped drastically, and we watched our savings account balloon—something we hadn't been able to accomplish prior to the pandemic, no matter how hard we tried.

I wondered where all the money was coming from. I wondered about universal health care. I wondered about the inherent waste built into the economic system. I wondered about million-dollar bombs perennially dropping on brown people in the Middle East.

I wondered about the clockwork crises of capitalism and the deep fake of perpetual austerity.

I wondered why the stock market kept climbing, why the filthy rich were getting filthier and richer while a million people died from the virus, and everyday commerce ground to a near-halt.

Like a lot of folks, I smelled a rat. During the pandemic, it felt like we were being appeased and led by the nose at the same time, a carrot pounded up our asses with the stick of enforced obedience.

I felt scarcely more affinity with the smug bumper-sticker liberals touting proper distancing behavior as a superior moral virtue than I did with the anti-maskers cooking up crazy globalist conspiracies about a mass contagion fabricated in order to tighten the screws on a New World Order.

Rabid skepticism—once the domain of the so-called Left—and establishment loyalty—traditionally a conservative posture—flipped sides, without anybody noticing.

And yet both sides missed the point.

Whatever the final cause of the COVID pandemic—global warming, laboratory leak, bioterrorism, nature's revenge, evolutionary winnowing, alien invasion—the old pyramid scheme of capitalism was going to plop itself down atop this new catastrophe as readily as a carnival barker collaring another rube.

The origins of the crisis didn't really matter. Was it the Chinese? Was it Big Pharma? Was it King Leoplold's ghost?

Most likely it wasn't a manufactured crisis, but that didn't stop it from being a boon to those in control, from top to bottom—including the pinchpenny twats running Cosmodemonic Transportation Authority.

DO NOT
STOP
ON
TRACKS

"You know," I said at last, "I've had quite a few crushes on you."

I couldn't tell if my therapist was shocked, pleased, uncomfortable, or repulsed. She just continued looking at me, smiling.

"I mean, it's stupid, I know," I said. "I'm not under any illusions about what this is"—making a circling gesture with my hand, taking in the whole office—"but I figured if I can't get honest here, then I'm just fooling myself."

"This is a safe space," she said.

"I appreciate that," I said, taking a deep breath. "So I've been thinking a lot about this. It's like I'm watching myself watching myself. I've never had any difficulty grasping the idea of being in love with two people at once, and the one having nothing to do with the other. But this isn't about that."

"Okay," she said.

"Like when you asked me to lean into my feelings of trust? At that moment, I felt immediately like I was going to cry, but I also felt this enormous sense of gratitude, and I didn't know where to put it, so it became affection toward you. A warm feeling. I don't know if affection is the right word, but there it is."

"If this feeling you have presents problems," she said, "we can explore other solutions."

I looked at her. "You mean like me getting a different therapist?" She shrugged. "Is that what you're suggesting?" I asked.

"I'm not suggesting anything," she said. "It's my job to offer appropriate options to you as a patient, and that's one option."

"I get that," I said. "Listen, here's the thing. I don't think I want that. I don't. There's too much water under the bridge already, and I'd be really sad to lose everything we've established here. I like working with you. It's been incredibly helpful. I trust you. And I trust myself with you, oddly enough. I can honestly say that if we did decide to end our working relationship, or whatever you call it, I'd be okay with that. It doesn't create any panic in me to contemplate that."

"Okay," my therapist said. "That's good."

"I actually feel better just telling you about it, this crush," I said. "It's like I moved it out and away from me. I feel free of it, to some extent. If that makes any sense. The reason I told you in the first place was to, I don't know, exorcise this emotional response in me that mistakes one thing for another. The attention of a pretty woman for affection, for instance."

"That's your anxious attachment," she said. "The part of you that seeks validation, and when it gets it, or even thinks it's getting it, jumps all in."

"And when it doesn't get it," I said, "goes completely ballistic, or gets suicidally depressed."

She nodded. "How are things with Clare?"

Well played, I thought. "Pretty good, I think," I said. "Things have been good lately. I asked her the other day if she's noticed any change in me. She looked at me for a second, and then said, yeah, absolutely. With a little smile on her face. She doesn't exactly excel at offering praise, that's not her strong suit, so that felt pretty good."

My therapist seemed genuinely pleased about this. "So that's good, right?" she said. "Even acknowledging that she might not be so quick with praise is a form of progress. She expresses her love in other ways."

"Sure," I said. "I mean, sometimes it all feels like two steps forward, one step back, and that one step back can feel devastating, like all the progress has been lost. When you're fighting all the time, one more fight is just one more fight. But when things have been slowly getting better, one fight can feel just terrible. Like a relapse."

"All couples have disagreements," she said. "The goal is to increasingly identify and understand the triggers, for both of you, and find ways of stepping back when that happens."

"Like a time out?" I asked.

"Sure," she said. "That's one option."

"I like the option where I stop being an asshole," I said.

Working-Class Hero

And then, about half a year into the layoff, Cosmodemonic called me back to the fold. I had mixed feelings, to say the least.

On the one hand, I understood that none of this could last indefinitely and that, eventually, out of sheer economic necessity, I'd be forced back into wage work, either with Cosmodemonic or some other bullshit organization. On the other hand, fuck, I had to go back to work.

And not just any work. I was a neophyte bus driver heading straight into the shitstorm of sociopolitical unraveling, replete with growing mass protests sparked by the open-air execution of an unarmed Black man by a psycho cop in Minneapolis, record-ed on a bystander's cell phone and broadcast nationwide.

With the murder of George Floyd, and the riots that fol-lowed, you could practically hear that trap snapping shut for the last time. Game over.

The reason for my rehiring, as I vaguely suspected at the time—and which actually proved to be the case—is that the good folks in charge at Cosmodemonic Unified Northwest Tran-sit had laid off a massive chunk of their low-end workforce in a faux-panic of fiscal austerity, only to saddle the remaining high-seniority drivers with a brutal workload that was now grinding them to gristle.

It was a classic business move, no less predictable for being altogether counterproductive. By which I mean, idiotic. Cut workers, save money to make money, slam the grunts at the bottom to secure funding at the top, and then sit back and wring your hands in phony concern as the only people doing any real work start falling off the cliff.

Oh, the humanity! It's like a street corner game of three-card monte applied to running a massive corporate entity, and the asymptotic arc it sends hurtling toward total failure does nothing to stop the managerial classes from employing it as a ramshackle strategy every time.

And then, as the workers commence to burn out and quit—dropping like proverbial flies—and the company suddenly finds that it can't conscript new peasants fast enough to keep the wheels spinning, literally and figuratively, the bosses start caterwauling about worker retention, bewailing the sad fact that no one wants to do an honest day's labor anymore.

You actually saw this on billboards during the pandemic: "Sorry. We're closed. Nobody wants to work anymore."

It was so shoddy. This horseshit was widespread in the aftermath of the pandemic. One massive bait-and-switch meant to keep your eyes off the money piling up in the vaults.

At least they gave me fair warning. The call back to work came as we were heading into the holiday season, and they informed me that I wasn't due to return until after the New Year. I had a couple of months to prepare myself.

As much as I dreaded going back to work, I will confess to experiencing a tinge of relief at now having something solid and visible on the horizon—it was like the salvation of punctuation finally dropped into a run-on sentence.

Whether the punctuation being plunked down was a period, an exclamation point or a question mark, I had no idea. Maybe it would be a semi-colon. Or a long dash—

—and lest, dear Reader, you have mistaken me for some degenerate slugabed whose treasonous anti-establishment leanings have led him to reject every last vestige of his beloved society's ideological championing of hard work, individual achievement, and upward mobility—completely reasonable suppositions at this point—let it be said that the prospect of re-entering the workforce after an unforeseen hiatus did in fact have a moderately salutary effect on my chronically aggrieved masculine identity.

I am not immune to the visceral call of the Protestant work ethic, nor am I somehow above equating earning power with vitality. If I am an existentialist by experience and an anarchist by sentiment, I am also a pragmatist by training.

A nagging guilt hounds every endeavor not aimed at the material betterment of my life situation. Knowing I was being recalled to gainful employment put a little pep in my step.

I was sexy and potent again, a working-class hero.

Straight time might be lame and pointless and often downright painful, but it grants you a pass for your extracurricular pursuits. It pays the bills, and gives you something to say at parties. It keeps the vultures from circling.

It staves off the stink of desperation. Or so you think.

Suddenly the days of unemployment remaining to Clare and I became precious. The clock was ticking again. My number was up.

We took a road trip south into the California Redwoods, to eat fast food, hike park trails, and have dirty sex in roadside motels. We drove out to the coast for a long weekend.

We did a bunch of stuff we'd had plenty of time to do but had failed to do. It's funny. No matter how many times you hear the spiritual dictum to live every day like it's your last, you never take it seriously until a gun is pointed at your head.

With work now looming on the not-so-distant horizon, things came back into focus—a quickening, a sharpening of the scenery. The time left now felt like a long vacation rather than an endless accusation of inaction.

Days once more became actual, distinct days. I started getting dressed in the middle of the afternoon for no particular reason other than to get out of my pajamas, which had been my uniform for the past six months.

It was like a dress rehearsal for the great return.

Ding!

Driving the bus during the height of the COVID pandemic was like wheeling a mobile M.A.S.H. unit through the festering wasteland of a fallen state locked in an undeclared civil war, complete with the bedraggled and besieged citizenry flailing through institutional collapse in its most desperate final stages—anger, confusion, mania, addiction, aggression, despair, paranoia, derangement.

In its infinite wisdom, Cosmodemonic tasked drivers with the responsibility of single-handedly policing the organization's confused and sometimes contradictory mask policy, meaning that along with the enormous burden of operating a bus in an ongoing national crisis, we now had to make sure that every single passenger was wearing mandatory face covering. In the best of circumstances, this would prove nearly impossible. Given the infantilized and violent proclivities of the American public, it was also fraught with very real dangers.

I was argued with, screamed at, and spat upon for merely requesting that folks riding my bus put on a mask.

One old man actually walked onto my bus with a plastic sack tied around his head at the neck. I watched him in my mirror, the flimsy skin of the bag expanding and then pulling tight against his skull as he panted in the back seat. I picked up my intercom. "Sir, a plastic bag is not a proper mask," I said.

I watched as he sat up straighter, his head swinging from left to right.

"Sir," I said. "Please. I can't have you dying on my bus."

He reached up and tore a hole in the top of the bag, then pulled it down over his mouth, leaving his nose exposed. I felt my heart break. "Thanks," I said into the intercom. At least he was trying.

Other passengers didn't even try. They wanted to debate me about global conspiracies and scientific facts, about libtards and snowflakes, about international conspiracies and communist takeovers. They wanted to kill me. It was madness. And the thing is, the majority of my colleagues actually agreed with the politics trumpeted by these extremist turds. When it came to enforcing the mask policy, however, they were furiously on board, using it to exclude and abuse riders left and right.

First comes irritation, then comes ideology.

"We the people" is apparently as far as a lot of these fuckheads got.

"I mean," I said to Doyle Claggart one day, "you think the pandemic is horseshit, and yet you enforce the mask rule with a vengeance. All I hear is everybody bitching constantly about having to wear masks while we're driving, but we're beating the shit out of riders who aren't masked up. Isn't that the definition of hypocrisy?"

"Rules are rules," he said.

A very drunk man staggers onto my bus. He holds up the mask hanging in his left hand. "I 'spose you wan me to push this on my face?" he says.

"Yes sir, please."

He grunts, rummaging through his front pocket with his free hand. "And I 'spose you want me to pay, too?"

"Yes sir, that would be good."

Tinny Christian rock is blasting from the speaker of the cell phone in his shirt pocket. "I know, I should turn the music off, too, right?"

"I'd appreciate that."

He pauses, takes a deep breath, and shudders from head to toes. "Jesus Christ!" he screams. "Quit fuckin' hassling me! You want me to do this all at once! It's too much! Give me a break! Jesus fuck!"

He stumbles down the aisle and plops down in a seat, having done none of the things he suggested he should do. He's singing along to the music. I get on the intercom. "Hey, sir," I say. "How about just putting the mask on, ok?"

I drive along, listening to him cuss me out to the other riders around him. The Jesus music keeps playing. All of a sudden he yells out: "I put my mask on, okay?"

I say nothing.

"The proper response is thank you!" he yells.

Nausea—that is my overwhelming response whenever I stop to contemplate work in all its grotesque dimensions.

It makes the soul sick, this perpetual grind of working-class reality.

Time for money, health for money, love for money, freedom for money. It's a terrible substitute for a life.

It absorbs everything, becomes your dominant identity, your only identity.

What do you do?

What do you do for a living?

What is you?

Who is you?

You is minus time plus money.

Your job asserts itself as a fait accompli that you futilely bargain away with the most vital and creative parts of yourself. Your soul.

And then, eventually, you forget those parts ever existed, and you make bitter fun of their evidence in others.

Or you try to squeeze those parts into the margins, after hours, like glue, trying to keep yourself together.

The object of the company is to prevent you from under-standing this, even if that means encouraging you to hate the object of work itself, ironically enough.

This is the great truth of class politics, and our denial of it. Money is a poor anodyne. It doesn't cut it. It doesn't cover the loss.

But, you know, we'll take it.

May I have another dollar an hour? No? Well, thanks anyway for the pizza feed, boss!

Real swell of ya.

Ding!

I was sitting in my living room, watching TV with the cats. Out the window facing east I noticed a huge wall of black moving in from the mountains, heading directly toward me. I stood up from the couch and walked to the window. It was definitely smoke. There'd been no warning at all. Here we go, I thought.

The fires that burned up a massive chunk of forestland running along the river raged for weeks that summer, blanketing the entire region in a permanent fug of smoke and ash. It didn't just look like the apocalypse—it was the apocalypse. It is the apocalypse.

You are here.

Driving the bus through that shit was a nightmare—and not just in the physical sense. Bus driver mortality rates are already alarming—we tend to croak somewhere between ten to fifteen years younger than the national average—and among the leading causes of driver illness and death are heart disease and lung cancer.

We are continuously exposed to a cloud of car exhaust farting into our faces all day long, not to mention the fumes pouring from our own buses. Add to this a miasma of smoke so thick you could almost hold it in your hands, and we're talking about serious health tolls.

But there is also the stress involved, and it should not be minimized —the subliminal stress of operating a bus as your world burns. You bear witness to a catastrophe in real time, and there is no escaping it.

In fact, not only is there no escape, but you are required to perform a public service that demands every ounce of your attention. It taxes your nervous system to the utmost.

Your eyes are wide open, and you have no significant time to process what you are seeing.

You are unwittingly absorbing something so intense, so dire—a novelty of Armageddon in real time—but you are also trapped on a treadmill of service regulated by an outmoded system of discipline and punishment, and therefore you are a soldier without a gun, on a mission without a distinct goal other than to keep moving and not die.

The evening of that first day of the fires, Clare and I ventured out in the car. We wanted to see just how bad things had gotten. We drove a few miles up the highway, toward the fires. The lanes heading east were empty, but soon enough we encountered a steady parade of headlights moving toward us, winding westward through the dark, for miles and miles, like the dim bouncing lanterns of pilgrims fleeing Gomorrah—a bumper-to-bumper procession of cars, motorhomes and trucks, some carting livestock, all of them fleeing the fire's devouring progress. It felt like a prophecy of a future that just so happens to be right now.

I'd get off work, my lungs ravaged and my eyes burning, and draw a bath. The water coming out of the faucet stank heavily of smoke.

Clare and I would administer an inhaler to our cat Blaze, whose asthma was going through the roof. And we hunkered down. We put up a few people who were in the immediate evacuation zone, their homes at risk of immolation, and we provided a temporary headquarters for a crew of friends who were running drinking water and used clothing back and forth to a school up the road that was providing temporary shelter for all the displaced folks, many of their homes already burned to the topsoil.

It was touch and go for a while.

They expanded the evacuation zone, putting our house directly in the line of fire. All of a sudden, we were pulling down cat carriers from the rafters and packing bags with essential items. Survival prep became an all-consuming occupation.

We moved with uncommon deliberation, unhesitant in our decision-making capacities, focused intensely on one thing, then the next, then the next. Shit had to get done.

The amorphous anxiety of everyday existence was brought to a pinpoint of urgency. It was the opposite of driving in circles.

Something in me looks back on this time, not with fondness but with a sense of greater meaning, as though the catastrophe—as awful as it was—worked to bring us together as a community. It granted a heightened sense of purpose to our actions.

And I wonder to myself why we cannot realize that these catastrophes are not distinct and momentary but perpetual and constant—always with us now, despite our inability or our unwillingness to plumb and compass them.

Can we please stop waiting for the next shitstorm to hit? It's here. Can we please start stitching ourselves a new, more helpful, more hopeful reality right this very moment? Or is it all just too much anymore?

It tells me everything I need to know that not once did Cosmodemonic halt service during the fires—not even when smoke levels surpassed their highest rating, pegging out on the top end of the human health-risk scale.

Nor did they ever prove willing to park their buses in any but the most inclement weather situations, often forcing drivers into the snow and ice despite nearly impassable roads. Perhaps this indicates an admirable determination to maintain a public service regardless of all obstacles—something akin to the Postal Creed. But I'm not buying it.

Because, more than once, the organization did opt to stop service—for instance, when the Black Lives Matter protests were taking to the streets.

Politics is everything here. Given how driven the bigwigs were to keep those buses moving in bad weather, despite obvious risks to the health and safety of its drivers and passengers, I am led to suspect that the cancellation of service due to a couple hundred unarmed people marching in civil disobedience was a pointed comment on the part of the administration—a chickenshit, Red Scare baiting maneuver that came down from the Proud Boys at the top of the Cosmodemonic hierarchy.

"Look what those communists are doing! They've disrupted bus service! How are people 'sposed to get around, fer God's sake?"

Or maybe Cosmodemonic really believed those "woke" antifa subversives were intent on tearing apart society in an un-American hurricane of violence and destruction—despite the fact that it was only the cops who were shooting rubber bullets and hurling flash-bang grenades.

Either way: Weak sauce.

Even anarchists and subversives deserve bus service—nay, especially anarchists and subversives! They are doing God's work. They are our only hope!

I drive the bus for the people!

I pulled into the station with an express bus. A lovely summer day, and my routes had been pretty chill. I was in a decent mood for a change.

I spotted Sam, my favorite security guy, standing on the platform nearby, looking a bit lost. I had five minutes to kill, so I walked over to shoot the shit with him for a few.

"Sam, what up? Quiet day, eh?"

He turned to look at me. I noticed at once that he was not his usual jovial self—no smile, kinda pale. In fact, he looked downright scared.

"Not really," he said.

"Oh, shit," I said. "Sorry, man. Is shit poppin' off for you?"

"Not me," Sam said. He shook his head. I watched as he reached up to flip a switch on his security vest.

It's a move I'd seen him make a dozen times—turning off the built-in mic so our conversation went unrecorded and unmonitored by Ops.

"Listen," Sam said. "I shouldn't be telling you this, and please don't tell anybody else yet, but one of our riders on the express was just attacked. Like, bad. I just watched the footage. I don't think he's going to make it."

"Fuck," I say. "That's horrible."

"Yeah," he says. "It's really bad."

It was my colleague Sheila who was driving the bus. The victim, an older gentleman on his way to the store, was sitting quietly in his seat.

It's unclear whether there was a precipitating event: certain rumors indicate a brief conversation between the attacker and his victim, perhaps a confrontation.

Either way, this lunatic—a younger guy, recently sprung from jail for assault—executed a vicious, bare-handed assault of such speed and violence that he snapped the guy's neck, severing his spinal cord.

The old man died on his way to the hospital.

"This could change everything," Sam said.

I recall as though it was yesterday the sudden darkness that fell over Seattle after The Gits singer Mia Zapata was found brutally murdered on the streets of the Central District.

Overnight, the lights went out on that city, and they've never really come back on. It was a solitary tragedy that changed absolutely everything—a random, senseless act of violence that somehow seemed inevitable, fated, and which cast an irrevocable pall not only over the present and the future, but all that had come before as well.

Innocence was gone.

And we wondered just how innocent it had all really been, anyway. Had we gotten carried away? Had we been naive?

The dank, druggy, euphoric games we'd been playing now looked incredibly reckless in retrospect—games played for keeps, full of nasty consequences, with life and death as the actual stakes.

Things would never be the same again, we understood, and that knowledge contained an undeniable element of guilt.

ROAD CLOSED

A similar feeling seized me, in microcosm, after that guy was murdered on one of our buses.

A lot of drivers were justifiably furious that their safety concerns had gone tragically unheeded by the administration. Here, at last, their worst nightmares had come true. It was only a matter of time, they'd said over and over again, and that time had arrived. Several drivers were unrepentantly vocal about it.

I didn't blame them for their "we told you so" mentality, though there were moments when it seemed like the whole thing was degenerating into a morbid objectification of the deceased— it's a sad day when the dead are forced to prove our point for us.

And, I'll confess, I was not above feeling vindicated. My anxiety grew fangs. It was a shitty situation all around.

Mostly, though, I just felt empty inside. I felt hollowed out.

I failed to channel any satisfying schadenfreude from the

situation, or to whip up any significant rage at Cosmodemonic's inability or—much worse—unwillingness to protect us. That had been made abundantly evident to me pre-homicide.

I realized that incompetence, inaction, and callous disregard closely resemble intentional neglect and outright evil at the administrative level, and the result in the end is exactly the same.

I didn't give a flying fuck why or how it had happened. It had happened.

End of story.

No—it was something else that got me. It felt like I'd hit bottom again. It wasn't drugs this time, it wasn't alcohol, though the results were oddly similar. I felt sad and trapped. Depressed.

Time got weird—or, rather, even weirder. My concentration faltered. My anxieties took up residence in that hidden secret private space inside, they settled in like a colony of barnacles, making themselves right at home. I was going chronic. It wasn't long after all this that I first got myself into therapy.

It was also at this time that I started seeing glitches in the matrix. Glitches like film footage burned through, the reel repeating itself, something right out of the vaults of David Lynch. You will think me mad, no doubt—and I don't blame you. It still freaks me out to contemplate the irregularities I was perceiving.

It's as though my rattled consciousness collaborated with the cosmos itself in order to produce little Lovecraftian rips in the scrim separating everyday reality from the nightmare lurking just beneath the surface.

Studies have shown that the leverage of constant stress on the human psyche—the nonstop triggering of the fight-or-flight mechanism, the constant shock of trauma—has the capacity to physically alter particular regions of the brain's functioning, mostly in the amygdala and the hippocampus.

Imagine your gray matter being squeezed like a blob of clay. The neurons seek new paths, they take zippy shortcuts or, sometimes, they are forced to trudge the long way home. The lens cracks, the shutter clicks. The world has changed. But has it?

Anyone who's taken psychedelics understands the convincing weirdness of suddenly seeing through the solidity of everyday things and events—the bark of a tree begins to breathe, two voices exit one mouth, a body in motion stutters through time like a nickelodeon, leaving observable traces of its passage.

The senses are deranged, and perception is upended—which is not to say that the things being perceived are illusory or false.

Madness and sanity do not exist on a spectrum; they are a closed loop.

My therapist suggested that I was disassociating due to stress. And that may be true. Trees really do breathe, though, right? That's an incontrovertible truth.

Would you rather know this, or see it for your own self?

I'm cruising along on the interstate, heading inbound from one of the longer rural routes served by Cosmodemonic. Early morning, light traffic, so I have the opportunity to take in all the cars in my path.

Wal-Mart semi truck, aqua Prius, red-and-white motorcycle, black '93 Ford F-150 with a wired-up back bumper.

I exit the freeway and make the ten-minute loop through town for pickups. And as I merge back onto the interstate, I see the same four vehicles that surrounded me before I exited, in the exact same arrangement.

Wal-Mart semi, aqua Prius, red-and-white tanked motorcycle, black '93 Ford F-150 with a wired-up back bumper.

It's as though the freeway stopped when I exited, and restarted the moment I entered again, like a motorized scroll.

As though it was waiting to prove, to me alone, my existence in time and space.

Or I deboard a pair of passengers and watch them begin strolling down the sidewalk, hand in hand. Twenty minutes later,

I drive past them, on the other side of town, strolling down the sidewalk, hand in hand.

I'd get a thought in my head, a simple phrase, or a snippet of an idea, and the very next passenger to board my bus would speak that exact thought aloud to the person beside them. I'd start humming a particular song, and then, half a minute later, drive past a car with that song blaring out the window.

These things happened over and over. I was coming unstuck in time. Or, rather, time was being revealed to me as a cheap joke, a movie on endless repeat featuring a finite cast of characters whose job it was to convince me that I was progressing in unrepeatable sequences through my differentiated days, advancing in linear historical time, when actually my minutes and hours and weeks were beginning to resemble a tedious tumbler of randomized sameness featuring just enough mixed-and-matched items to create a reasonable facsimile of the world in flux.

Yes, it did occur to me to wonder whether this whole thing—and by whole thing, I mean the universe itself—is not in fact one gargantuan simulation, a fabricated web of virtual reality we're all stuck inside—assuming we even exist at all—and that I had been struck just the right amount of fucked up to catch an unapproved glimpse of the gears in motion behind the scenes.

I had my Philip K. Dick-*Wizard of Oz*-*Brave New World* moments. But, as usual, and not necessarily to my benefit, I was also able to compartmentalize this suspicion, and to realize, on the other hand, that I was merely responding, physically and neurologically, to an inordinate amount of stress, and that there was nothing particularly unique or special about what was happening to me.

I do not, however, consider these two possibilities to be mutually exclusive. Everything is only a metaphor for something else, or maybe it's just metaphors all the way down. Who knows?

All I know is that, in my experience, there's far more in heaven and earth than is contained in my philosophy, etc., etc., … and if solipsism is the ultimate truth of our experience here on earth, it doesn't automatically follow that our isolated experience has zero to say about the broader truth of existence, even on the grandest scale.

NO
MOTOR
VEHICLES

I pulled into the bay at the downtown station after my final run of the day. I had a Vietnam vet in a wheelchair in the mobility bay behind me, so I set the parking brake, put the bus in neutral, lowered the chassis and picked up my receiver.

"Ramp coming out, watch your step."

I checked the aisle, swung the doors open and began to deploy the ramp. Just as it hit about 20 degrees deployment, a rough-looking chick in white shorts and a white tank top with a bandage across the bridge of her nose comes barreling past.

She attempted to leap the ramp, but her left foot got caught. And she began to fall forward, her right foot came down atop the ramp, slamming it back down and sandwiching the other foot with all her weight.

"Oi, chingada!" she screamed. "My foot! My fucking foot!"

"Okay, okay," I hollered. "Don't move!" In my panic, I flipped the ramp switch in the wrong direction, bringing it down harder on her foot.

"Oh Jesus!" she hollered, grabbing her left ankle with both hands.

"Hold still!" I shouted.

I flipped the switch in the other direction. The mobility ramps beeped and beeped, but nothing happened. The woman continued to squirm.

Finally, the ramp rose slowly from her foot and she fell backward on her ass. She stood up and limped off the bus, followed by the guy in the wheelchair and then the passengers waiting behind him.

I watched as she took a seat on one of the station benches across from my bus. She pulled off her shoe and began rubbing her foot.

Once the bus was completely deboarded, I walked over to her. "Are you okay?" I asked. "Do you need medical assistance?"

"I don't know," she said, continuing to minister to her foot. "Jesus fuck, that hurts."

I decided to call it in, just to be safe. I let Ops know that a woman tripped on my ramp and that she may or may not be requesting medical assistance, I don't know, I'm just following procedure, what should I do?

Claggart and a couple security guys showed up. Doyle gave me a curt nod, his face expressionless, and then he walked over to the woman. He bent down to talk to her, but I couldn't hear what was said.

The two security dudes circled around me, faces expectant. They wanted the story. I gave them the basics, without editorializing. It felt to me like all three of us should be holding donuts and cups of coffee.

"Yeah," one of them said. "Sounds about right. Just another idiot."

"I'm sure you're good, dude," the other said.

"Yeah," I said. "I don't know about that. I hope I didn't do anything wrong."

"Nah," chirped the first guy. "It ain't your fault. These people are total morons. She's probably jacked up on meth. Don't worry 'bout it. We see this shit every day."

"Yeah, maybe," I said. "I just hope she isn't really hurt."

"No blood, no foul," the other one chimed in.

"Yeah," I said, "that's not really how broken ankles work, but whatever."

"You okay, dude?" he asked.

I looked at him. He seemed genuinely baffled at my attitude. "Yeah, I'm just bummed out," I said.

He chuckled. "Yeah?" he said, arching his eyebrows. His voice was oozing sarcasm. "Maybe you need to take a couple weeks off? Get yourself some federal leave? Get some therapy?"

I decided to play along. "Yeah," I said. "Better call the whambulance. I think I've been traumatized. Best if I take a month or two off. With pay, of course."

The two of them erupted in laughter.

"Stupid bitch'll probably show up in a fake cast tomorrow," I went on. "Here comes the lawsuit, right?"

They both continued to laugh, circling around me tighter. "These people," the second guy said, shaking his head. "Don't worry, bro. We've got your back."

There is a hurt, a vulnerability, so deep and so buried inside me that I cannot find a language to let it begin to speak. I cannot begin to find a language to find the language to let it speak.

Sheila was given administrative leave after the murder on her bus. She came back after a few weeks, first on light duty, then going back to full-time driving.

But she wasn't right. She seemed haunted. Sheila had never been a big fan of Cosmodemonic, to say the least, but something in her had changed—she'd lost her feistiness, her vigor, replaced by a condition that looked an awful lot like deep and unprocessed grief.

"I'll be driving along," she told me, "and suddenly I'll just start shaking. I can't get it out of my head. I mean, it's been months, but I don't feel … I don't feel safe. And these fuckers don't seem to care. I mean, nothing's changed, right?"

"A couple press releases," I said. "A bunch of hot air, but no, nothing's really changed. Just sweep it under the rug and roll on. It's all optics."

"I actually had a meeting with Jack the other day," she said. "I just wanted him to know that this shit isn't going away for me, that I'm still having a really hard time."

"How'd that go?"

"It felt like I was talking to a brick wall," she said. "I mean, he tried to fake empathy, but it was all business. It's like he couldn't wait to get me out of his office. Do you know what he said to me?"

I shook my head.

"At the end of the meeting, he actually said to me, 'Well, this job isn't for everyone, you know'" she said. "Can you fucking believe that?"

"Yeah," I said. "I actually can."

So let your hearts break, comrades, and grieve. Grieve it all. Make peace with your grief. It's the fighting off of the grief that turns us bitter and cruel. It's okay. Let it go. Free yourself from the prison of death. Break the hands of the clock. Tell the boss off, make your move. Become tender, and get ready to die. Let it go. Everything—let it go. Your world, your society, your culture, your job—all of it has become one enormous insane asylum, a locked warehouse of chronic lunacy and irreversible decay, and it's impossible at this point to distinguish the inmates from their keepers, the convicts from their guards, the doctors from their wards.

We face each other in a fun-house mirror, cracked. Us and the mirror, the mirror and shadows. We are Stockholmed and anxietized, hogtied and brainwashed, pushed to the brink. We are so over it. A great storm is brewing on the horizon. The pendulum is making its final swing. The noose is tightening. The river beds are running dry. Winter has become summer, and autumn is now spring. Your politics are bone gristle and rotten teeth. Blood sport. Shit's getting medieval again. The people want a king. They are sick and tired of it all. All of it. They want the gallows, the shock treatment, the game of thrones. There will be blood. It's inevitable as the day is long. Even those of us who don't feel it coming, feel it coming. It is written in our cells, locked in the destiny of our DNA. Denial only hastens its arrival. It's okay. It's alright. What are you gonna do?

There is no escape, nowhere to go—not anymore. As if there ever was anywhere to go. Because you are here. You always were here. You are in and of the world, nothing more. And you are already dead. So give yourself a big hug. Enjoy every sandwich. Take the dog for a walk. Keep your promises to yourself, and tell your secrets to the cosmos. The time is nigh. Because let me tell you, tender comrades, that the things I see through the windshield of my bus would make Jesus think twice about getting up on that cross for us a second time. Ravening, mad, violent things, endorsed by the void, underwritten by the fear.

Nobody is having a good time anymore. It's the age of monsters. Everyone is a suspect, everyone is a victim, everyone is a potential murderer now. We are acting on principle alone. We are acting on impulse, we are acting on orders. Nobody is sorry for anything, everyone wants an apology. Shoot first, apologize later. Or never. We're all terribly busy, and no one is doing anything. All the people are in a mad dash to get somewhere else they don't want to be. I drive the bus for the people! The people are standing on two feet, immobilized, jackknifed in half, awake asleep. The people are on bad drugs. The people are on bad information. The people are on bad religion. The people are naked from the waist up, naked from the waist down. They are carrying bats and swords. They are locked and loaded. The people are broke. They are pushing shopping carts full of electronics and bike parts. They are standing in the middle of the street talking to God. They want answers, they need someone to blame. They are looking at the other guy and shaking their heads.

The people want food. They want money. The people are cashing checks everywhere and watching them bounce. The vaults are empty. They've been looted. The market is crashing. There is shrinkflation, stagflation, inflation, recession, depression, reform, retaliation, austerity, fear and trembling, perpetual war. It goes on and on. There is horseshit and hogwash. There are hallelujahs and hallucinations. All these dead fetishes, the commodities aren't selling. Nobody can afford them anyhow. The market is moribund. The culture is stagnant. The queen is dead. This is no country for anyone, except maybe old men.

Your neighbor hates you. Your coworkers are insane. It's okay. It can't be helped. Let your heart break. Become childlike, even childish—but not infantile. We've had enough of that. No more know nothing. Or grow old. Become ancient. Become as timeless as the universe itself. Become spacetime bending. Become the asymptote. Become the puckered asshole of the world. Become the symptom and the cure. Become the end of all things. It's okay—the grave is okay, it was your destiny all along. It's the ending of the whole thing that demolishes you. It's the waiting for it. The arc of your story has been hammered flat. The narrative has been blown to smithereens. And it hurts really bad. It's a pain without pain. It's a pain that is synonymous with the impossibility of describing it. It baffles you. You can't put your finger on it. You can't speak yourself back to life. Meaning is upended. Work sucks. Not working sucks. Hope feels like an insult. Let the nihilist celebrate it all. Let the politicians wring their hands. Let the reformers suture the rot. Throw them a parade. Join the procession. It's not your fault. It all feels so shoddy and dull and desperate. Spread the blame forward and back. Give yourself a hug. Kiss your ass goodbye. And let yourself grieve.

"I can't tell if I'm doing relatively well, all things considered," I say to my therapist, "or if I'm totally falling apart."

My therapist looks at me for a long couple of seconds. "Well," she says calmly, "maybe this kind of questioning is another good example of those extremes you tend to fall into. You want to paint everything as black and white, where some people might see a lot of gray. Could it be that this is the way you learned to avoid getting surprised or getting hurt in childhood?"

"Yeah, maybe," I say. "Seems feasible to me."

I look at her and grin, rolling my eyes—my trademark warning to her that I'm about to say something so very much like me.

"I mean, on the one hand," I say, "it seems obvious to me, and I think to anyone really paying attention, that his whole thing is falling apart. The system, the empire, the planet. Fascism is spreading everywhere. And it's just going to get worse. The wheels have come off. Denying that seems pretty silly to me, and even kind of dangerous, really. Nothing is going to get better ever again."

I take a breath.

"On the other hand," I continue, "I actually still really like being alive. I mean, less so lately, but my will to live remains pretty strong. I don't know where I find hope, but I've always been able to find it. I've always felt like there was something to look forward to, even if I couldn't really name it at the time. There's just something about right now ... I don't know, it seems like hope is going away, really fast. Like the future is being erased right before our eyes. I feel like I'm on a treadmill that's moving faster and faster. I mean, one day of driving the bus feels like an eternity, but the years are flying by. Time is just a big vacuum. I'm not moving toward anything. Does that make sense?"

"Sort of," she says. "I'll just point out that right now you offered two different scenarios, but both of them were pretty, um, negative."

I start laughing. "I don't know what to say," I say. "Despair's a bitch."

"There's lots of people experiencing despair these days," she says. "That's for sure. But there are also a lot of people who are not living in despair, even though they understand that the world is terribly broken right now. For them, it's not an either/or proposition. They continue living their lives, finding hope."

"I'd sure like to meet these people," I say.

When a friend asked whether he thought there was any hope to be found in this world or beyond, Kafka responded, "Oh, plenty of hope … an infinite amount of hope. But not for us."

It's such a perfect answer.

I trudged from my bus toward the Ops building. It felt like a million miles. Limping like a crippled pilgrim across that acre of asphalt with an offering to leave at the walls of Mecca. The song playing in my head was pure madness. I could feel my heart pounding in my chest. I felt all of it.

Bernie was sitting behind the counter. I set my backpack on the floor and signed in my bus on the lined sheet. I dumped my leftover day passes in the recycle bin.

"Hey, Bernie," I said.

"Wassup, buddy?" he said without looking up from his computer.

"I've got something for you," I said. I reached into my back pocket and fingered out the baggie of dope. Held it up for him to see. His eyes got wide.

"Hoo, yeah," he said, shaking his head. "I'm not touching that, man."

I put it on the counter. "I don't know, Bernie," I said. "It looks like pretty good stuff."

He chuckled. "Not for me, man. Did you call it in?"

"Nah," I said. "I just found it on my prep-out. Figured why

bother, right?"

"Okay," he said. "I'll take care of it."

I watched him reach under the counter for a pair of blue latex gloves.

"Hey, Bernie," I said, watching him pull the first glove over his fingers. He paused and looked at me. "I just want to say thank you," I said.

"For what?"

"I think you just saved my life, brother," I said.

He shrugged. "What did I do?"

"Everything," I said.

JCT

Driving home that night, I thought about all the things I didn't know. I thought about all the things I thought I'd known for sure but had been forced to unlearn, usually the hard way, things about myself and things about the world. Things about my wife.

I tried to place that new information, or lack thereof, in a different context—one where I wasn't constantly adjudicating my own existence. One where intimations of meaninglessness made truce with my strong need for meaning.

One where tenuous, contingent, hard-earned hope was still hope, and gestures emanating from goodness and love spread outward in time like ripples in a pond, beyond my own death.

Clare had told me during an argument that she could tell simply by the sound of my footsteps coming through the back door what sort of day I'd had at work, and how she might be made to pay for it. This information shattered me. I myself had heard those footsteps in childhood and cowered, awaiting the violence that came like a roll of the dice.

I slipped my shoes off and walked into the hallway. I looked at the family portraits Clare had hung there when we first moved in. Not one of them hung true. It looked like a fun house gallery, each photo slightly askew, slightly off.

I reached up to straighten a black-and-white portrait from our wedding day, but my hand froze. A sudden surge of affection broke my heart in half. I felt like a ghost. I beheld my wife from an impossible distance, my wife without me, alone, in all her infinite striving—her beauty, her failures, her desires, her love, her meanness, the heartache she couldn't share, the words that stopped in her throat and the ones that escaped, the crooked angles of her life that spoke to a wholeness beyond the limits of perfection.

She was on the couch in the living room, reading. I walked in quietly, bent over and kissed her on the forehead. She smiled. "Hi," she said. "How was work?"

I plopped down beside her on the couch. I didn't say anything.

"Yikes," she said, smiling nervously. "That good, huh?"

I looked at her. Everything in my being wanted not to scare her, no matter what, ever again. I smiled as gently as I could manage. "Don't worry," I said, "it's not bad."

"Okay," she said, raising her eyebrows and drawing out the two syllables. She closed the book in her lap.

"We should talk," I said.

During those early days, I was often forced to drive the express bus, which made one huge, wiggly loop through the entire region served by Cosmodemonic. The express was rough-going. It had the feel of an inner city subway. Many drivers refused to drive it. Certain passengers called it "the shame train," because it was the scene of so much violence and otherwise shitty behavior.

At the end of the day, when I came to my final loop on the express, I learned to tell myself I was rolling up the scroll—meaning every inch of ground I covered on this final run I would not cover again, as it rolled up behind me like a story told for the last time.

It's corny, I know. But it worked.

Inside that scroll I put all the animosity, aggression, heartbreak, and raw human badness I encountered while driving my appointed circles. In my head, I tried to suture it all shut with all the love and forgiveness I could conjure, in order to be at peace with yet another day—to find some sort of convalescent beauty in it, so it didn't stay open like a festering wound.

So it didn't kill me. I needed to do this.

I needed to tell myself a story.

Yes, Clare and I finally investigated the sailboat abandoned in front of our house. Curiosity got the better of us.

We hauled the big ladder out of the garage and anchored it in the gravel, propping it against the hull. I climbed to the penultimate wrung and leaned into the thing, testing it for stability. It rocked mildly on the trailer, but I figured it would hold my weight.

I was pretty high up there—a good seven or eight feet off the ground. From this vantage, I could see how dinky the thing actually was. The surface of the boat was littered with a debris of twigs and desiccated pine needles, brittle and brown. The mast lay flat over the top of the cabin, all the rigging tangled up in piles.

It was a mess.

I rubbed the corner of my hand against the narrow cabin window, trying to clear a view. The glass was smeary, with white mold edging in from the corners. I leaned over the boat's gunwale and peered inside.

No bodies. No cocaine. No bundled stacks of unmarked bills.

"What do you see?" Clare half-shouted up at me.

"Nothing," I said. "Garbage. There's a portable heater sitting on the cabin table. A flare box. A medical kit. A bunch of rumpled up plastic sheeting. Just random shit. It's mostly empty."

"I figured," she said. "The people who left it here knew it was going to stay a long time. Or forever."

I noticed that the entire bottom of the cabin was percolating with a tapioca of green mold floating on stagnant water—the opposite of Gatsby's green light. I felt a lump in my throat, a sadness for whoever's derelict dream this now represented, ship-wrecked and festering on the shore of the American continent.

Climbing down, I asked Clare if she wanted to take a look. "I'm good," she said. "Unless you actually want to break into it."

"I'm afraid of what's been cooking in there," I said, stepping to the ground. "We might unleash the zombie apocalypse."

"Yeah," she said, "but that might be an improvement, don't you think? A zombie apocalypse I'm prepared for. We might even stand a chance. But this shit?"

"Well," I said.

"At least we've got a boat now, right? In case of the flood?"

I clapped my hands together. "You're right," I said. "We're all good. Come hell or high water."

"Or both," she said.

"Or both," I said.

Acknowledgments

Writing is a lonely business for sure, but no writer writes a book in a vacuum, and I certainly could not have wrestled this beast to the ground without significant support. Thanks, first and foremost, to my fellow writers, and dear friends, in the Stonecutters Union, who for years now have been providing endless encouragement, inspiration, editing, goading and ego-correction; I am proud of you all, and humbled by your talent.

Throughout its evolution from anguished yelp to short story to fledgling full-length manuscript, this novel has benefited from a series of talented and perceptive readers who offered invaluable support and feedback: Andy Valentine, Patrick Newson, Benjamin Ficklin, Dante Zuniga-West, Emerson Brady, Nate Lippens, Nathan Johnson, Trask Bedortha, Wes Barstad, and Steve Lafreniere. Thank you all for your eyes and brains and loving-kindness.

Thank you especially to Jeff Bolkan and Sharleen Nelson at GladEye Press for believing in me and the work, and for pushing me to bring it to fruition and seeing it through at every stage. You have no idea what your faith and hard work mean to a small-town hick like me!

Thanks to the folks at Dark Pine Coffee, where I wrote most of this book and also performed passages from it.

Finally, thank you to my amazing wife Liz, who endured me through this whole process, offering unwavering support, and whose curt, knowing nod when she finished the manuscript told me like nothing else that I might just have done okay. I love you.

About the Author

Rick Levin is an award-winning journalist and critic whose work has appeared in *The Stranger, The Seattle Weekly, The Village Voice,* and the *Eugene Weekly,* among other publications. His short fiction and essays have been published in a handful of literary journals over the years, including *Oyster Boy Review, Timberline Review,* and *Blue Collar Review,* where an early excerpt of this book first appeared. He is an active member of the Stonecutters Union, a writers collective in Eugene, Oregon that he helped co-found in 2011.

In a spasm of romanticism and blue-color solidarity, he abandoned his journalistic career in 2019 to become a city bus driver in Oregon's Willamette Valley, where he lives with his wife and varous animals. *Off Route* is his first novel.

MORE BOOKS FROM GLADEYE PRESS

Follow the adventures and missteps of time-traveling PI Imogen Oliver as she recovers lost items and unearths long-buried stories and secrets from the past in this exciting series! (*The Time Tourists is available on Kindle Unlimited.)

The Time Tourists Trilogy
Sharleen Nelson

The Extraordinary Journey of a Tall Ship in a Tiny Pool Far from the Sea
Donevon Reves

With gentle absurdity and copious humor, author Donovan Reves weaves a whimsical yarn entwined with a tender love story all set in a ridiculous landlocked tall ship built in a tiny pool. As hard to describe as it is to put down, this tender fable evokes the magic of *The Princess Bride*.

I am the Wind
Cullen Cantwell

In GladEye's first YA novel, adults as well as teens will be inspired by the journey of a young long-distance runner who receives advice and encouragement from an unlikely source.

Join 19-year-old Ben Tucker for a passionate and revolutionary tale of protests, parties, trials, and a band of idealists who set out to build a countercultural utopia in the southern mountains of Oregon.

The Risk of Being Ridiculous Trilogy
Guy Maynard

*Available as an ebook on Kindle Unlimited.

All GladEye titles are available for purchase from
your local bookstore and www.gladeyepress.com.

*Federation of the Dragon
*Footman of the Ether
Jason A. Kilgore
Enter the ancient world of Irikara for
high-stakes epic fantasy adventure
in a mythical land filled with dragons
and demons, dwarves and elves,
magic and mages and gods.

Far Side of Revenge
Anne Dean
*A tale of two brothers, bound to each other but fol-
lowing divergent paths, this Booklife Editor's Pick,*
traces the life of Brian Boraime from his childhood
as a son of a clan king until *he was named King of all
Ireland.*

Coastal Coffee Club Mysteries
Patricia Brown

Six cozy mysteries follow retired poet
Eleanor Penrose and her band of
quirky friends as they solve mysteries
along the Oregon coast.

Black & Tan Fantasy
Randall Luce
A Booklife Editor's Pick, this gritty historically accurate
tale of racial identity and life in the deep South during
the turbulent early days of the Civil Rights Movement is
engaging and hauntingly relevant today.

COMING SOON *from*  GladEye Press

The Parable of Sam
Jason A. Kilgore
What if the biblical stories in Judges 13–16 were set in modern times? The Old Testament wasn't all gardens, apples, and manna from heaven. When Sam draws upon his supernatural strengh to save his friend from being mauled by a lion, his behavior begins to change, not for the better.

The Kingdom Brothers
Mike van Mantgem
Out on parole, white-collar grifter Cornelius Tayler finds himself enmeshed in a multi-level maelstrom of brutal neo-nazis, pseudo-religious gangsters, and unreliable allies who may be out to con the con-man.

So Much for a Safe Landing
Susan Solomon
With a dash of humor, action, empathy, and truth, a recently retired woman finds herself enmeshed in the polarizing and perilous world of women facing tough decisions in a post-Roe v. Wade world.

Friday Night at Atonement Cafe
Jim Currie
When Native American rock musicians awaken from a coma at a hospital in the Columbia Gorge, downwind of the Hanford Nuclear Reservation, the group's charismatic leader and his followers set out on a mission to protect sacred lands and get to the bottom of the accident at Hanford.

RERELEASES FROM JASON A. KILGORE
Around the Corner from Sanity: Tales of the Paranormal
Fourteen short stories of spine-tingling horror that will scare you AND tickle your funny bone!

Guide Me, O River and other poems